Broken Vows

Book Six of the Barrington Family Series

Chris Taylor

LCT Productions Pty Limited

LCT Productions Pty Limited

18364 Kamilaroi Highway, Narrabri NSW 2390

ISBN: 9781925441093 (eBook)

ISBN: 9781925441109 (Print)

Broken Vows is a work of fiction. Names, places, characters, brands, media and incidents are either the product of the author's imagination or are used fictitiously. Any resemblance to persons living or dead, events or locales is entirely coincidental.

Other books by Chris Taylor

The Munro Family Series (in order)

The Profiler
The Investigator
The Predator
The Betrayal
The Deception
The Negotiator
The Christmas Vigil (A novella)
The Ransom
The Defendant
The Shooting
The Maker

The Sydney Harbour Hospital Series (in order)

The Perfect Husband

CHRIS TAYLOR

The Body Thief
The Baby Snatchers
The Final Bullet
The Debt Collector
The Lab Test
The Stolen Identity
The Cliff-top Killer
The Likeable Fraudster

The Sydney Legal Series (in order)

An Accidental Murderer
At the Hand of her Father
A Woman Scorned
Lies and Deception
Ordinary Evil
The Ties that Bind
The Perfect Crime
A Toxic Inheritance
Malicious Love

The Craigdon Family Series (in order)

Callum
Joel
Isabella
Nicholas
Sophia

Flynn
Noah
Logan
Elizabeth

The Barrington Family Series (in order)

Broken Lives
Broken Promises
Broken Bonds
Broken Spirits
Broken Minds
Broken Vows
Broken Hearts
Broken Dreams
Broken Homes

The Fairfax Family Series (in order)

A Cattleman in Disguise
A Cattleman's Quest
A Cattleman's Daughter
A Cattleman's Secret Baby
To Catch a Cattleman
The Doctor and the Cattleman
To Rescue a Cattleman
A Cattleman's Heart
For the Love of a Cattleman

CHRIS TAYLOR

Bachelors and Brides Series (in order)

Matilda
Austin
Farrah
Benjamin
Verity
Denver
Ebony
Tyrone
Willow

Books by Chris Taylor
Writing as Bella Christian

This Is Where It Ends Series
(in order)

Jessie's Story
Ryan's Story
Holly's Story
Sarah's Story
Veronica's Story

Love audiobooks? Check out Chris Taylor Books on audio
iTunes   Amazon   Audible

Join Chris Taylor's Facebook reader group/fan page and be among the
first to receive news of book releases, read and review books prior to release
and other amazing offers.

Join Now!

This book is dedicated to Patricia Thomas, editor extraordinaire and my friend. You've been with me from the very beginning... Fifty books and counting... But all good things have to come to an end and I thank you from the bottom of my heart for everything. It was a wild ride.

And as always, to my husband, Linden. My best friend, my soul mate. I love you to the moon and back.

Chapter One

His body thrummed with excitement. The night cloaked his office in a pervasive darkness that titillated his senses. The place was still and quiet. He'd locked the door, but the possibility he might be discovered, however slight, gave him an added thrill. He drew his keyboard toward him and logged onto the website, relishing the surge of anticipation and guilty pleasure.

The screen filled with erotic images, dazzling his senses and swelling his cock. Impatient to see her, he entered his credit card details, messing up the numbers and having to start again. The tremor in his hands gave him pause and he breathed deeply in an effort to still them. Care was needed. The longer it took, the longer it would be before he saw her.

Agonizing seconds passed while his credit card was processed. Of course, he could have allowed the site to save his details, but he was wary of having them stolen. The Internet was a haven for scammers and thieves. But he was too smart for that.

A few moments...then finally... *Yes! I'm in.*

She was waiting, looking as sexy as always. Black leather bra with strategic cutouts to display her long, erect nipples. High-cut leather boy shorts that showed off a tight, toned ass. A black mask. A riding crop she flicked impatiently against a thigh-high black leather boot. Another wave of excitement rushed through him. He struggled to loosen his belt. He popped the button on his pants and eased his zipper down.

His cock was hard and pulsing, desperate for release. But he'd learned to pace himself. Delaying gratification heightened the experience. Besides that, the minute he blew his load, the show was over, no matter how much he'd paid. If he wanted to extend his time with the woman on the screen, he'd be forced to enter his credit card numbers again. Sometimes he lost count of how many times he did that in a night. Not that he cared. The rush was worth any cost.

The woman on the screen greeted him with the glare of a dominatrix accompanied by a saucy pout. White-hot desire pulsed through him and he relished the guilty pleasure. She stood front and center on the screen, her legs spread wide, sliding the riding crop up and down her leather-clad pussy.

"You want this, don't you?" she taunted in that husky voice that drove him insane with desire. "You want to reach right through that screen and touch this," she purred as she slowly lowered the zipper on her shorts.

"You know I do."

His voice was rough and ragged. He tugged at his shirt collar which was suddenly too tight. Her slow striptease with the zipper suddenly revealed her gleaming pink lips to his avid gaze. Moving closer to the camera, she tantalized her flesh with the tip of the crop. With a groan, his hand went to his cock. Unable to resist temptation a moment longer, he began to stroke.

Emily Wilson tucked an errant strand of loose hair behind her ear. Though her younger self had spent hours in front of the mirror perfecting a lifetime's worth of sophisticated hairstyles, her work as a pediatric oncology nurse in the reputable Sydney Harbour Hospital meant ponytails were much more practical. The simple style worked well for her when she was short on time and often physically and emotionally exhausted. Having a few extra minutes in bed was the priority these days.

Her shift had almost ended. Another long but fulfilling day. The courage and high spirits of her young patients never ceased to amaze her. They motivated her to get up each day and be grateful for her life. The truth was, she had nothing to complain about. The challenges her patients faced so bravely put any minor troubles she might have into perspective. Their positive attitudes never failed to inspire her.

She thought of going home to her solitary life and felt a momentary pang. At least she had Leo. Okay, so it would be nice to have someone to come home to who could answer her when she shared her day, but the little Scottish terrier did provide unconditional love and relatively undemanding company.

She hadn't had a serious boyfriend since high school and though the emotions she'd felt for Zac Barrington all those years ago had been genuine and strong, it was so long ago she barely remembered what being in love felt like.

They'd graduated high school and gone their separate ways and that was that. She and Zac Barrington were history.

Well, not quite...

Her mind shied away from the decision she'd made six years ago. A decision that still haunted her. She'd learned over the years not to think about it. That was the only way to cope with the guilt. It also helped that she hadn't seen Zac since they'd left high school six years earlier. And of course, after what had happened to her brother, anything to do with the Barrington name was now anathema. She couldn't stand the thought of her path ever crossing a Barrington's again. And yet...

She went on a final round of her patients, checking to make sure they were all right before she left for the day. Her last stop was with Izon Fernando. The ten-year-old had been battling cancer for most of his short life. He was no stranger to the oncology ward. Over the years, they'd become close. As she walked into his room, she smiled at the sight of a half-finished jigsaw puzzle laid out on his table.

"Don't tell me you've been working on this without me," she teased.

The young boy offered her a weak grin. "You always take too long to come back. I don't have all day you know."

Emily arranged her expression into mock outrage. "Izon Fernando! Anyone would think you were my only patient!"

He giggled. The sound of it warmed her heart. The truth was, he wasn't doing so well. The doctors had recently started him on a new drug regime, but so far things hadn't improved. It was a concern for everyone. Still, it was important for them to remain positive. Miracles did happen.

"I just wanted to let you know I'm finished for the day," she said.

Izon pulled a face. "Do you have to go?"

"I'm afraid so, buddy. And then I'm having a few days off."

His face filled with disappointment. "So I won't see you again."

She forced a smile. "Not for a few days. But after that, I'll be back. You better promise not to finish that jigsaw in the meantime. I want to be here when you put in the last piece."

He gave another half-hearted smile. "Okay. I promise."

She moved closer and touched his arm. "How are you feeling?"

He looked at her solemnly with his big dark eyes. "Sore. Sick. Sad."

Her heart clenched. Her voice was husky with emotion. "I get it, Izon. I really do. It must feel like you've spent all your life in hospital. It gets you down. But look on the bright side. The doctors have just changed your medication. We're all hopeful it's going to make a difference. Don't give up on us now."

He gave her another sad smile. "I won't."

She squeezed his arm. "That's the spirit. Now, is there anything you need before I go?"

"No thanks, Emily. See you round."

Hating to leave him in such a low mood but knowing there was nothing more she could do for him right then, she waved goodbye and left the room. She sat down at the nurses' station and finished making the final notations on her patients' charts. Once she was done, she leaned back against her chair, stretched her arms above her head and sighed.

"How's Izon doing today?" her best friend and work colleague, Jane Radcliffe, asked quietly.

Emily closed her eyes on another sigh. "He's had better days. Doctor Barker was so confident about this new drug, but so far it hasn't had much effect. Izon's blood work was all over the place today and he's feeling miserable."

Jane compressed her lips, her expression one of sadness and understanding. "Give it time."

Emily nodded. "Yes. You're right. And if I've learned anything after working in the pediatric oncology ward all these years it's that time can make all the difference. Along with miracles. I haven't given up on those either."

"Atta girl." Jane turned to glance at the clock on the wall behind them. "Nearly time to go home," she commented with a smile.

Emily rustled up a weary grin. "You bet. I've just worked seven days straight. In ten minutes or so, I'm on three days' off. And just as well. Leo's forgotten what I look like."

Jane chuckled. "You're lucky he's happy to stay at home all day without you. My Missy barked the house down whenever I walked out the door. In the end, I had to take her to live with Mom."

Emily sympathized with her friend. "At least she only lives a couple of blocks away. You can visit whenever you want."

Jane winked. "Of course. Why do you think I stop in there every day on my way home from work? I'm just lucky Mom's at home most of the time and can keep my baby girl company."

Emily understood Jane's attachment to her fur baby. Like Emily, Jane was a twenty-something single woman. While both women were open to the idea of falling in love, so far it hadn't happened. In the meantime, they devoted all their attention and not an inconsiderable part of their salaries to their dogs.

Pushing away from the desk, Emily headed for the tearoom to deliver an accounting of her patients' day to the incoming shift. As soon as she was done with her handover, she was free to leave. It had been a long stint of emotionally draining shifts. She was beat. She looked forward to a relaxing soak in her tub, accompanied by a glass of chilled white wine and some relaxing music. Right now, that pairing sounded sublime.

Hours later, with her skin freshly exfoliated and moisturized and two glasses of crisp, cold Sauvignon Blanc under her belt, Emily wrapped herself in her favorite thick terry robe and padded into the kitchen. Leo jumped up from his bed and came over to sniff at her bare feet. His little pink tongue stole out and licked her toes.

She chuckled. "You like the taste of mango body scrub, do you little guy?" She picked him up and buried her face against his warm fur. "I don't blame you. I think it smells pretty good too."

Carrying him into her open plan living room, she paused in front of the windows that faced the street. Night had fallen. The velvety darkness was pierced only by the streetlights and the occasional car that passed in a gentle hum far below her. Situated on the seventh floor of her building, she had a good view of the houses and other buildings that filled almost every foot of the inner-city suburb of Camperdown. Many had been warehouses, abandoned with the changing times and now gentrified, sleek one- and two-bedroom apartments like hers.

From her kitchen window, she had a glimpse of the city skyline. The modest scattering of skyscrapers, the Sydney Tower, the Sydney Harbour Bridge—a masterpiece in architectural design and an icon recognizable around the world. She couldn't see the Opera House from her vantage point, but it was there, tucked around the corner.

Leo squirmed in her arms. With a quick kiss to the top of his head, she lowered him to the floor and released him. He padded back to his bed. She glanced at the clock on the living room wall. A little past eight. Not too late to call home. She spoke to her parents every couple of days. Sometimes it was more often than that, especially if her mother was feeling needy. Since the tragic death of her older brother, Emily was now their only living child.

Her mother hadn't come to terms with the loss of her son. It made her over-protective of Emily. She sought reassurance about her daughter's welfare every spare moment she had. Emily understood her mother's need to stay in regular contact and tried not to get irritated. It had been a year since Evan's accident, but her mother said it felt like yesterday. It seemed grief worked to no one clock. Emily knew that better than most.

She'd seen her fair share of grief at work. It was sad that not all of her patients got better. More often than not, they spent their final days in hospital, often on the same ward where they'd spent so much of their short lives. Some people couldn't handle the stress of being surrounded by a disproportionately high probability of death and sometimes Emily also struggled. She was human after all. Forming close relationships with her young patients during countless rounds of cancer treatment was something she had no control over. Neither was the grieving that followed their loss.

Still, she wouldn't change her job for anything. The immense satisfaction she got from helping to make a young person's time in hospital easier—no matter how long or short the stay—was worth the pain that far too often followed the loss. Her patients needed her. They were facing the scariest moments of their lives with such tremendous courage. The least she could do was provide a friendly, cheerful face and offer hope.

The death of her brother had come as an unexpected blow and even though a year had passed, the circumstances surrounding Evan's accident still made her blood boil. He should never have lost his life. It was that simple. The ensuing cover-up by Barrington Mining had made things even worse. Thank God the insurance company had finally settled, but her family should never have been forced to litigate what was clearly Barrington Mining's fault.

Aside from the emotional trauma, having the case dragged through the courts had been an expensive and unnecessary drain on all of them. Most of all, on her mother. Emily was just grateful her parents had each other to help process what had been and what continued to be a heartbreaking time. Bob and Lorraine Wilson had been married thirty years. They still held hands whenever they went out. They still kissed each other goodbye. Emily prayed that one day she'd know that kind of enduring love.

Her father was the pastor at a local church in Broken, where Emily and her brother had grown up. It was a small rural town about ninety minutes' drive south of Sydney with a population of less than five thousand. She'd spent her childhood living in the rectory, exploring its expansive grounds. It was while she'd been marveling one afternoon about the ancient Moreton Bay fig tree in her backyard that she'd first met Zac Barrington.

Emily hadn't even known he was there until he called out to her. Discovering him seated high above her on a sturdy branch had frightened her out of her wits. She'd had no idea he was there. When he eventually deigned to come down, they'd spent the afternoon getting to know each other. She discovered they were the same age and attended the same school. What surprised her was that she hadn't noticed him before.

With his thick dark hair and intense brown eyes, he had an aura of confidence that drew her. Of course, she'd heard of the Barringtons. Everyone in Broken knew of them. They were a prominent family in the town. Not only was Frank Barrington wealthy beyond anyone's comprehension, but he was also a father to nine children. Those things alone tended to draw people's attention. But until that time, Emily had been oblivious that there was a Barrington in her year.

She suspected it had more to do with the fact Zac was undeniably good looking, sporty and popular and she was the complete opposite. While Zac spent his lunchtimes playing football, Emily was in the library, or under a tree with a book. She didn't have much interest in sports and even less interest in boys. But at ten years old, she couldn't deny Zac Barrington had sparked her curiosity.

That chance meeting in grade four had been the beginning of a close friendship that had eventually—some would say inevitably—led to love. They'd dated during their senior years. A magical two years of her life. Most people expected them to be together forever. She was pretty sure Zac had thought that.

But she'd wanted more than to settle down in Broken and raise a family, even if that meant breaking the heart of the man she loved. She wanted to explore the world, make her own mark, forge her own path. At the time, she'd felt like she had no choice but to break things off with him. She was also a firm believer in the whimsy of fate. If they were meant to be together, somehow they'd find their way back to each other.

Evan's death had changed everything. Her world had been turned upside down and she couldn't see past the fact it was Zac's family who was responsible for her brother's death. And by association, it was Zac's fault.

I need to let it go... I need to put Evan's death behind me and move forward... It isn't healthy for me to bottle up this anger... I need emotional strength for my patients...

The heavy thoughts weighed her down. She sighed wearily. What she wouldn't give to feel carefree again. To have nothing more pressing to concern herself with but what to cook for dinner or what to watch on TV... It didn't help matters that her mother, in her grief, had become needy and depressed. She hadn't been herself since Evan's death. And that worried Emily.

Two days earlier, she'd called home. When she'd asked to speak with her mother, her father had told her she wasn't there. She'd expected to hear from her later that day, but her mother hadn't called. Busy with back-to-back shifts, Emily had forgotten until now.

Pulling out her phone, she dialed her parents' landline. Despite Emily's repeated requests, her mother insisted she didn't want or need a mobile phone.

"I'm at home most of the time," she'd say. "You know where to find me."

Her mother was right. She did her fair share of volunteer work, though she was mostly a homebody who gained satisfaction from seeing to her husband's needs. Emily's father spent most of his time in the small office attached to his church. As pastor, he spent hours finessing his sermons, answering correspondence, dealing with the finances, meeting with his flock. The small parish of Broken only catered to a couple hundred parishioners, but her father took his duties as their shepherd seriously. He was always available to those in need and his parishioners loved him for it.

As Emily listened to the call dial out, she pictured the phone that hung on the wall in her parents' modest but cozy kitchen. Its strident ringing would disrupt the peace and quiet of their evening. No doubt they were gathered around the fire. Her mother would be knitting. Her father would be reading the bible. The phone rang three times, four times, five before it was answered.

"Hello? This is Pastor Bob. What can I do for you?"

"Hi, Dad. It's Em."

"Emily! How are you?"

"I'm fine Dad. How are you?"

"Yes, can't complain. Not like Mrs Whitcomb. Did you hear her cancer's come back again? Poor old thing. We're all praying for her."

Emily made sounds of commiseration. She'd known Eileen Whitcomb all her life. The woman had been Emily's first Sunday School teacher. She held a fond place in Emily's heart.

"Oh, poor Mrs Whitcomb. Let's hope she sends the cancer packing like she did last time."

"Yes. You have that right. What's been happening with you? How are your babies?"

Emily knew he meant the young patients in her care. She always referred to them as her babies and that's exactly how she felt about them. Most of them spent enough time on her ward that she got to know them well, along with their families. It made it even more heart wrenching when one of them didn't make it.

"Not too bad. Some days are better than others, but we never give up hope."

"Your patients are always in my prayers, Em. You know that."

"Yes, Daddy. I do. And thank you." Her voice was husky with emotion. She swallowed past a lump in her throat and then got to the reason for her call.

"Can I speak to Mom?"

"Well, you could if she were home."

Emily frowned. "What do you mean? Where could she be this time of night?"

"That's the thing," her father responded slowly. "I don't know."

Emily's frown deepened. A stirring of unease filled her stomach. "What do you mean, you don't know? You two are joined at the hip."

Her father's answering chuckle sounded strained. "Well, not quite at the hip."

"You know what I mean, Daddy. Did Mom say where she was going?"

"No."

"What time did she leave?"

"I don't know. When I got home from evening prayers at the church, she was gone."

"Did you see her earlier?"

There was a pause on the other end of the phone. "Em, I haven't seen your mother for a couple of days. It seems she's...disappeared."

Shock held Emily immobile. "A couple of *days?* Daddy! What are you saying?"

He gave a weary sigh. "Just that. Two nights ago, I arrived home after evening prayers and she was gone. There was no sign of her. Not a note, not a message on my phone. Nothing. I thought she'd gone to the shops or something. Her handbag wasn't in its usual place. When she didn't come back that night, I thought she must have gone to visit one of her friends. She'd mentioned in passing that Rosie Murray was doing poorly since her surgery."

"Did you call Rosie?"

"Not that night, but I did call her the next day. She hadn't seen your mother."

"Did you call anyone else?"

"No. I don't have the contact numbers for her other friends."

"What about going to see them?"

"I asked a couple of people who attended church this morning if they'd seen your mother, but no one had. I haven't spoken to her closest friends. I didn't want to alarm them unnecessarily."

Emily shook her head, aghast. "It's been *two days*, Daddy. Why didn't you call me?"

"You have a lot on your plate. I didn't want to worry you. I'm sure she'll turn up soon. Maybe she needed some time alone?"

"Why would she need time alone? That doesn't make sense. She hasn't left your side for thirty years. Is anything missing? Her clothes? A suitcase?"

"I don't know," her father replied in a small voice. "I... I just wish she'd come back."

Emily heard the fear and confusion in his tone and her heart clenched. "Daddy, you need to call the police. Something might have happened to her. She might be hurt."

"You're right," her father said in the same dazed voice. "Did you hear about that poor Webster boy? Murdered by his school friend. I can't believe something like that could happen in Broken. Terrible. Just terrible."

Emily's heart thumped in panic and she tried her best to keep her voice calm. "Yes, it was terrible. I feel so sorry for Oscar's family. I remember Cassie from school. She was always so sweet. But Daddy... I'm not suggesting Mom's been murdered. Still... It's strange she's been away two days without letting you know her whereabouts. Something's wrong. If only she had a mobile phone so we could call her."

Her father sighed. "You don't know how many times I've tried to get her to carry one."

"You and me both," Emily muttered.

"Will you...come with me to the police? To file a missing person report?"

All of a sudden, he sounded every bit of his sixty years. He also sounded scared. Perhaps the thought of going to the police made his wife's unexplained absence that much more real. Emily could only imagine the scenarios playing through his head right now. No doubt they were the same ones playing through hers.

"Of course Dad, but the Broken Police Station isn't manned twenty-four hours a day. It's already late. There won't be anyone there. I'll drive down first thing in the morning and pick you up. We can go there together."

"Okay." He sounded relieved.

"In the meantime, if you hear anything from Mom, call me, okay?"

Chapter Two

The mid-winter sunshine poured through Detective Zac Barrington's windscreen and hit him square in the eyes as he parked in his usual spot in the staff carpark of the Broken Police Station. The empty carpark signaled he was the first officer to arrive. Either that or the others had already been called out to an incident, which would be unusual but not unheard of in a town the size of Broken. He thought briefly of the recent murder of Oscar Webster and grimaced.

Climbing out of his car, Zac drew in a lungful of crisp, fresh, country air. He loved working in the community where he'd grown up. Broken was where he'd been born and bred. He'd even gone to high school there, along with his brothers and sisters. He'd excelled at cricket, hockey and swimming and had enjoyed a glorious time as captain of the winning football team three years in a row. Those were good memories.

The small rural town was a ninety-minute drive south of Sydney in the beautiful southern highlands. Far enough away from the city that he could enjoy all that a country life had to offer, but close enough that he could easily venture up to

Sydney for a weekend of fun. As far as he was concerned, it was the best of both worlds, and he was pleased he'd made the decision to transfer there from the central coast.

Working at Broken Police Station also meant he got to work alongside his brother. Trace was a couple of years older than Zac and had been a detective for that much longer. Zac had always looked up to his older brother and that hadn't changed over the time they'd been working together. Zac had great admiration for Trace's dedication to keeping his community safe and his ability to follow leads and catch the bad guys. Zac hoped to learn as much as he could from his brother. In fact, Trace had been instrumental in tracking down Oscar Webster's killer. The fact the perpetrator was the teenager's best friend had been doubly shocking.

That murder had shaken the town. Crime ranked lower in Broken than in many other towns throughout the state. It was one of the things Zac loved about the place. That, and the fact his parents lived only a short distance away. He was one of nine children and although his oldest brother was technically only a half-brother and his second oldest brother was adopted, all nine of the Barrington siblings remained close. Apart from his brother, Vaughan, who'd gone AWOL for the past three or four months, they caught up on a regular basis.

Family gatherings had become even more interesting recently, with some of his siblings meeting and falling in love with their soul mates. Christopher, Trace, Charlotte, Lincoln and most recently, Wade all now had significant others. Zac felt a little envious of their closeness to their partners. They'd created their own secret world of tender glances and wordless communication with the merest brush of a hand. It would be nice to feel that kind of love someday.

Unbidden, memories of his one and only high school girlfriend flooded his mind. As seniors, he and Emily Wilson had been inseparable. He'd spent many a night dreaming of forever with her by his side. But right after graduation, she'd accepted a position to study nursing at a Sydney university and had bid him farewell with hardly more than a kiss on the cheek, a squeeze of his hand and a fond smile. She'd broken his heart. Of course, he'd never told her that, but he suspected she had a fair idea about the dreams he'd had for the two of them. They'd talked about a future together.

He sighed. So much for that. It was so long ago he couldn't believe he was still wasting time thinking about what could have been. She'd left Broken and gotten on with her life. Moved to the city, never to be seen or heard from again. And though she'd finished university a few years ago, she'd never returned to Broken to live.

No doubt she'd hooked up with a flash guy from the city. A fellow nurse, or maybe a doctor. It wasn't unusual for people to find love in their workplace. After all, so many hours of every day were spent there. The only female officer stationed at Broken was a nineteen-year-old probationary constable who talked incessantly about nothing of importance and irritated Zac to death. Some of his colleagues had teased him about the fact Kate liked him, but even if she did, the feeling wasn't mutual.

In fact, he did his best to avoid her, which wasn't easy. It seemed wherever he turned she was there. Like right now. Standing in front of him while he took a seat at his desk and opened the morning newspaper. He ignored her for as long as he could, then with a muffled sigh, he gave her his attention.

"Hi, Kate. How are you this morning?"

She gave him a wide smile. "I'm absolutely fantastic! I had the *best* sleep!" She stretched her arms up over her head. The action pulled her uniform blouse tight across her modest chest. He remained unmoved and forced a semblance of a smile.

"I'm pleased for you. Now, is there something you wanted?"

She shook her head and smiled. "No. Not really. Madge asked me to tell you there are some people out front who want to file a missing person report."

"Okay." Zac pushed away from his desk and stood. He reached for his jacket that hung on the back of his chair and shrugged it on.

"Who is it?"

"I don't know. An older man and a younger woman. That's all I saw."

Zac made his way past the empty desks of the two other detectives—one of whom was Trace—and walked into the reception area. Madge sat behind the counter, guarding it like her life depended on it. In her early sixties, with graying hair and an expanding waistline, Madge had been working as a receptionist at the Broken Police Station for as long as Zac could remember. She'd been there so long she felt like a permanent fixture.

He nodded in her direction by way of greeting. "Kate told me someone wants to file a missing person report."

Madge lifted her gaze from her keyboard and looked at him. "Yes. Pastor Wilson and his daughter, Emily."

Zac felt like he'd been sucker punched. He tried to breathe, but air was suddenly in short supply.

Emily Wilson is here?

He hadn't seen her since high school.

I wonder what she looks like… Has she changed? Will she recognize me?

The questions rushed through him, filling his head with noise. He looked down at his pale blue business shirt. It was clean and freshly pressed and tucked neatly into the waistband of his navy-blue pants. A muted gray-and-red striped tie completed his outfit. Though he'd filled out since high school, he was as fit as he'd always been. His heart thumped in anticipation of seeing her again.

Madge gave him a strange look. "Zac? Are you okay to speak with them?"

He wasn't sure if she was aware of his connection to Emily. Knowing Madge, she probably was. She was an institution in Broken. Nothing got past her.

He quickly recovered his aplomb. "Of course. I'll take them into Interview Room One."

Zac drew in a quick, fortifying breath, smoothed back his hair and opened the door that led into the waiting area. He wasn't sure where to start. Should he offer condolences on the loss of a brother and a son? Emily stood with her back to him beside her father. It gave him a few seconds to take in the fact her blond hair was as long as it had always been and was pulled back in a simple ponytail. She was just as slim as she'd been in high school, but there was a maturity to her lush figure that sent a *zing* of awareness through his body, along with an even deeper need. Doing his best to tamp down the instinctive surge of desire, he greeted them.

"Pastor Wilson? Emily? Hi. It's Zac Barrington. It's nice to see you both again."

At the sound of those familiar, deep tones Emily tensed in shock. She'd know that voice anywhere. With her heart thumping, she forced herself to turn around and face the boy who'd stolen her heart all those years ago. Of course, he wasn't a boy any longer. He was twenty-four. A full-grown man. And boy, did he look it.

His boyish good looks had matured into something that was sure to gain attention wherever he went. Thick dark hair, dark chocolate eyes framed by thick lashes, a neat beard. Shoulders that looked impossibly broad, a wide muscled chest that tapered to slim hips and long legs. He'd always been taller than her, but now he towered over her. Six foot two or three, at least.

She couldn't believe he was here in Broken. Last she'd heard, he was working somewhere on the central coast. Though she didn't make a habit of inquiring about him, he came up in conversation with her parents every now and then. After all, they'd been well aware she'd dated him in high school and how serious the two of them had been. They hadn't said anything, but she was sure they'd expected the two of them to marry right after graduation, like most of the people who knew them in Broken.

God! She hadn't seen him since she'd walked away. Her busy work schedule meant she didn't come home all that often and when she did, she mostly spent the time with her parents. She hadn't heard Zac was back in town. The fact he looked even better than he had in high school only irritated her now. She didn't want to see any Barrington, let alone the one who used to own her heart.

She thought of the decision she'd made all those years ago and quelled the swift stab of guilt. Averting her gaze, she willed away the heat that flooded her face and focused on the fact the Barringtons were responsible for her brother's death. Anger poured through her. She glared at him.

"We'd like to see somebody else."

Zac's eyes flared with surprise at her response and something that looked very much like hurt, until he covered it up with a bland smile.

"I'm sorry, but there *is* no one else. Everyone's out. Unless you want to wait for someone to return, then I'm all you've got."

Emily tamped down her frustration. "How long will they be?"

Zac continued to regard her with that same bland expression. "Who knows? If they've been called out on a case, it could be all day. Feel free to wait if you like."

With that, he turned away, dismissing them. He took a step toward the door from which he'd appeared. Emily bit her lip. She glanced at her father. He looked pale and drawn. He'd been frightened at the thought of attending the police station. He was even more concerned another night had passed and his wife had failed to return. She wasn't sure he had it in him to wait around for another officer to arrive.

"Wait," she called, hating herself but having no choice.

Zac came to a halt and slowly turned back to face her. One dark eyebrow was raised in silent query.

"This is important. My mother's been missing for more than two days. We'll talk to you," she added reluctantly.

"Your mother?" Once again, surprise momentarily widened his eyes. Then he nodded briefly, all business. "Okay. Follow me."

He led them through the doorway from which he'd come and into a small windowless room. It was painted a depressing shade of gray. The walls matched the color of the industrial-strength carpet and the vinyl laminate on the table that stood in the middle of the room. Four plastic gray chairs completed the room's sparse furniture.

Zac took a seat across from them and dragged a blank notepad toward him. He pulled out a pen from his pocket.

"Let's start with the basics. Name, address, age."

Emily stared at him for a moment. So, he was all business. She guessed that was just as well. The less personal the better. She glanced at her father. He remained mute beside her. She turned back to Zac. "Lorraine Wilson. 445 Brunswick Street, Broken. She's fifty-eight," she supplied.

Zac wrote the information down. "When did you last see her?"

Once again, Emily looked at her father. "Dad?" she prompted.

Her father blinked. "Um… It was three nights ago now. I got home from evening prayers and she wasn't home."

"What time was that?" Zac asked.

"About eight o'clock."

"Were you expecting her to be there?" Zac asked.

"Yes. She's always home once the sun goes down. She doesn't like walking around on her own at night, even in Broken."

Zac frowned. "She doesn't drive?"

"No," Emily responded. "I thought you might remember that. She doesn't have a license. She wasn't interested in learning to drive. She always said she could do whatever she needed to do on foot."

"What about shopping for groceries?" Zac asked.

"I mostly did that," Emily's father responded. "If there was something Lorraine needed at short notice, she'd usually just walk to the shops."

"So, she wasn't there when you got home from evening prayers. When was the last time you actually saw her?" Zac asked.

Emily's father stared down at his hands where they were clenched in his lap. He still looked so pale and distraught. Her heart ached for how hard this must be for him. As far as she knew, her parents had never spent a night apart in the thirty years of their marriage. She couldn't imagine how disorientating this must be for him.

"Dad?" she prompted softly once again.

Her father sighed and looked at her with eyes that sparkled with tears. "Earlier that day. At lunch time. I came home for lunch, like I usually do. She was there. We sat and ate and talked. Then I went back to my office."

"What did you talk about?" Zac asked.

Her father shrugged. "I don't know. Nothing much. Just conversation, you know?'

Zac scribbled a few notes. "How did she seem?"

Emily's father shrugged again. "I don't know. Just like she always is."

"And how is that? Was there anything to indicate something might have been troubling her?"

"No. Not that I recall."

"Did she mention she intended to go somewhere? Down the street? To visit a friend?"

"I don't think so."

Emily frowned. "I thought you told me last night she mentioned Rosie Murray?"

"You're right. But not at that lunch. Besides, I talked to Rosie. She hasn't seen her."

"Is there anything missing from the house? Her handbag? A suitcase?" Zac asked.

Emily's father frowned; his expression grew confused. "I don't know. I don't think so."

Zac sat forward. "Her handbag is still there?"

Her father shook his head. "Yes. No. I don't know. Maybe. I'll have to look."

"Did she usually share her daily movements with you?" Zac asked.

"Yes. Most of the time. But sometimes things came up... A phone call from a parishioner in need, a sick friend. You know how it is." He gave Zac a pointed look. "She didn't need my permission to leave, Detective."

Zac felt the heat from his blush all the way up his neck and across his cheeks. He ducked his head and pretended to write additional notes. All the time, he was acutely aware of Emily's gaze on him. He wondered if she'd noticed any changes in him. If she remembered how it had been. Remembered how she'd broken his heart and left without a backward glance...

Get a grip... I'm taking down a missing person report... Focus....

"Have you tried calling her?" Zac asked, directing his question to Bob.

"No," he said.

Zac frowned in surprise. "No?"

"She doesn't own a mobile phone," Emily explained. "We've both tried to give her one countless times. She's always refused."

"Okay, so no mobile phone." He looked at Bob. "Is there any reason you can think of why she might want to leave?"

The flare of anger on Emily's face told him he might have overstepped the mark and in truth, what he remembered of Mr and Mrs Wilson, they never had a cross word to say to each other. In fact, they'd seemed completely devoted to one another. Still, it had been years since he'd been in their circle and the question needed to be asked, if only for the sake of thoroughness.

"What the hell?" Emily exploded. "Of course she didn't have a reason to leave!"

Zac kept his composure and merely nodded. He looked at Emily's father again. "Bob?"

"Don't answer that, Dad! Zac's being incredibly rude and arrogant. If he remembered anything at all about you and Mom, he could never ask such a question." She shot him a disgusted look. "I wouldn't expect anything less from a Barrington."

The last comment she mumbled under her breath. Zac tensed with surprise. "What's that supposed to mean?"

Emily glared at him. "As if you don't know!" She shook her head, her eyes blazing. "How dare you insinuate there was some issue between my parents! You'll never meet two more loving, devoted people. They've been together thirty years! Thirty *years!* And never a cross word between them. I should know. I lived with them most of my life."

"But not in the last six years." Zac couldn't help the gibe.

Angry color blazed across Emily's cheeks. She glared at him. "Don't go making this personal. This is about my missing mother, Zac. We're worried about her safety. She's never stayed out all night before. Something's happened."

Zac drew in a breath and nodded. "What about her health? Any issues to be concerned about?"

"No," Emily answered. "She's fighting fit."

"Okay. I'll file the report and put out a BOLO—be on the lookout—for her." He turned back to Bob.

"Can you give me a list of her friends and their contact details?"

Bob nodded. "I can give you names. I don't have contact details. Lorraine mostly visits in person."

Zac handed him a sheet of blank paper and a pen. Then he turned to Emily. "Do you have a recent photo of your mother?"

With a tight nod, Emily pulled out her phone and scrolled through her photos. A moment later, she airdropped one to him.

"Thank you," he murmured. "I'll start making some inquires." He looked at Bob. "Write down your contact details." His gaze slid to Emily. "Is the number attached to this photo the best to contact you on?"

She nodded curtly. Bob slowly wrote down his details and then slid the piece of paper back to him. Zac glanced down at it and then looked at the two of them again. "I'll make a few inquires. I'll be in touch as soon as I have anything to report. In the meantime, if Lorraine shows up, please let me know."

In silence, he showed them out. Animosity continued to wash off Emily in waves. Her attitude surprised and confused him. Okay, so they'd parted on less than amicable terms, but that had been more than six years ago. And *she'd* been the one who rejected *him*.

So, what's she so mad about? Is it because of Evan? Maybe I should have offered my condolences... Gotten it out in the open...

She'd been obviously reluctant to have him involved in the case, even to the point where she'd tried to get someone else to take the report. Then there was her anger at his very reasonable question about whether there might be a reason why her mother might have left. Emily knew that Zac had known her parents from years earlier and he'd always had a great deal of respect for them. She must realize he wasn't trying to disrespect them now; merely trying to get some clarity on her disappearance.

Maybe her hostility was due to their past history. Nothing else made sense. He hadn't seen nor spoken to her since their breakup. She'd already cut him completely from her life. And that was her decision, not his.

Chapter Three

Emily settled her father on the couch in the living room and then went into the kitchen to put the kettle on. He'd barely spoken on the journey home. Instead, he'd stared out the window, looking pale and scared. Her heart went out to him. She couldn't imagine the agony he was going through. His wife of thirty years was missing and no one knew where she was.

Not knowing if she was lying injured somewhere, unable to go for help, was the worst of it. Every time Emily's mind wandered in that direction, she forced her thoughts elsewhere. She couldn't allow herself to think like that. No, for everyone's sake, she needed to stay positive.

Leo jumped out of his bed and padded over to her. She'd left Sydney too early that morning to call and arrange to leave him at a kennel and she hadn't wanted to do that anyway. Her parents loved Leo as much as she did. This wasn't the first time she'd brought him home with her.

She crouched down beside him and patted his head. "Hey there, buddy. Whatcha doing?"

He whined and licked her hand. His soft tongue tickled her skin. She picked him up and stood, burying her face against his soft fur.

"It's okay, buddy. We're going to find her. I know we will." She wasn't sure which one of them she was trying to convince.

Waiting for the kettle to boil, she wandered into her mother's room. She hated to admit it had been months since she'd been there. She'd been so busy at work and on her rare days off, she was usually too exhausted to make the ninety-minute drive through heavy Sydney traffic down to Broken. Now she looked around for a clue, anything that might indicate where her mother had gone, but everything looked like it always had.

Recalling what Zac had said about anything missing, she set Leo down and opened her mother's wardrobe. The racks were filled with clothes. There was nothing out of place. No empty hangers. No gaping spaces. She stepped inside the master bathroom. Two toothbrushes sat in a cup on the sink, along with her mother's hairbrush. It only reinforced Emily's fears that her mother was hurt and unable to go for help. One thing was for certain: Nothing in the room indicated her mother had planned a getaway, no matter what Zac might have implied.

She frowned. She was still mad at Zac for asking that question. He knew her parents. Had known them for years. He knew as well as she did how devoted they were to each other. Asking such a question had been downright rude and insensitive. Okay, she understood he was trying to do his job and eliminate possibilities. The more he eliminated, the closer they got to finding her and that's what they all wanted. Still... It was unnecessarily offensive just the same.

Her mind shied away from the possibility her parents' perfect marriage might have hit a rough patch. She couldn't bring herself to ask her father if they'd argued that last time. The truth was, she didn't want to know. Shame burned through her. She cared for the bravest, most courageous kids she knew and here she was, scared of asking a question because she didn't want to know the answer. She was a coward.

The thought wouldn't have even occurred to her if Zac hadn't posed that stupid question. This was his fault. He'd grown annoyingly more good looking with age. She would have felt better if he'd grown soft and fat, or shown some signs of having pined for her! But that was churlish thinking and, if she were honest with herself, unfair. After all, she'd done the leaving.

The fact he still looked so good was just another reason to steer well clear of him. She'd broken up with him because she was moving away and didn't want the hassle and stress of a long-distance relationship. She'd also wanted to give herself the freedom of dating others, enjoying single life at university. That didn't mean she'd stopped caring about him; just that she'd wanted to experience more, and in the broader world.

The fact she'd used him as the measuring stick against her relationships that had followed, she chose to ignore. She'd allow herself to acknowledge that she hadn't stopped caring about him, but she'd been scared of being stuck in small-town Broken and had taken the first opportunity to get out.

Though she'd accepted her future no longer included Zac, she'd been unable to completely obliterate the memories of how he'd made her feel. Then the accident at the Barrington mine had happened. The attitude of the Barringtons had enraged her and her anger had put an end to any lingering tender feelings. She firmly believed the Barringtons were the reason her brother was dead.

Okay, so Zac hadn't been personally involved, but it was impossible to separate him from what his family had done. The irony of the situation wasn't lost on her. She wanted nothing to do with him, but she needed to deal with him because he was her chance of bringing her mother home.

Please, Mom. Please, come home... Where are you?

Zac almost collided with his brother on the way out of the station.

"Whoa!" Trace said, neatly sidestepping him. "Where are you off to in such a hurry?"

"Sorry," Zac mumbled. "I was miles away."

Trace grinned. "So I gathered. You nearly ran right into me. What's going on?"

"Emily's back in town. Her mother's missing."

Trace's expression filled with surprise. "You saw Emily again?"

"Yes. She came in with her father, Bob. I assume she was with him for moral support."

"How is she?"

Zac was flooded with images of Emily looking every bit as beautiful as she'd been at eighteen. "She's okay."

Trace gave him a look. Zac averted his gaze. His meeting with Emily was still fresh in his mind. He hadn't had time to analyze every minute detail. There was no way he was up to talking to his brother about her.

"Wait. You said her mother's missing. For how long?"

"She hasn't been seen since the afternoon of the twenty-third."

Trace frowned. "That's three days ago. Does anyone have a clue about where she might have gone?"

"No. Emily was adamant her mother wouldn't have just walked away from her life. Bob doesn't have a clue where she might be. He's pretty shaken up about the whole thing. According to Emily, they haven't spent a night apart in thirty years until now." Zac frowned. "Come to think of it, Bob made no comment either way."

"I remember Lorraine Wilson. Sweet, gentle, softly spoken," Trace said. "Of course, there was a lot of grief when Evan died."

"Yes. That was tragic. Still, in all the years I knew her, I've never heard an angry word escape her lips. She's always been kind and helpful. I haven't seen her since my return to Broken, but back when we were young, she was always supportive and interested in me and my future. I think she approved of me."

"Why wouldn't she?" Trace chuckled. "You were a catch for her daughter."

"It wasn't just that," Zac protested. "She saw the good in everyone. Still, the mine incident devastated the family from all reports." He paused and then added, "Let's hope she's okay. She doesn't have a mobile phone, which is going to make it more challenging to track her down."

"Wow. I didn't think people like that existed in the twenty-first century, but it's probably more common than we think with the older community."

Zac grimaced. "Yeah, well apparently Lorraine's one of them."

"Have you checked with her friends?"

"There's where I'm going now. Door knocking. Bob didn't have any contact numbers for her friends." At Trace's frown, Zac explained. "Lorraine preferred to catch up face to face. I guess that's why she didn't keep phone numbers. I could go online and get contact details, but I prefer to talk face to face anyway. It's impossible to read body language over the phone."

Trace winked. "You've learned your lessons well. Let me know how you get on. I guess without any signs of foul play, we're going to have to treat this as a straight missing person's case and do the due diligence."

"Right. I'll go and talk to her friends, see if anyone knows anything about where she might be and when they last saw her. I'll see you later."

With that, Zac headed toward the police cruiser. He checked the piece of paper where Bob had written down the names and addresses of his wife's friends. The first one lived only a few blocks away. Entering the address into his GPS, he pulled out onto the road.

As he cruised along the quiet streets of Broken, his mind went back to Emily. The shock of coming face to face with her after so many years was still reverberating. He couldn't believe she'd appeared in the station like that. She'd looked just as surprised to see him there. He wondered if she'd known he was a cop.

Did she keep tabs on me, like I did on her?

Not that he'd gone out of his way to inquire about her. A casual question here or there to his family was about as intrusive as he'd gotten and of course, they'd told him about Evan's death.

He was curious, that's all. There had been a time when he thought they'd spend the rest of their lives together. Feelings that strong didn't dissipate overnight. In fact, if he were brutally honest, his deep feelings for Emily were still there. They'd never really gone away, despite him having had a number of relationships since.

Emily was one of the reasons, if not the key reason, he'd left his stressful job in the Drug Enforcement Agency on the central coast for a quieter life in the country. He could have relocated anywhere, but his carefully placed questions to his family and friends had helped to ascertain that Emily wasn't married. He'd dared not push his luck and spark too much curiosity by asking if she were seeing anyone. It was enough that she was still single.

A marriage would have killed off all his dreams for good. As it was, he still harbored hope. He'd returned to his hometown because it was where the only woman he'd ever loved used to live and a part of him wanted to do whatever he could to rekindle their romance, given half a chance—or say goodbye to her forever.

Closure. That's what he needed. That's what he'd come home for. Emily had never given him closure. He was determined this time she would.

He'd known their paths would cross again. Even though she lived in Sydney, her parents were still in Broken and she'd always been close to them. Broken was a small town. It was only a matter of time before they ran into each other on one of her visits home. Now that day had come, and he was topsy-turvy with emotion. All the feelings he'd had for her had come rushing back, leaving him uncertain. One thing was for sure: seeing her had confirmed he was still in love with her. Now he had to figure out how to reconnect. They weren't off to an encouraging start.

If their initial meeting was anything to go by, any tender feelings she'd had for him had long since died. Aside from the death of her brother, which had had nothing to do with him, he couldn't explain her overt hostility. Did she really blame him?

He didn't know much about the case, other than it had been an accident and that the company had eventually settled.

Regardless of her antagonism, he intended to get to the bottom of it. In the meantime, he needed to find her mom.

He remembered how devoted Emily's parents had been to each other. Not only had he spent many a weekend with Emily at their house, but he'd also attended Pastor Wilson's church every Sunday, along with his brothers and sisters. Lorraine Wilson had always been there, seated off to the side, looking at her husband with adoring eyes, ready to assist where she was able.

Zac also remembered Emily's older brother. Evan had been three years ahead of them in school. Zac hadn't known him well. Evan had barely acknowledged him whenever he was at the Wilson residence and had mostly kept to himself. The accident had been unfortunate and while Zac hadn't been in Broken at the time, he'd heard from family that it had devastated the Wilsons and shaken the town. He hadn't been able to offer condolences earlier because Emily had beaten him to the punch and knocked him off balance.

Arriving at his destination, Zac shelved the thought and climbed out of the cruiser. According to Bob Wilson, the house belonged to Anita Marshall. Zac had a vague recollection of an older woman with a walking stick who grew prize-winning roses. The neat front garden certainly bore evidence of an abundance of rose bushes, all winter-bare and pruned back, ready for the spring.

Zac climbed the steps to the front veranda and knocked on the door. He was immediately met with a chorus of loud barking and yapping from somewhere inside the house. As he waited for the occupant to answer, he looked around him. The *circa* 1950s weatherboard cottage was in good repair, with fresh paint and new window trims. The butter-yellow color on the timber contrasted nicely against the white trim. It was a picture-perfect cottage and spoke volumes of the pride its occupant took in her home.

A moment later, an elderly woman met him at the door. By her feet were two fluffy white Maltese dogs. As they caught sight of Zac, their barking increased to a frenzy.

"Snowball! Archie! Be quiet," the woman ordered.

The dogs stopped barking but remained close by their master's feet, their big dark eyes ogling him distrustfully. Though he'd never met Anita Marshall, he knew her in passing from years ago. He greeted her with a smile.

"Mrs Marshall? I'm Detective Zac Barrington. It's been a long time. Do you mind if I come in?"

The elderly woman smiled and pulled open the screen door. "Zac Barrington! You're one of Frank and Evelyn's boys."

"Yes, I certainly am."

"I remember you all when you were children. All nine of you perched up together on those hard wooden pews! I used to marvel at your mother, keeping you all so quiet."

Zac grinned. "Not always so quiet. There were more than a few squabbles Mom and Dad had to referee."

She looked aghast. "Surely not in church!"

"Afraid so. I hate to disillusion you, but we weren't always perfect." He winked.

She laughed and waved away his comment. A becoming blush stained her wrinkled cheeks. "Get on with you. I don't believe it."

He grinned and gave her a wide-eyed look of innocence. "Would I lie to you, Mrs Marshall?"

She chuckled. Her gaze moved over him. "So, you're a police officer. Imagine that!" And then her expression sobered. "Is there something I can help you with?"

He saw the mild look of concern in her eyes and hastened to reassure her. "I'm just making some inquires about Lorraine Wilson. Her husband told me you and Lorraine are friends. Is that right?'

"Yes, we've been friends for years. Of course, she's at least a decade younger than me, but we get on like a house on fire. Is she all right?"

The concern was back in her eyes. Once again, Zac tried to reassure her. "I hope so. The thing is, Bob hasn't seen her for a few days. He's worried. She didn't say anything to him about going away. I was wondering if she said anything to you?"

"No, not at all. In fact, I ran into her down at the supermarket on Monday and she told me she was buying ingredients for a new recipe. She was going to cook it for dinner that night."

He pulled out his notebook and jotted the information down. "Was that Monday the twenty-third?"

"Yes. That's right. The twenty-third."

"What time was that?"

"Oh, it must have been around half-past eleven. I remember I'd just finished at the hairdresser. Got a new rinse." She primped at her hair self-consciously before adding, "What time did Bob last see her?"

"He said he came home for lunch that day and they ate together. Then he went back to his office. When he returned later that evening, she wasn't there."

A frown appeared on Mrs Marshall's forehead. "That's very strange. Lorraine isn't keen to go anywhere at night. She doesn't drive, you see. She walks everywhere. And as safe as Broken is, nowhere is completely safe, right? I mean, a young boy was murdered a couple of months ago. Murdered! Here! In Broken!" She shuddered.

"Was there anything unusual about her demeanor the other day? Did she appear distracted? Upset?"

"No. Nothing like that. She was her normal self."

"How long have you known Lorraine?"

"Oh, it must be going on twenty-five years! I used to babysit her children when they were young. Little Evan and baby Emily. Such a shame about Evan, wasn't it?"

Zac frowned. "Yes. An accident, I believe."

The woman gave him a sideways look. "I'm not sure the Wilson family would agree with that."

Zac's frown deepened. "Why would you say that?"

"The family blames the mine for the accident. There was a court case and all. Oh dear. That was your family wasn't it. Oh dear. I'm so sorry. And you and Emily used to be so tight."

"Mrs Marshall, I've only recently moved back to Broken. The courts found it to be an accident. I didn't know the Wilsons blamed my family."

"Yes. Well, the courts might have determined it was an accident, but let me assure you, the family thinks differently."

Zac felt like he'd taken a punch to his stomach. That was the last thing he'd expected her to say. He'd thought Emily's earlier animosity had arisen from his failure to offer condolences. It hadn't occurred to him she blamed him for her brother's death.

"I didn't know. It was ruled an accident..."

"Lorraine and Bob took it hard," Mrs Marshall continued. "Lorraine especially. She's still grieving. Of course, it doesn't help when her only remaining child lives so far away. And poor Emily! She's so busy at the hospital! She hardly has time to visit anymore."

Zac nodded, still feeling dazed. "What about Bob? How's he been since Evan's death?"

The old woman compressed her lips. "Bob's always been a pillar of strength. I guess he gets that from the Lord. He was devastated by Evan's death, but he seems to be able to handle that kind of thing better than most."

"How was he with Lorraine? Did he understand her grief? It must have been difficult, counseling her along with his parishioners and dealing with his own loss."

"Oh, yes. I'm sure it's been tough on Bob. And you're right; he's so busy running his parish. But the two of them have always been inseparable. He'd do anything for Lorraine and she feels the same. They might be grieving over the death of their son, but their relationship's as strong as ever. At least, that's what she's always led me to believe."

"So, Lorraine never confided in you any concerns she might have had?"

Mrs Marshall frowned. "Concerns? What do you mean?"

"Nothing in particular. Just canvassing all options."

"No. She never expressed any concerns. Like I said, she was her usual self. Of course, some of her zest for life has dimmed since Evan's death, but that's understandable."

Zac gave her a tight smile. "Yes, of course." He looked down at the piece of paper in his hands. "Bob gave me a list of Lorraine's friends. Unfortunately, he didn't have any of their contact numbers. You wouldn't be able to help me out there, would you?"

"Let me take a look," the woman said.

Zac handed her the paper. She reached for the glasses that hung around her neck and put them on. She scanned the names.

"Yes, I think I have most of these ladies' numbers. Hold on a moment. I'll get my address book."

She turned away and disappeared down the hallway. The dogs padded after her. A few minutes later, she reappeared, dogs in tow. Zac pulled out a pen while she flipped through the book and found each phone number.

"Thank you," Zac said when she was finished.

"No problem. Happy to help. I hope you find her. She's a dear friend. Is it okay if I help? Ring some of her friends? I'll let you know if I find out anything."

"Of course. The more people looking for her, the better." Zac reached into his shirt pocket and pulled out a business card. He handed it to the woman.

"If you hear anything or think of anything else that might be relevant, please call me."

She took the card and nodded, her eyes once again filling with concern. "I will. And please, if you find her, will you let me know? We're expecting her to be at the Country Women's Association meeting on Saturday. She was baking a cake for morning tea."

"Yes, of course."

With that, Zac turned away. He dropped the notebook back in his pocket, along with his pen. He was halfway down the front porch steps when she called out to him.

"Oh, I just remembered something. I don't know if it's important or even worth mentioning..."

Zac turned and paused. "What is it?"

"I was walking Snowball and Archie to the park on Monday afternoon. The one at the end of Brunswick Street. The path there takes me right past Lorraine's house. I saw a man outside her house. He was just kind of standing there by her front gate."

Zac moved closer and pulled out his notebook and pen again. "Did you recognize him?"

"No. I've never seen him before."

"What did he look like?"

"Dark graying hair, dark eyes. Unshaven. A bit unkempt. I kind of got the impression he might have been homeless." She paused and then added with a delicate twitching of her nose. "He smelled."

"How old was he?"

"I don't know. Mid-fifties. Maybe a bit older."

"Was he Caucasian?"

"No. He looked Aboriginal."

"What time was this?"

The woman's brow furrowed in thought. "It was after lunch. Maybe around three."

Zac made some notes. "Did you speak with him?"

"No. Snowball and Archie began barking at him and I was a bit embarrassed by their fuss. He looked scared of them, even though they wouldn't hurt a fly." She looked down at the dogs at her feet. "Would you, my sweet babies?" She returned her attention to Zac. "We just kept on walking by."

"Did you look back at all?"

She nodded. "Yes. It was strange seeing him outside Lorraine's house. I wondered what he was doing there."

"Was he still there when you looked back?"

"Yes, but as soon as he saw me looking at him again, he walked off."

"Which direction did he go?"

"He crossed the street and headed east."

The poorer part of town was located on the eastern side of Broken. Zac made a mental note and then thanked the woman for her time, along with a repeat of his earlier request that she contact him if she thought of anything else that might be helpful. Armed with the best clue he'd received all day, Zac said goodbye and left.

Chapter Four

After spending time with her father sharing a pot of tea and a plate of freshly made sandwiches but not much in the way of conversation, Emily excused herself to collect her suitcase from the car. Until now, she hadn't had time to get settled. Her only thoughts had been on reporting her mother missing. She left her father staring vacantly at the floor in the living room and slipped outside. Leo followed her.

She'd parked behind her father's car, inside the fenced front yard. She retrieved her suitcase and a winter coat she'd draped over the back seat and then headed back inside. She set the suitcase down on the floor in her childhood room. Leo padded in behind her. She looked around her and was hit by a sudden wave of nostalgia. Though she always stayed in this room whenever she came to visit, somehow this time things felt different. She knew what it was.

Mom's not here. That's what's different... The place feels empty without her... I can't remember a time when she wasn't here... Not even when I was a child...

Her mother had always been home when Emily and her brother arrived back from school. She'd always been there to ask about their day, pour cold lemonade in the summer and hot chocolate in the winter. There was always a plate of freshly baked cookies to eat. Emily had taken it for granted that everyone came home to a mom like that. She was in the third grade before she discovered that some kids came home to an empty house—no freshly baked cookies, no lemonade, no hot chocolate, no mom. She remembered feeling sad for those kids and incredibly grateful for her mom.

Her room appeared much the same as it had when she was a teenager. The same pink-and-white bedspread, the same pink walls. The glossy posters of Brittany Spears, Miley Cyrus and One Direction she had plastered around the room, an indication of the music she'd have blaring from her speaker. The love letters from Zac Barrington she kept hidden in a shoe box under her bed which remained there to this very day. Somehow, she hadn't been able to part with them.

So many memories... They'd had such a fun, carefree time... So much love and laughter...

It all seemed so long ago. It was six years since she'd left Zac and if she were honest, had broken his heart. She knew, because she'd broken her own in the process. Broken *them*. It felt like a lifetime ago. She thought back to the way he'd reacted to her antagonism at the station. He'd appeared shocked and genuinely hurt and confused. It wasn't possible that he hadn't heard about Evan. It might have been years since Zac had lived there, but she was sure he would have kept in contact with his family and something as big as that, especially when it involved the Barringtons...

No, there was no way she'd believe he didn't know about Evan.

But perhaps he doesn't know how much I blame his family?

That was possible. Zac had also spent quite a few years away from Broken. He hadn't been in town when it happened, nor seen the toll the court case had taken on them. He might not be aware of what she considered the Barrington "pay-off" to go away. Perhaps that explained his confusion over her anger? Still, that didn't absolve him of responsibility. He wasn't directly liable for the decisions of his family, but they were *his* family.

As far as she was concerned, he was guilty by association. He hadn't even reached out to express condolences, even back then. It was likely unfair, but she couldn't think about any Barrington without linking them to what had happened to her brother, and sadly, she didn't think that would ever change.

How fickle was fate in putting her back in Zac's orbit? She'd be forced to engage with him for the foreseeable future, or at least until her mother was found. Had Emily known he was back in Broken, she would have avoided him altogether but now that wasn't possible. He was the lead investigator and she desperately needed him to find her mother. At the very least, they were going to have to talk on the phone.

That reminded her she hadn't heard from him since she and her father had left the station earlier that morning. She could only assume that meant he hadn't yet found her mother, but she was going crazy not knowing what was going on. He'd said he was going to talk to her mother's friends, see if they could shed any light on her whereabouts. As much as she didn't want to speak with him again, she needed to put on her big girl panties and make that phone call. Drawing in a fortifying breath, she scrummaged in her handbag on the bed and dialed his number.

Zac had spent most of the day interviewing Lorraine's friends, systematically moving down the list. Luckily for him, almost all of the women had been home. Everyone he'd spoken to had been equally confused about Lorraine's disappearance. They had nothing but good things to say about the pastor and his wife. They not only loved each other; they were loved by everyone in the town. Always holding hands. Very affectionate with each other. Always together. This confirmed what Zac remembered of them from years earlier. No one could offer any reason why Lorraine might have left.

Zac thought back to the pastor's demeanor at the police station. There was no denying the man was distressed. He'd been pale and shaking, obviously upset. But he'd also been very quiet. Had only responded to questions after prompting. Zac wasn't quite sure what to make of that. Of course, not everyone expressed their distress aloud. Some people went into themselves.

Is that how it is with Bob?

And yet, Anita Marshall had said the pastor had been so stoic over his son's death. Had Bob only put on a brave face for the sake of Lorraine? He didn't appear stoic now. In fact, at the station, he looked like he was barely coping with his wife's disappearance. Until that last remark about Lorraine not needing his permission to venture out. That seemed to have gotten him fired up. What had that been about?

So where is she?

As Zac turned away from the woman who was the last name on his list, his phone rang. He checked the screen, but the number was unfamiliar.

"Zac Barrington."

There was a pause. "Zac. It's Emily."

His heart skipped a beat. Now he knew she blamed his family for Evan, he wasn't sure where to start. Some of his confusion about her earlier antagonism had faded, but he was still puzzled about what Evan's death had to do with *him*. Before he had a moment to put the question to her, she spoke again.

"What have you been doing to find my mother?"

Her aggressive tone took him aback, but he remained calm. "Hello, Emily. I've interviewed most of her friends. No one knows where she is. Nor did anyone have any knowledge of an upcoming trip."

"I already told you my mother didn't go away! There's no way my mother would up and leave without telling my father—or me, for that matter. Besides, she doesn't have a license, remember? To get anywhere out of Broken, she'd have to take a bus or the train. We both know that. Have you checked the security cameras at the train station and the bus depot?"

Once again, Zac ignored her demanding tone. "Not yet. I've been caught up all day interviewing her friends. There were quite a number of them on the list."

"Of course there were. My mother's well-known and well-loved. Their pastor's wife. I shouldn't have to tell you that."

Zac bit back a retort and drew in a calming breath. "Have you found anything at your parents' house that might give us a clue as to her whereabouts?"

"No. Not as far as I can tell. Everything's where it should be, including her toothbrush."

A feeling of unease stirred in Zac's gut. No one left town without their toothbrush. "What about her clothes? Anything missing?"

"Not that I can tell."

"Any missing suitcases?"

"How the hell would I know? I haven't lived here for years. You should be here asking my father those questions. Where are you, anyway?"

Zac's patience shredded. "And yet earlier you were adamant they'd never spent a night apart! For God's sake, Emily! Why are you being so antagonistic? Is this about Evan? I'm sorry I didn't say anything earlier, but I had no idea you're blaming my family for the accident."

"You're *sorry?* Is that all you have to say?"

Her tone had become more strident. Zac closed his eyes briefly and drew in a deep breath, striving to hold on to his temper.

"What do you want me to say? Losing a brother so young is terrible. I'm sorry for your loss. I would have offered my condolences at the time, but I didn't know where to find you." It was a low blow, but it was also the truth.

"*Your* family's responsible," she hissed.

"Emily, be reasonable. Yes, my family own the mine, but the courts ruled it a terrible accident. I understand how difficult that might be for you to accept, but that's the truth."

"Bah! The truth's for anyone who can afford it. Evan's death was no accident."

Zac was stunned. Did she think it was murder? He wished his older brother, Vaughan, was around to talk to about it. Vaughan had until recently run the day-to-day operations of Barrington Mining. For sure he'd know what had gone on. The only problem was, Vaughan had gone AWOL. Was apparently living up life in Bali.

No one knew why he'd suddenly dropped out of life and abandoned everything to holiday in a tropical paradise, but what if his leaving had something to do with Evan's accident? He'd been gone for nearly four months. No one knew when he might be back. What if something had happened to make Vaughan feel he could never come back? Zac couldn't bear to think about that.

I need to talk to Dad...

As head of Barrington Mining, Frank would have deeper insights into Evan's death. He'd also know if something more had gone on than a tragic workplace accident. He might even know the extent, if any, of Vaughan's involvement in the court case. Swallowing a sigh, Zac made a mental note to raise the issue with his father as soon as he could.

From the silence on the other end of the phone, Zac could tell Emily wasn't satisfied with his answer. He didn't know if they could move on when she had a fundamental belief that his family, and he by association, was responsible for her brother's death. It was untenable.

He sighed.

So much for moving back to Broken to win back her heart...

Up until now, he'd thought all he had to do was convince her she still had feelings for him. He'd had no idea she'd already drawn up the battle lines over her brother. He wasn't sure he'd ever be able to convince her otherwise.

One thing he did know was that there was no point rehashing the issue any further. Her mother was missing, and he was determined to do everything he could to find her. Finding her and bringing her home might go some way to redeeming him in Emily's eyes. He could only hope.

He cleared his throat in an effort to get the conversation back on track. "Like I said, I've found nothing yet to indicate where your mother might be or why she left. I haven't yet checked the public transport options, but I'll follow up on that. There's also the possibility she left with someone else. Or of course, she could have hitchhiked."

"Really?" Emily's tone was incredulous. "You really think my mother might have hitchhiked?"

Zac flushed. "You're right. I can't imagine Lorraine doing that."

"Besides," Emily continued. "Why would she feel the need to leave? We've already been over this, Zac. You're going around in circles."

He heard the frustration in her voice and understood it. "You're right. According to one of her friends, your mother was planning to try out a new recipe for dinner that night. She was seen in the supermarket buying the ingredients earlier that day. That's hardly the actions of someone planning to disappear."

Along with the fact her toothbrush was still there...

Nothing made sense. Someone must know where she was. He needed to do more digging into the man Anita Marshall had seen lurking outside Lorraine's house. Though there was no evidence linking him to her disappearance, he was definitely a person of interest and someone Zac wanted to talk to. Maybe he'd find a clue to Lorraine's whereabouts at her house.

"Did your mother do any work with the homeless? Someone who looked homeless was seen in the vicinity of her house the day she went missing."

"Mom's involved with a number of charity projects, but I don't know about the homeless. Dad might know. She does volunteer at a soup kitchen."

"Do you mind if I stop by your house and take a look around? Maybe take the opportunity to ask him?"

"I already told you nothing's missing."

"I understand, but I'd like to see for myself."

He heard her sigh. "Sure. Whatever helps."

"Is it all right if I drop by now? I'm already in the neighborhood."

"Come whenever you want."

"Great. I'll see you soon."

Less than five minutes later, Zac arrived at Pastor Wilson's church. Right next door was the rectory. The place was pretty much as Zac remembered it. Not even the cushions on the couch in the living room had changed.

Zac looked around. "Where's your dad?"

"He's been moping around the house all day. I've never seen him like this, not even when Evan died. I finally convinced him to go to his office next door. He always has so much to do there. Parishioners often drop in to see him, needing assistance. Besides, there's nothing he can do here except sit around and get himself worked up over the fact Mom's not here. That can't be good for him."

"This must be very difficult for him," Zac said.

Emily merely nodded. A little ball of white fluff came bounding toward him, barking madly. Emily bent and picked the dog up and cuddled him to her chest.

"This is Leo," she said.

Zac gave the dog a scratch. "Hello, Leo. You're a bit cute."

"Yes, he is," Emily agreed.

Zac moved around the living room and into the kitchen. The place was neat as a pin, with everything in its place. He went back to the front door and examined it for any signs of forced entry. He did the same thing with all the windows and the back door. Everything looked intact.

"Do you mind if I look in your parents' bedroom?"

"No. Follow me."

Emily led him to a room in the back of the house. Along the way, they passed her old room. He refrained from letting his gaze stray in that direction. Though her parents had forbidden her from ever taking him to her room, he'd been there once when they'd found the courage to break the rule—while her parents had been out. All Zac remembered was a profusion of pink before guilt got the better of Emily and she'd hurried him out. They'd giggled about it afterwards.

The bedroom Lorraine shared with her husband was also neat and tidy. The queen-size bed was made. There were no clothes on the floor. He poked his head into the bathroom. As Emily had said, there were two toothbrushes in a cup on the sink. He pulled open the door to the medicine cabinet above the vanity. A few bits and pieces—face creams, antiseptic, a cake of unused soap. Band-Aids, cold sore cream, a razor, over-the-counter pain medication. Nothing unusual and nothing that indicated where she might be.

His shoulders slumped on a sigh. Despite his efforts thus far, Lorraine Wilson's disappearance remained very much a mystery.

"I think I'll pop next door and ask your dad about your mom's charity work."

Later when he questioned Bob that proved to be a bust. The pastor didn't know the specifics of his wife's charity work, including whether she worked with the homeless. She might have worked in a soup kitchen, but he couldn't say for certain. She had her projects, and he was busy with his parishioners.

Defeated, Zac headed back to the station.

Emily came awake all of a sudden. She'd dozed off after spending much of the night tossing and turning. Leo jumped up on her bed and snuggled in beside her. She kissed him on the head and gave him a pat.

"How are you, buddy? I hope you had a better night than I did."

She'd spent the night dreaming about her mother. She'd also dreamed of Zac. Both dreams had left her feeling unsatisfied and yearning for something more. She wanted her mother found. She needed to know she was safe and unhurt. She didn't want anything to do with Zac, but she was struggling to suppress the feelings which had been dormant but were now making themselves known.

What's with that? It was like they were just waiting for an excuse to be fanned back to life. She didn't want to have anything to do with the Barringtons. Not even one she'd once been in love with and who still had the power to increase her pulse rate.

Leo whined and licked her hand. She tapped on the screen of her phone.

Seven o'clock.

As much as she wished she could linger in bed a little longer, she needed to get up and let him outside and then fetch his breakfast. She wondered if her father was awake. Last night, they'd shared a quiet dinner. They didn't talk about her mother. There was no point. Neither of them had any further information to add and re-hashing what little they knew seemed like an exercise in futility and one that would only make them feel worse. It was bad enough that they had so little to go on.

Zac had spoken to most of her mother's friends. No one had anything useful to add; no one had been given any indication she'd intended to leave.

And of course they hadn't! My mother isn't the kind of person to just up and go somewhere overnight without telling my father. She wouldn't have left him like this.

Which left other, much darker possibilities to consider. Possibilities she'd shied away from contemplating and she still wasn't ready to consider now. The more constructive thing to do would be to re-trace her mother's steps the day she'd disappeared. Fortunately, her mother's schedule was very predictable. Even better, she kept a diary.

Emily grimaced. Damn! She wished she'd remembered that when they were at the police station. They could have saved valuable time. Her mother was always meticulous about recording her daily movements. When the diary wasn't in her handbag, she kept it stowed in the top drawer of her bedside table. It could contain a vital clue to her whereabouts.

With a feeling of urgency driving her forward, Emily threw off the covers. She set Leo on the floor and padded down the hallway toward her parents' bedroom. The door was open. She stepped inside. The bed was made. The room was neat and tidy. In fact, it looked the same has it had the day before.

Did Dad even sleep in here last night?

He'd been quiet and morose when she'd left him seated in his armchair before the fire in the living room late the previous night. Her earlier attempts at conversation had been met with monosyllabic replies. She hadn't pressed him. It was obvious he was taking her mother's disappearance as hard as she was. In the end, she'd kissed him goodnight and had gone to bed. Now she wondered if he'd spent the night on the couch.

She walked over to her mother's side of the bed and pulled out the top drawer. Her mother's red leather-bound diary sat on top.

More confirmation she didn't just up and leave...

Taking a seat on the edge of the bed, she opened the diary and flipped to the day her mother had last been seen.

July 23rd...

According to the diary, her mother had the morning free. No doubt she'd kept herself busy doing household chores. Zac had mentioned someone had seen her at the shops. The rest of the morning was usually spent reading the bible or doing needlework until it was time to prepare lunch. Her father had confirmed they'd had lunch together. That was the last time he'd seen her.

Emily's gaze moved lower down the page. A notation with the words "*Joe—kitchen*" had been scrawled in the diary between two and three. Emily knew from days gone past her mother's afternoons were usually spent doing volunteer work. She always ensured she allowed plenty of time to cook dinner for her husband before he left again to conduct evening prayers at church.

Most often, her father ate beforehand, but occasionally he got caught up with a parishioner and didn't get home until later.

That must have happened the other night. That's why Dad said the last time he'd seen her was over lunch... He said the next time he was home was after evening prayers...

Emily made a mental note to ask her father if he remembered what her mother had prepared for dinner that night, if anything. That would give a more accurate timeline as to when she'd disappeared. According to someone Zac had spoken to, her mother had been going to try a new recipe. It would be interesting to know if she'd had time to follow through with that. A half-cooked meal, or one that was in the early stages of preparation, could be important in helping to narrow down the timeline. Likewise, it would be good to know if she had disappeared before she prepared the evening meal at all.

Had there been groceries left out that indicated she might have left in a hurry?

At her feet, Leo whined. Absently, she reached down and patted him. Her gaze was drawn once again to the notation about Joe. Mondays were one of the days her mother volunteered at the soup kitchen a couple of blocks from the church. She helped to prepare and serve the food, along with talking to the patrons, listening to their stories, offering support and understanding, as she kept them company.

When Emily was younger, she and her brother used to accompany their mother to the soup kitchen. Her mom had impressed upon them their good fortune in having a roof over their heads and food on their table. Not everyone was so fortunate.

Is Joe someone she knows from the soup kitchen? Did she meet with him that day as planned?

She had to call Zac and tell him about the diary. They needed to go to the soup kitchen and see if her mother had showed that day. If only that didn't mean coming into contact with Zac Barrington again.

The thought of calling him again filled her with a mixture of emotions. Being around him brought back so many good memories, but alongside that was the recent year of angst and anguish in the wake of Evan's death. It was difficult to reconcile the conflicting emotions that warred inside her.

Leo whined again. "I'm sorry, sweetie. I got distracted. Come on. We'll go outside now."

Even though her father had installed a doggy door in the kitchen, Leo insisted on waiting to go outside with her. It was a pain in the neck sometimes, but that's the way her fur baby liked it. With a sigh, she closed the diary and stood. The house was still and quiet. Her father must have left for his office already. Either that, or he'd fallen asleep on the couch.

She made her way toward the kitchen. She'd steel herself with caffeine before she called Zac. Then she'd go and find her father and see how he was holding up. But first, she'd deal with Leo's needs.

Chapter Five

Zac had arrived early at the rectory in the hopes he'd catch Bob Wilson in his office. Zac recalled from years ago the pastor was an early riser and was usually in his office by seven. During their school days Zac had admired the pastor's work ethic. Not everyone would have been so dedicated to the cause, day after day, year in year out. He wondered if that were still the case or if the loss of his son and now the disappearance of his wife had affected his routine.

Climbing the two concrete steps that led to the front door of the church office, Zac gave a perfunctory knock and then pulled open the door. The hinges squeaked loudly, announcing his arrival. He grinned wryly, wondering if the pastor kept the hinges in that condition on purpose. It gave him a few moments warning of the arrival of a visitor. No doubt as a well-known and well-respected pastor, Bob had plenty of those.

Emily's father was seated behind his desk, his head in his hands. He looked up as Zac appeared in the open doorway of his office. His face was pale. His eyes were puffy and red.

His hair was disheveled and his tie askew. It wouldn't have surprised Zac to discover the pastor had slept in his clothes. Upon seeing Zac, he blinked with surprise.

"Zac. What... What are you doing here again?" The question was quickly followed by another. "Do you have news? Have you found my wife?"

Zac shook his head, walked further into the room and lowered himself into a chair opposite Bob's desk.

"No. I'm sorry, Bob. I don't have any news and Lorraine is still missing. I take it you haven't heard from her?"

"No." Pastor Bob slowly shook his head from side to side. He stared down at his desk, looking bewildered.

"I wondered if I could ask you a few more questions," Zac ventured.

"Of course. What do you want to know?"

"I spoke to nearly all of Lorraine's friends yesterday. One lady I spoke to said she ran into Lorraine at the supermarket the day she went missing. Apparently your wife was planning to try out a new recipe for dinner. I was wondering if you ate dinner with Lorraine the night she disappeared?"

Bob shook his head. "No. I already told you. The last time I saw her was at lunchtime. I... I didn't come home for dinner. My afternoon meeting ran overtime and by the time it finished, people were arriving for evening prayers." He shrugged apologetically. "I don't always make it home for dinner."

"Okay. So what time were you there for lunch?"

"One o'clock."

"And what time did you leave?"

The pastor scrubbed at his face and scrunched up his eyes. "I can't remember the exact time. Probably around two. I usually take an hour for lunch."

"Okay, and when you did get home later that evening, it was about eight o'clock, right?"

"Yes."

"And that's when you realized your wife wasn't home?"

Tears filled the man's eyes. "Yes."

"Did you see any evidence that Lorraine had been cooking? Was there anything in the oven? On the stove?"

"No. There was nothing. I remember thinking at the time that was a bit strange. Lorraine prided herself on cooking me a hot dinner every night, even the nights when my work ran late."

"Was there any sign she'd been to the shops? Any groceries lying around?"

"No."

"What about when you came home earlier for lunch?"

"No, I don't think so."

Zac frowned in thought. A witness had seen Lorraine buying groceries earlier that day for a meal she'd been planning to cook that night. Surely she hadn't packed everything away when she intended to use it only a few hours later? Then again, perhaps she had. The house was scrupulously clean and tidy. Perhaps Lorraine was a bit of a neat freak and had packed the groceries away.

"Bob, I understand Lorraine didn't like to be out after dark. Didn't you think it was unusual when she didn't come back that night? You waited two days to report her missing. Why? Is there something you're not telling me? Did the two of you have a fight?"

"No! No! No! No! No!" Bob cried, holding his head in his hands.

The sound of Zac's phone ringing interrupted before Zac could question him further. He checked the screen.

Emily.

His heart skipped a beat. He glanced at Pastor Bob and fought a blush. Quickly turning away, he mumbled an apology and stepped outside of the office before answering the call.

"Emily."

"Zac. Sorry to call you, but… I… I might have found something."

Zac's pulse leaped. "What is it?"

"I'd rather show you. I'm at home. Can you call around and see me?"

"I'm here with your father, in his office. I can be there in a few minutes."

With that, Zac ended the call. He re-entered the office and found Bob in the same position in which he'd left him. He was quietly sobbing. Deciding the questions could wait, Zac reassured Bob he was doing everything he could to find his wife and reiterated that if he thought of anything that might help the investigation, to call him. Then he headed next door to Emily. She met him at the door.

"Talk to me," he said.

She let out a sigh. "I don't know if it's important or not, but I thought you should see this."

"What is it?"

Instead of responding, she turned her back on him and walked into the house. Zac followed her in silence. They walked all the way to the end of the house and then into her parents' bedroom. He watched as she crossed the room and opened a bedside drawer and withdrew a leather-bound book. She handed it to him.

"What is it?" he asked again.

"My mother's diary. She kept a record of all her daily appointments."

Excitement leaped in Zac's veins. "Why didn't you tell me about this earlier?"

"I didn't think of it. I was so distressed about Mom missing, then you turning up." She grimaced.

Zac said nothing but opened the book and flipped to the date Lorraine had disappeared. There was a single notation.

"Who's Joe?" he asked.

"I don't know, but she's also written the word "kitchen" next to his name. I'm assuming he's someone she met at the soup kitchen."

"The one on Brand Street?"

"Yes. It's been there for decades. You probably remember it from when we were kids."

Zac shook his head. "I'm afraid not. We lived outside of Broken, remember? We used to catch the bus home right after school. We didn't get to wander the streets like you did."

"I didn't walk the streets!" she protested. "I only know about it because Mom used to take us there. Evan and I. She used to volunteer at the soup kitchen and we sometimes helped out."

"Does she still volunteer there?" Zac asked.

"According to her diary, yes. A couple of days a week. The last time I accompanied her there was probably about six months ago or more." Emily had been a bit slack lately. Work had consumed her life. "It would be in her journal if you need specifics."

"I need to check with the people who work there. See if anyone saw her on the twenty-third. I'll also ask about this Joe guy. If he's a regular there, someone should know him."

"Do you mind if I tag along?"

Her question took him by surprise. He would have guessed he was the last person she'd want to spend time with. As much as he longed for her company, he found himself shaking his head.

"I don't think that's a good idea. I'll be there in a professional capacity. I'm investigating your mother's disappearance."

"Exactly!" she said. "She's *my* mother. No one has more reason for her to be found than I do. And my father, of course. But this has hit him hard. He's not really up to doing anything substantive as far as searching for her goes. In fact, he doesn't seem to be up for anything."

Zac had come to the same conclusion, but he didn't comment. Instead, he opened his mouth to argue again, but Emily beat him to it.

"I'm a familiar face at the soup kitchen. Okay, so it might have been six months or so since I've been there, but I'm guessing you've never stepped foot inside the place. Am I right?"

"Right," Zac reluctantly agreed.

"I might be able to help ease the natural suspicion many of the patrons have of the police. I mean, look at you. You're dressed in a five-hundred-dollar suit. And you have an air of authority about you. It's obvious you're a cop. That's hardly going to put these people at ease. How do you expect them to open up to you?"

Zac thought about what she'd said and knew she was right. Again. Having a familiar face alongside him to break the ice and make introductions might be the difference between getting a real lead or nothing.

"Okay," he grudgingly agreed. "You can come with me."

"Yes!"

She grinned for a sweet moment. Her beautiful blue eyes shone with enthusiasm before clouding again. Zac forced himself to look away. While he waited for her to collect her handbag and lock the front door, he tried not to remember how close they once were or notice how attractive she looked.

She was dressed simply in Levis and a long-sleeved, floral-patterned, peasant blouse, but the soft cotton of both garments melded to her body and drew attention to her shapely curves. Her thick blond hair was plaited and artfully wound around at the nape of her neck in a thick coil. His fingers ached to sink into it.

He remembered a time long ago when they'd spent hours lying on a blanket by the river, talking and laughing and making out. Sharing their hopes and dreams. Lying on their backs, staring up at the sky, fingers entwined, Emily's hair spread out like a fan beneath her. Even back then, it had been long and thick and silky and had always smelled good.

She climbed into the front seat of the police cruiser and Zac shifted the car into gear. He went to put the address of the soup kitchen into the GPS but Emily stilled his hand.

"It's all right. I can direct you there."

His hand tingled from her touch. He resolutely ignored it. An uneasy silence fell between them. It seemed to get the better of Emily. She grudgingly asked him about his work as a cop and what he'd been doing in the years since they'd left school. Relieved that she seemed to have moved on from her accusations about Evan's death, he skimmed over his time at the Police Academy and the years he'd spent working for the DEA. It was hard to share the challenges and trauma that work had inflicted on him over time. He'd burned out.

She asked a couple more questions. Though her tone was less antagonistic than it had been earlier, it was more detached curiosity than friendly warmth. Still, it was better than cold silence and he was quietly pleased that her attitude toward him appeared to be thawing. He didn't know what that meant, but he was going to take whatever olive branch she extended.

He glanced toward her. She sat quietly, her gaze directed forward. Her profile was just as beautiful as he remembered: the slim nose, the full lips, the shapely jaw. He wanted to ask her if she was seeing anyone, but he didn't want to upset their fragile truce and it was none of his business.

There was another reason he held back. He wasn't sure if he could handle knowing she had a boyfriend or a significant other in her life. The very possibility filled him with jealousy. It was ridiculous, because of course, she had every right to have a boyfriend. A woman like Emily Wilson was a catch for any man. And let's face it, he hadn't exactly lived the life of a monk in the intervening years.

Thankfully, they arrived at the soup kitchen before his thoughts could turn too morose. He and Emily climbed out of the cruiser and headed inside.

As it turned out, they were there ahead of the lunch queue and the place was empty except for the kitchen manager and a handful of volunteers who were busy peeling vegetables in preparation for the usual crowd.

They approached the woman who appeared to be in charge. Zac introduced himself and Emily.

"You look familiar," the woman said to Emily. "Have you been here before?"

Emily nodded. "Yes. It was about six months ago. I was with my mother. Lorraine Wilson. She volunteers—"

"Lorraine?" the woman interrupted. "Of course I know Lorraine! So she's your mother?"

"Yes," Emily replied.

"Lorraine's an angel. She comes in here to help a couple of times a week. She's amazing. One of those people who are happy to roll up their sleeves and get to work. And she loves the patrons. Always has a kind word for them. They love her just as much."

"When was the last time Lorraine was here?" Zac asked.

The woman frowned in thought. "Let me see. She was here last Friday. She was supposed to be back here on the Monday, but she didn't show."

"You mean the twenty-third?" Zac asked.

The woman nodded. "Right."

"Did you try calling her?" Zac asked.

"No. She's a volunteer. Though she's usually regular as clockwork, we don't keep tabs on our volunteers. We appreciate whatever time they can give us."

"Do you know a man by the name of Joe?" Emily asked.

The woman frowned again. "Joe who?"

"We don't know his last name," Emily said. "My mother had his name written in her diary, along with the word 'kitchen.' We think she might have intended to meet him here that day."

"Why don't you ask her?" the woman asked.

Zac gazed at her. "She hasn't been seen since the twenty-third. Her family is concerned."

The woman's frown deepened. "You mean, she's missing?"

Once again, Zac responded. "We're not sure of the details yet, but if you know where she might be, we're very keen to talk to her."

"I don't have a clue. I only ever run into her here."

"Is there anyone here by the name of Joe? Someone Lorraine might have known?" Zac asked.

"The only person I can think of is Joe Sampson," the woman said slowly. "He's been coming here ever since he got out of jail."

"What did he serve time for?" Emily asked.

The woman shook her head. "We don't ask questions like that. This is a safe place. No judgement, only support and understanding."

"Of course," Emily mumbled.

"What else can you tell us about Joe?" he asked.

The woman compressed her lips. "He and Lorraine struck up a friendship. She treated him with kindness and compassion, like she does everyone. He took a shine to her."

"Was he here on the twenty-third?"

"I think so. I don't pay that much attention. I'm usually too busy in the kitchen, making sure we have enough food to go round."

"What about last Friday, when Lorraine was last here?" Zac asked.

"I'm sorry. I can't say for sure."

"Is there anyone else we could talk to who was working here that day?" Zac asked.

The woman nodded. "Yes. Linda was here. She might have noticed Joe. She's usually on the serving line, so she sees most of the patrons that come in."

"Is Linda working today?" Emily asked, her tone giving away her growing anxiety.

"Yes. She's just over there. She offered to peel the carrots today."

They looked over to where the woman pointed. A slight, gray-haired woman with wrinkled skin and glasses stood at the long counter, a vegetable peeler in one hand and a carrot in the other. Zac thanked the woman for her time and he and Emily made their way over to Linda. Once again, Zac made the introductions.

"You're Lorraine's daughter, aren't you?" Linda asked.

Emily nodded. "Yes. Do you know my mother?"

"Of course I do! She talks about you all the time and shows me pictures of you. You look so smart in your nurse's uniform."

"You seem to know Lorraine well," Zac said.

Linda chuckled. "I ought to. We spend enough time together. She volunteers here almost as much as I do! We usually do the peeling together. It's a lot faster with two of us."

"That's why we're here," Zac said. "We're looking for Lorraine. She seems to have disappeared and her family is worried. When did you last see her?"

"She was here last Friday," Linda replied, confirming what the other woman had said. "She volunteers Mondays and

Fridays. "I expected her this past Monday, but she didn't show."

"Do you know someone by the name of Joe Sampson?" Emily asked.

Linda nodded. "Of course. Joe's been a regular here these past few months. He and Lorraine get along well. He's always disappointed if she's not here."

"Do you know where Joe lives?" Zac asked.

"No. We don't ask any personal questions. All I know is he's not from here."

"Do you think Joe would ever hurt Lorraine?" Zac asked.

He heard Emily's sharp intake of breath and wished he'd taken the woman aside and asked the question privately. But it was too late for that now. He waited for her answer.

"Joe? No. Joe's a sweetie. He really likes Lorraine. They get on well. Sometimes they sit and talk half the afternoon away."

The woman sounded confident. Zac saw the relief fill Emily's face and was glad she didn't feel the same unease he did.

"What does he look like?" Zac asked.

Linda thought for a moment. "Tall, thin build. Dark hair. Graying. A nice smile."

"Is he an Aboriginal?" Zac asked.

"Yes."

"How old is he?"

The woman pursed her lips. "Maybe in his fifties."

Zac acknowledged her responses with a nod. The description sounded like the man Anita Marshall had seen outside Lorraine's house the day she'd disappeared. Once again, the fact the man knew her—and it appeared from the notation in her diary that she had a meeting with him—didn't prove he was involved in her disappearance, but it certainly pushed him higher on Zac's list of people of interest.

Of course, they didn't have any evidence of foul play. For all he knew, Lorraine might have hopped a bus or train out of Broken and was safe and sound enjoying a holiday. The fact she'd told no one of her plans and had left behind her toothbrush and most, if not all, of her clothes cast doubt on that, but they had no evidence to indicate anything to the contrary.

However, he had a name and that was a lead. As soon as he returned to the station, he'd run Joe's name through the database. If he'd recently been released from jail, they would have received some notification of that, along with a copy of his parole conditions. He would have also had to supply an address where he'd be residing once he left jail. That would be a good start.

"When did you last see Joe?" Zac asked.

Linda frowned in thought. "He was here briefly on the Monday. He ate lunch and left shortly afterwards. I haven't seen him since."

Emily was quiet on the journey back to her parents' house. Zac kept glancing at her, trying to gauge her mood. She wasn't stupid. He could only imagine the kind of things that were going through her head. He had his own suspicions about Joe, but he'd keep them to himself until he talked with him, got his background details and had more concrete information.

In an effort to cheer her up, he invited her to lunch. She appeared just as surprised as he was by the spontaneous invitation, and to his relief, she agreed.

Chapter Six

Emily wasn't sure if Zac's decision to take them to the same café they used to frequent as teenagers was deliberate or if he'd made the turn and parked there merely from habit. Either way, she was bombarded with memories as he held open the door for her to the Café on Main and waited for her to enter. She hadn't been there since high school, but the place hadn't changed at all.

The same black-and-white checkerboard linoleum floor, mint-green Formica counter and red vinyl booths were a throwback to an earlier time. The décor had been deliberately styled to suit. Black-and-white framed photographs of Hollywood icons littered the pink pastel-colored walls. The place looked like something out of a *Happy Days* TV set. Being there again made Emily smile.

That time of the day, the place was buzzing. Though the teenagers were still in school, professionals and blue-collar workers filled the tables. Pop music blared from a jukebox. The conversation was loud and upbeat as people enjoyed their lunchbreak. A mother with three young children took up a booth near the door. She looked tired and stressed and defeated as the kids started arguing back and forth over their meals.

"Ray! Quit that now!" the mother said, as the boy pulled his little sister's hair.

"Ow! That hurt!" the girl cried and slapped her brother hard.

The young mother juggled the baby on her lap while she tried her best to intervene. The kids ignored her. They were moments from erupting into a full-on fight when Zac closed in on them and smiled. He crouched low beside the table so that he was at eye level with the kids.

"Hey, guys. What's going on?"

The two children stopped fighting and turned to stare at him in surprise.

"That hamburger looks delicious," Zac continued. "And what about those fries? What kind of milkshake do you have?" he asked the little girl.

"Chocolate. My favorite," the child said shyly.

"Yum. Chocolate's my favorite too," Zac replied with a grin.

He looked at the girl's brother. "How about you? Do you like milkshakes?"

"Nah. I like juice."

"Hey, juice is good too." Zac stood and brushed off his pants. "Well, you all enjoy your meal. And take it easy on your mom, okay? She brought you here for lunch. The least you can do is be kind to each other." He looked from one child to the other. "What do you think?"

The children mumbled agreement and had the grace to look abashed. The young mother shot him a grateful look.

"Thank you," she said.

Zac waved it off. "No worries. Have a nice day."

The only available seat was a booth in the back. Emily's stomach somersaulted as more memories overwhelmed her. It was the same booth they'd claimed as theirs all those years ago. It hadn't mattered if the place was empty. They'd always made a beeline for the very last booth. It had offered the most privacy for when they wanted to make out.

As they made their way toward it, Zac flashed her a grin, his eyebrows raised. She quickly averted her gaze, annoyed at the sudden rush in her pulse. From the knowing look on his face, she could tell he also remembered the significance of that booth. Still, there was no way she was going to comment on it. She had no intention of renewing their relationship. The last thing she wanted to do was draw attention to what they'd once meant to each other. It was just that there was nowhere else to sit. Better to act like there was nothing of significance about the back booth.

Zac slid into the seat. Emily sat across from him. Just like old times. Except six years had passed and they were no longer dating and never would date again. He was her past, not her future. She'd made that decision a long time ago and that had been reinforced this last year. She'd be wise to remember that the next time her pulse leaped when he smiled.

"What are you having?" Zac asked, scanning the menu.

Emily dragged her gaze away from him and picked up another menu. Though it had been updated since the last time she'd been there, the usual café fare of fried food, hamburgers, coffee and milkshakes were still on offer.

"I'll have a burger with the works and a strawberry milkshake," she said.

Zac's eyes twinkled and she suddenly wished she'd ordered something else.

"Some things never change," he teased.

"That's not true!" she said indignantly, fighting a wave of embarrassment. "I've changed a good deal. I'm sure you have too. We're not teenagers any longer," she added.

"Too bad," Zac said softly. "I enjoyed every moment of my teenage years."

The look he gave her was so intense, her heart stopped momentarily. It was all she could do to remember to breathe. She remembered how they'd been back in high school, so young, so innocent, so in love. The first time they'd made love had been on her seventeenth birthday. It had been the most magical night of her life.

Her decision to break things off at the end of high school hadn't been made lightly. Zac wasn't the only one who'd nursed a broken heart after their breakup. But as much as she'd been in love with him, she'd wanted more from life than being a wife and mother in Broken. She hadn't wanted to look back with regret that she hadn't spread her wings and made her mark on the world when she had the chance. And so she'd left.

She shook her head. "Zac..."

To her relief, the waitress arrived, sparing her the need to continue. They put in their orders. As Zac returned the menu to its place between the salt and pepper shakers, Emily's gaze slid involuntarily to his left hand. His ring finger was bare. Her heart leaped reflexively. She frowned with annoyance, both at her heart's reaction and her brain's willingness to jump to the automatic conclusion he was still single.

Just because he has no ring doesn't mean he's not married. A lot of married men don't wear wedding rings... Particularly those in law enforcement. It gives them some protection from having their families targeted...

During her infrequent visits to Broken over the years, she'd deliberately refrained from asking her parents about Zac. Occasionally they'd volunteered information, such as the fact he'd gone into the police force. At some point she'd been made aware that he was living on the central coast. By and large, apart from their brief conversation earlier, she didn't know much about the life he'd led after graduation and that's the way she wanted it. She'd made certain decisions which had brought their relationship to an end once and for all. She refused to regret them.

But now she couldn't help but wonder what might have happened if their relationship had gone down the path most people had expected it to. That thought was quickly followed by another. She wondered if he was married or had a special someone in his life. The only way to know for sure was to ask him. Her palms went sweaty at the thought. Her pulse picked up its pace. Before she lost her nerve, she drew in a breath.

"Are you married?" she blurted. "It's just that you don't wear a ring... I know law enforcement officers sometimes don't, even if they are..." Oh, God. She was babbling.

Zac's eyes widened in surprise. Heat exploded across her face. She waited tensely for his answer, wishing desperately that she didn't care one way or the other.

Zac blinked, completely taken aback by Emily's unexpected question. Just as quickly, hope surged through him.

Why would she ask such a personal question if the answer meant nothing to her?

"No. I'm not married." He sucked in a breath and found the courage to ask her. "What about you?"

"No."

"Are you...seeing anyone?"

"No. You?"

"No. Slim pickings in a town the size of Broken," he joked.

She gave him a strained smile. "I haven't had much better luck in a city of five million."

The knowledge that she was single burned inside him. His heart thumped. Unable to stop himself, he reached across the table and squeezed her hand. Her slim fingers were warm and soft against his. To his relief, she didn't immediately pull away. Instead, her mouth came open on a sudden intake of breath.

A faint blush stained her cheeks. She looked away and her tongue stole out to lick her lips.

Desire bolted through him and centered in his groin. Just like that, the attraction he'd felt toward her all those years ago flared back to life. Then she eased her hand out from under his and he was filled with disappointment. All he wanted to do was drag her into his arms and kiss her, taste her, familiarize himself with the feel of her until the world faded away and there was no one but the two of them.

Of course, he did none of those things. They were sitting in a café waiting for lunch. They were no longer a couple. They hadn't spoken for six years. As much as he longed to be with her, to love her like he used to, right now it was nothing more than a beautiful pipe dream.

She cleared her throat and his heart stopped. All of a sudden, he didn't want to listen to what she had to say. He was sure it wouldn't be what he longed to hear.

Emily's heart pounded, both from the feel of Zac's fingers closed around hers and the way he looked at her like she was the most desirable woman in the world. It was heady stuff and reminded her of the way she used to feel whenever he was near. Giddy with excitement, nervous with anticipation, filled with desire at the thought of them making love.

She wasn't surprised there was still a powerful attraction between them. Once, a long time ago, they'd been inseparable. As close as two people could be. Being here with him now was familiar, comforting, safe. It felt like coming home. He moved in his seat and she caught a whiff of his cologne. Sweet and spicy. The same as he'd always worn.

More memories came flooding back. Their passionate kisses, the feel of his strong arms around her. The warmth of his skin. He'd filled out since high school, broadened in the shoulders and chest, grown a beard. But he was still the same Zac. With eyes the color of rich chocolate, clear and uncomplicated. Ever ready with a smile. Seeing the positive in every situation. She'd been surprised when he'd gone into policing. Now, in an effort to divert his attention away from the two of them, she chose to ignore the tumultuous beating of her heart and told him as much.

He shrugged. "I understand why you might be surprised. After all, I was such a dreamer in high school." He grimaced. "If I recall rightly, you called me sweet and sensitive more than once."

"Hey!" she protested. "That was a compliment. I liked sweet and sensitive guys."

"No eighteen-year-old guy wants their girlfriend to describe them as sweet and sensitive." He paused. "But I did want to make a difference. I wanted to make the world a better place. That sounds ridiculously naïve, but I thought I could do that by being a cop."

With her chin propped on her hand she gazed at him. "And have you?"

"I'd like to think so. At least in a small way." He sighed quietly. "I didn't feel that way so much when I was working with a DEA taskforce. We'd put one drug gang behind bars and another three would pop up. It felt like we were fighting an endless war, one we couldn't win. Of course, that's no reason to give up. We need to keep up the fight, but my heart wasn't in it. It was no longer a fight I felt I could be a part of."

He offered her a disparaging smile. "Trace was already working in Broken. He encouraged me to give it a go. So I came home. And I'm glad I did. Community policing has so much more to offer. It's a tight-knit community where most people know each other and they look out for each other. They're really grateful for the presence of the police. And unlike big city taskforces, we really feel like an integral part of the community."

He gave an embarrassed shrug. "I could never have imagined I'd think like that a few years ago. I couldn't wait to leave my hometown, but it's funny how some places have a way of calling you back."

She smiled softly. "No regrets?"

His gaze caught and held hers. The intensity in his eyes snatched her breath. When he spoke, his voice was rough with emotion. "About returning to Broken?"

She swallowed. "Yes."

"None."

His gaze remained fixed on hers. She cleared her throat and forced a smile. "That's good then. And I'm sure the town's happy to have their hometown hero back."

He looked away. An adorable flush stained his cheeks. "Hero?" he scoffed. "I don't know about that."

She grinned. "But of course! The captain of the football team! You won three years in a row! You put Broken on the map!"

Once again, he shrugged off her praise. "It wasn't just me. The whole team made that happen."

"Still so modest. So humble. It's nauseatingly refreshing." Her laughter sounded brittle.

Thankfully, their conversation was interrupted by the arrival of the waitress with their food. They took refuge in their meals. Zac took a huge bite of his hamburger, chewed slowly and swallowed.

"So, how about you? A nurse in the big smoke. Is it everything you thought it would be?"

Her stomach clenched. Given that her need to make a mark on the world was the reason she'd given him for breaking things off, she knew how much her answer would mean to him. She could be honest about that much at least. As for the other... No, that was over and done. In the past. Best to leave it there.

Aware that Zac waited expectantly for her reply, she pasted a smile on her face.

Chapter Seven

Zac watched the shadows pass over Emily's face, dimming the brilliance of her blue eyes. She shrugged and averted her gaze.

"Emily?"

She gave him another smile that didn't reach her eyes. "Is nursing everything I thought it would be? Of course."

Her tone was far from convincing. He reached across the table for her hand and squeezed it again. The contact sent an arc of electricity surging between them. He pulled his hand back. She curled hers into a fist.

"Hey, you can tell me," he coaxed. "We used to tell each other all kinds of stuff. Remember?"

She smiled sadly. "Yeah. I remember. That was a long time ago. And before you became the enemy."

"Not that long ago. And believe what you will, but I'm not your enemy. I'd like to be your friend," he said softly. "What is it, Em?"

At the use of her nickname, tears welled up in her eyes. His heart clenched in distress. "I'm sorry, Emily. I didn't mean to upset you. Forget I even asked. It's none of my business."

She looked up at him. Tears shimmered in her eyes. "No, no! You didn't upset me. It's just that... I gave up a life with you to pursue my career. I didn't take that decision lightly. I still don't." She swiped at her eyes. "The thing is, I love my job, but I don't get to talk about my work with many people. I work with dying kids, trying desperately to prolong their lives. More often than not, despite my best efforts, I only delay the inevitable. A lot of my patients leave in body bags. That doesn't make for polite dinner conversation."

His heart filled with compassion. He resisted the urge to move and sit beside her and draw her into his arms. He knew she wouldn't welcome that. Instead, he settled for once again reaching out and covering her hand with his.

"You can talk to me."

Something in his tone must have resonated. She drew in a deep, unsteady breath and began speaking.

"I always wanted to be a nurse. For as long as I can remember. I left you, and my family, my friends, so I could go to university and study. I could have chosen a different course, something I could study closer to home, but I wanted to be a nurse. I wasn't prepared to let anything or anyone hold me back. Not even you."

She flicked a glance in his direction. He nodded slowly. "I understood that. As much as I wanted to beg you to stay, I knew that wasn't fair. You had the right to forge your own path, find your destiny. I knew you'd make a wonderful nurse. You always were so kind and compassionate."

"Thank you. And you're right, I loved nursing. I loved everything about it. Eventually I decided to specialize in pediatrics. Then I moved to the oncology ward." Her gaze lifted to his. It was filled with a combination of hope and sadness and underneath all of that was a touching vulnerability that pulled at his heartstrings.

"Working with kids who are battling cancer is such a humbling experience," she continued in a voice that was husky with emotion. "They're so positive, upbeat, funny. They find humor in the silliest things and it's wonderful to see. They have every reason to be down on the world. To be furious with God at the lousy hand they've been dealt. And yet they're not."

A gentle smile lit up her face. "They're so full of hope and positivity. It's like they can't conceive they won't get better. That they won't skip on out of there and get on with the rest of their lives. They have such faith in us, the health professionals. It's inspiring, but it's also deeply wounding. Especially when the inevitable happens and some of them don't walk out of there. That's the hardest part of all."

A wave of compassion welled up inside him. He knew something about death. He'd told grieving relatives on more than one occasion that their loved ones had gone, especially during the years he'd spent policing in the city. A car accident, a drug overdose, a bar fight... Thankfully a town the size of Broken didn't experience high levels of violent crime.

Then again, only a couple of months earlier there had been the murder of a teenage boy in their town—fourteen-year-old Oscar Webster. Trace had been the lead detective. Zac had been with him when they broke the tragic news to Oscar's mother. And even though Trace had since fallen in love with Oscar's sister, Cassie, it was never easy bringing that kind of news to the relatives, even when those people were strangers. Particularly when the victim was a child. That was the cruelest cut.

Being the bearer of such grim news was something he'd never get used to and it always took a toll. He couldn't imagine how much harder it would be for Emily who'd actually gotten to know her young patients and their families, often over an extended period of time.

In an effort to lighten the mood, he tactfully steered the conversation back to her visit in Broken. He asked her how long she was staying. That inevitably led to a discussion about her mother.

"What do you think about this Joe Sampson guy?" Emily asked.

Zac acknowledged her question with a tilt of his head. He wasn't yet ready to share with her Anita Marshall's disclosure. No sense in heightening Emily's anxiety without concrete proof Sampson was involved. Still, she wasn't stupid and he wouldn't treat her as such.

"The fact your mom had his name in her appointment book the same day she went missing means he's definitely someone we need to talk to. As we discerned earlier, it seems they didn't meet at the soup kitchen that day, but it's possible they met somewhere else. I'll make some inquires and run his name through the police data base. If he's done time, he'll be in our system. At the least I should be able to get hold of a last known address."

"Will you let me know if you find out anything important?"

"Of course," he readily agreed.

"I only have one more day off and then I'll have to return to Sydney. When Dad told me Mom was missing, I came down as soon as I could. It was lucky timing if you can call it lucky, that I was about to go on a few days' off. I thought we'd have found her by now; that she would have turned up. I wasn't expecting this to turn into something so...difficult."

She sounded so lost and confused it was all Zac could do not to hold her tight and reassure her everything would be all right. He knew better than to make such rash promises. Right now, he didn't have a clue where Lorraine was or what was going on. Not that he'd tell Emily that. She needed to believe her mother would turn up alive and well.

"We'll find her, Em."

She gave him a searching look. With an effort, he held her gaze. She was the first one to look away.

"I need to return home tomorrow afternoon and check on things at my apartment, cover my rostered shifts and arrange for some additional leave so I can come back. That's if we haven't found her by then."

His heart clenched at the hope and fear that warred in her eyes. He silently vowed to do everything he could to bring the smile back to her beloved face.

Emily asked Zac to drop her off at her parents' house. The ride home was quiet, both lost in their thoughts. He left her with a promise to call the minute he knew anything. She managed a half-smile, grateful for his reassurances.

It was funny. Up until yesterday she hadn't wanted anything to do with Zac Barrington—with any of the Barringtons. But his kindness and compassion had started to thaw the ice around her heart. Now she was glad he was the officer who'd taken her report.

Who better to help? He knew her. He knew her parents. This was personal. Her mother wasn't a random stranger who'd gone missing.

Zac knew her as intimately as it was possible for someone to know another person. He also knew how much she loved her mother. Having him on her side, doing everything he could was surprisingly comforting. After what had happened to Evan, she never thought she'd put comforting and the Barrington name anywhere near each other. But she'd come to accept what she'd always known: that Zac wasn't responsible for the actions and responses of his family. Just like she wasn't responsible for those of her mom.

Where are you, Mom?

Though she'd been adamant her mother would never have just up and left without a word to anyone, she didn't know unequivocally if that was right. Over the years since she'd left for university and then later, when she secured fulltime work in the city, her visits home had been less and less frequent. Though she was still close with both of her parents, she wasn't as closely connected to their daily lives as she'd once been.

Once upon a time, she knew every minute of her mother's daily schedule, from the time she rose in the morning, to when she called it a night. But over the years, as life got busy and full of the demands of her job, she didn't have time to share every aspect of her mother's life. It was enough to know she was there, getting on with things, alongside Emily's dad.

Now she couldn't help but wonder if she was wrong. Was it possible her mother had gone away for a while without telling anyone? But what about her toothbrush? Had she left in such a hurry that she hadn't bothered to pack? If so, why? And how had she left? By public transport, or had someone picked her up?

None of her friends knew anything about a trip, planned or otherwise, but that didn't mean she hadn't involved someone else. Someone like Joe Sampson, maybe? After all, they'd arranged to meet the very same day she disappeared. No one at the soup kitchen had seen either of them since. Was that just a coincidence, or something else? And who was Joe Sampson? Where did he really fit into her mother's life?

The endless questions running around in her head threatened to overwhelm her. She blew out her breath on a weary sigh. She had to put her faith in Zac that he'd find her mother because she was all out of ideas. If she'd gone by choice, wherever she was and for whatever reasons she'd left, that was her decision. Emily respected that. All she really wanted to know was that her mother was safe. Nothing else mattered. They could deal with the reasons for her departure once she was home.

Please, Mom. Please come back home... I need to know you're okay... Why haven't you called?

Letting herself into the house, she walked through the quiet rooms. The place didn't feel the same without her mom. Her warm, constant, reassuring presence... It had always been that way but now the rooms felt cold and empty.

She walked into her bedroom and spied Leo asleep on his bed. Though she wasn't aware of making any sound, he opened his eyes and leaped off his bed and came running toward her, barking with excitement. She bent down and picked him up and snuggled him against her chest.

"Great watchdog you are. I'm already in the house," she chided. "How are you, buddy? Did you miss me?"

Leo lifted his head and licked her hand. He stared at her with his big dark eyes and her heart melted. Animals had so much love to give and they were so uncomplicated, even with their unique personalities.

Leo squirmed in her arms, wanting to be put down. She laughed and gently lowered him to the floor. He scampered around, wagging his tail and barking.

"I get it. You need to go outside, right? You do know about the doggy door, don't you? Of course you do. Come on. Let's go and find Dad."

Stepping outside again, Leo darted across the yard to do his business before scampering ahead of her toward the church next door. The winter sun was warm on her face. She tilted her head back to take in the clear blue sky. It was dotted with white fluffy clouds – one of those perfect winter days when you couldn't imagine anything dreadful happening.

But the sight didn't lift her spirits. The feeling of dread in the pit of her stomach which had formed the moment she'd learned her mother was missing had congealed.

With a sigh, she walked up the steps to her father's office. She wanted to check on him, make sure he was doing okay. Like her, he was taking her mother's absence hard. She was concerned he wasn't coping.

Last night she'd left him sitting in the darkness, staring despondently into space. He'd started blaming himself for the fact her mother was gone. She'd brushed off his confused mumblings as nothing more than a combination of fear and grief. They were both on edge, worried about where her mother was and what might have happened to her. Now Emily felt the need to try harder to reassure him, even though she felt just as helpless.

The hinges on the door protested loudly as she pulled it open. She stepped into the foyer.

"Dad? Are you in here?"

She was met with momentary silence. Then she heard a sob. Alarmed, she pushed open the door to her father's office. She found him bent over his desk. He looked up as she entered. Tears streamed down his face.

"Dad!" she cried. "What is it? Have you heard something?"

Her father merely shook his head from side to side and continued to sob, a helpless expression on his face. Emily kneeled down beside him and patted him gently on the shoulder.

"Hey, Dad. It's going to be all right. Please don't cry. This isn't your fault. We'll find her. Zac's out there looking for her now. If anyone can find her, he will. He knows us. He knows Mom. He knows how much we love her and how much we need to have her back."

Her father continued to cry quietly. She stood and hugged his head to her stomach, but the tears continued to flow. She'd never seen him so defeated, so utterly devastated. She tried once again to reassure him.

"*Shh*, Dad. It's okay. Don't upset yourself. Mom's fine. I'm sure of it. Maybe she went away for a while? Maybe she needed some time to herself. She gives and gives and gives to everyone. I hate to admit it, but I've taken her for granted. She's always been there for us. Maybe she felt ignored? Maybe she decided that by leaving for a few days, we'd realize how much she does for us and how much we need her. But she'll come back. She loves us and she knows we love her. And when she does come back, I'm going to hug her hard and tell her how much I love her before I yell at her for scaring us so much."

Her father's howls of distress only got louder. It sounded like his heart was being torn in two. Tears burned behind Emily's eyes. She hated seeing him like this. He'd always been the strong one. The one his parishioners relied on, turned to in times of need. She'd been there when he'd commanded the attention of more than a hundred people, hanging off his every word. They came to him for guidance, to hear his wisdom, to have him pray over them.

She barely recognized the man beside her. Broken with confusion and grief. She'd never felt so helpless, so powerless in her futile efforts to offer comfort. Zac had to come through for them. He just had to. Before her father's grief took him to a place so dark he might never come back.

Zac's gut was coiled with tension. He'd run Joe Sampson through the database and was alarmed at the man's extensive criminal history reaching back many years—possession and supply of drugs, serious assaults, B&Es. He'd recently been released from jail after serving time for a serious assault involving the infliction of grievous bodily harm on a housemate.

According to the police facts, Sampson had turned on his housemate in a violent rage after the man refused to share his six pack with him. The man had been left comatose. He'd remained that way for a week and now had residual brain damage.

Sampson had been given three years for the assault, with a two-year non-parole period. Now that time was up and he was back on the street. Though he'd previously resided in Sydney's western suburbs, for some reason, he'd found his way to Broken. Zac's concern for Lorraine Wilson continued to escalate the more he delved into Sampson's past.

According to his rap sheet, Sampson had been a drug user for a long time. There were arrests for drug-related offenses going back to when the man was fifteen. The most recent report submitted by his parole officer stated he was only violent when he was under the influence of ice. Similarly, it was his drug habit that apparently forced him to commit break and enters. Like that made a difference.

There was no sign of forced entry into the Wilson house, but Sampson was known to Lorraine. She could have easily let him in if he'd come calling. Had he gone there to rob her, and things had gotten out of control? Unlikely. There had been no sign of a disturbance in the house. Had he convinced her to go with him somewhere and had he hurt her there?

Zac scrubbed at his face. So many questions and no answers. He returned to the homepage and took down Sampson's last known address. He needed to track the man down as a matter of priority. Whether or not Sampson was involved in Lorraine's disappearance, Zac's gut told him the man was likely to know something about what had gone on.

He'd been seen outside the Wilson house the same afternoon Lorraine went missing.

His thoughts turned to Emily. He'd promised to keep her in the loop, but right now he didn't have anything definite to tell her. Best to wait until after he'd spoken to Sampson and see what played out. He didn't want to raise her expectations or her stress levels unnecessarily. She already knew of Sampson's existence and that he was known to her mother. He needed more information before he decided what, if anything, he'd say to her.

It wasn't that he was going back on his promise. It was more a need to protect her from unnecessary pain. That's what you did for the people you loved. Even if they didn't love you back.

Chapter Eight

Zac turned the police cruiser into the Lazy B Caravan Park on the eastern edge of town. He parked in one of the designated parking spots for visitors. It was nothing but a small patch of dusty, bare ground.

He climbed out of the cruiser and walked toward the rows of caravans and mobile homes lined up on either side of a dirt road. Long, yellowed grass grew on either side. The verges hadn't been mowed in some time. A snake haven in the summer, no doubt. Scattered piles of faded bark chips and a few straggling bushes that barely clung to life comprised the rest of the landscaping.

Dismal, depressing and drab. It was the kind of place where someone ended up when they were out of options. Cheap cash rates where there was no requirement for more than a nightly commitment and no paperwork involved. It was easy to see why the place would be attractive to a parolee.

Checking the number on the piece of paper in his hand, he walked past caravans in various states of repair. Some were in good order, likely owned by travelers passing through.

Toward the back were rows of more permanent structures. Most looked rundown, decrepit, falling apart. Rusted tin roofs of cabins and mobile homes bent under the weight of decades of fallen leaves. Junk of every description covered the ground. Car tires, spare parts, rusted scrap metal.

The mobile home that matched the address on Zac's paper was as equally decrepit as the structures that surrounded it. Sparse tufts of unkempt grass struggled to survive in the packed dirt, no doubt doubly challenged by morning frosts. A single red geranium growing in a small terracotta pot near the front steps caught his eye. It was incongruous among the filth and detritus. The glossy green foliage and bright red blooms were a testament to someone's love and attention. He wondered if that love and attention had come from Joe.

Zac rapped on the door and then stood back. A moment later, the door opened. A man who fit Joe's description filled the open doorway. He wore a wary expression.

"Joe Sampson?"

"Yeah."

Zac knew from Sampson's file that he was forty-three. The fact he looked a decade older than that was testament to the lifestyle he'd led for such a long time. His face was drawn and weathered and covered in wrinkles. His eyes were a piercing blue. His cheap clothes hung off his frame. They were at least two sizes too big. Either he'd lost a good deal of weight since leaving prison or else he was in borrowed clothes. Zac was betting on the latter.

As the man walked down the steps and came to a halt beside him, Zac held out his hand. "I'm Detective Zac Barrington. I'm with the Broken Police."

"What do you want?"

"I'm wondering if you know a woman by the name of Lorraine Wilson?"

The man's expression didn't change. "Yeah. I know Miss Lorraine."

"Where did you meet?"

"At the soup kitchen on Brand Street. She volunteers there."

"How long have you known her?"

The man scratched at the stubble on his cheek. "Three or four months."

"Someone at the soup kitchen told me the two of you are friends."

Joe nodded slowly. "Yeah. I guess you could say that."

Zac observed the man closely. Though his eyes were red, his gaze was clear. Zac couldn't detect the smell of alcohol on his breath. Neither did he appear to be under the influence of drugs.

"What else can you tell me about Lorraine?" he asked.

"She's a good woman. An angel. She really cares about people, you know? I told her about my struggles with drugs and alcohol. She promised to get me into rehab, but first I have to show her I'm willin' to get sober." He shot Zac a sideways look. "It ain't easy. I've been havin' trouble stayin' clean. Miss Lorraine's been helpin' me, prayin' for me."

"How are you intending to pay for rehab?" Zac asked, curious.

Sampson scowled. "Miss Lorraine said she'd speak to the pastor and see if they could raise the money." He paused and then looked directly at Zac. "I've been on the wagon for eight days now. I gave up the grog and the drugs the very same day I spoke to her about wantin' to get my shit together. She's the first person I've met who gives a fuck, to treat me with respect. She's the only person who hasn't given up on me."

He stared down at his feet and kicked at the ground. "I don't know why. Fuck, *I've* just about given up on me. I've done some bad shit over the years."

His honesty surprised Zac, along with his willingness to accept responsibility for his actions. Zac didn't cross paths with too many ex-cons who were willing to do that.

"When did you last speak with her?" he asked.

"Last Friday. Why?"

"Were you using that day?"

Joe lowered his head. Embarrassment and shame reddened his cheeks. "Yeah."

"Are you sure you saw her on Friday?"

"Yeah. I know it was Friday because that was the day I decided I was gonna get clean. I told Miss Lorraine and she was happy for me. Said she'd help me. We agreed to meet up again the followin' Monday at the soup kitchen so she could check on my progress, see how I was doin'."

"But you didn't see her on Monday, right?"

"Right. I went there, but she didn't show. Has somethin' happened?"

"She's missing. Do you know where she is?" Zac asked.

Joe frowned. "Missin'? What do you mean?"

"She went missing on Monday. The same day she was supposed to meet with you at the soup kitchen."

Joe's eyes widened with comprehension. He began to shake his head from side to side with increasing vigor. "Oh, no. No, no, no! You ain't gonna pin this on me! I got nothin' to do with it. I didn't even know she was gone."

Zac watched him closely. His distress appeared genuine. Still, Zac wasn't about to forget Sampson's violent past. Or the fact he'd been seen outside Lorraine's house.

"Have you ever been to her house?" Zac asked.

"No! I don't even know where she lives."

Zac narrowed his gaze on the man. "Don't lie to me, Joe. Someone saw you outside her house that afternoon."

Fear and panic flooded his face. He blinked fast and averted his gaze, but it was obvious the news had shaken him.

"Why were you there, Joe? Why were you outside Miss Lorraine's house on Monday afternoon?"

Tears shimmered in the man's watery eyes. His bottom lip trembled. He staggered away and stumbled and then sat down abruptly on the top step of his mobile home. He buried his face in his hands.

Zac squatted beside him. "Talk to me Joe. Tell me what happened. Tell me about Miss Lorraine."

The man only continued to shake his head slowly from side to side. "You're wrong. I wasn't there."

"You were there, Joe. I have an eyewitness."

His shoulders slumped in defeat. He dragged in a ragged breath and then slowly raised his head and looked Zac straight in the eye.

"Okay. I was there. When Miss Lorraine didn't show, I went lookin' for her. She told me she'd be there. She's solid, you know. Always keeps her word. She knew I was tryin' to stay clean. Monday was the day we'd agreed I'd check in. She goes there Mondays and Fridays. She should have been there. But she wasn't. I needed to see her. I was havin' the cravin's and I needed to see her real bad. I was desperate." His gaze slid away.

"So you went to her house."

"Yes."

"Why did you lie when you said you didn't know where she lived?"

Sampson's gaze remained averted. "Shit. I... I got scared, man. You just told me she was missin'."

"Why would that make you scared?" Zac's gaze narrowed on Sampson's face. He needed answers before the man closed down.

"You already knew she was missing, didn't you? Before I told you. You knew she'd disappeared."

"No! No! No! No! I didn't! I didn't know anythin'! I went there to see if she was home because she hadn't turned up when she said she would. I wanted to tell her I'd been on the wagon for three days. She'd told me I had to be clean for a week before she'd go to the church for money. I wanted to prove to her I could do it." He paused and scrubbed at his face. "But she wasn't there either."

"How do you know?"

He shrugged. "I stood outside her house for a while. I called out to her. She lives on a quiet street. No way she couldn't have heard me. When she didn't come, I left." He lifted his head and stared at Zac. "I swear, that's the truth."

Zac gave him a hard look. The piercing blue eyes were filled with fear and worry, but he couldn't discern any dishonesty. Still, appearances could be deceiving and as an ex-con, Sampson would be wilier than most.

"You want to hope so. If I find out you've lied to me, you'll go straight back in the slammer. Got it?"

Joe kept his head down and nodded. Zac pulled out a business card. "Call me if you remember anything else, or if you hear from Miss Lorraine."

Joe took the card. "I've got no phone, but I'll get a message to you if I hear anythin'."

"Good." Zac went to turn away and then looked at Joe again. "Oh, and don't go leaving town."

Emily finished packing her overnight bag and put it in her car. She needed to return home. She was due on the ward tomorrow afternoon and she needed time to do laundry, shop for groceries and catch up on all the other things she'd neglected during the few days she'd been in Broken. There wasn't much she could do to help here anyway, apart from keeping her father company, and she was pretty sure he barely knew she was there.

The sun had already dipped low on the horizon, painting the sky in purple, crimson and orange hues. She'd already left it too late to avoid hitting Sydney rush-hour traffic, but she hadn't been able to bring herself to leave yet.

Her father had come in for lunch and though he'd barely said a word and hadn't expressed any interest at all in eating, she'd forced him to finish the ham, tomato and cheese sandwich she'd made and a cup of tea. He'd barely eaten or spoken since she'd been there. She understood his concern for her mother but having him fall in a heap from lack of proper nourishment wasn't going to help him.

She'd also been hoping to catch up with Zac before she left. He'd promised to keep her updated with any news. She'd expected to hear from him by now, but her phone had remained worryingly silent. She'd restrained herself from calling him. She didn't want to interrupt his investigation, nor did she want to appear too eager to hear his voice. He'd promised to do all he could to find her mother. She had to take him on his word and trust that he'd call her if he had news.

As if on cue, her phone rang. She dug it out of the pocket of her jeans and checked the screen.

Zac.

Her heart skipped a beat and then a rush of nerves swirled in her stomach. She licked suddenly dry lips, cleared her throat and answered the call.

"Hi Zac." She frowned.

I sound way too breathless. For goodness sake, get a grip!

"Emily. How are you?"

"I'm... I'm fine. How's the investigation going? Do you have anything to report?"

"I'm following up a few lines of inquiry."

"Did you track down Joe Sampson?"

"Yes."

Her stomach clenched. "Has he spoken to my mother? Does he know where she is?"

"I'd rather not do this over the phone. Do you have time to meet with me?" There was a brief pause on the other end of the phone. "Perhaps we could talk over dinner? I could cook."

A fresh wave of nerves rushed through her. Her instinct was to refuse. She and Zac were over. What they'd once had in high school had been lovely, but that was in the past. She'd moved on, matured, focused on a future that didn't include him. But somehow the words got stuck in her throat. Before she knew what was going on and despite the fact having dinner with Zac at his house no less would further delay her return home, she heard herself accepting his invitation. She ended the call with a dubious smile on her face and her heart pounding with anticipation.

What have I done?

Zac tried to ignore the hope that had flared to life inside him the moment Emily agreed to having dinner with him. He'd spent the past six years getting on with his life, building a career, having fun… But all the time, Emily had been there in the back of his mind. He realized now he'd been in some kind of holding pattern… He still had hope of a future together and he was going to do his best to convince her they were meant to be together.

He was proud of all she'd achieved. The strong, independent woman she'd become only made her that much sexier to him. He'd never stifle her need to make her own mark on the world. But surely they could continue to do that together, as a couple? He was a modern man, willing to embrace every aspect of equality and support her in the way she needed. Being a small-town cop would enable him to have more time to give to the relationship.

But he had to convince her and that wouldn't be easy. In high school, he'd had it all planned out. They'd live together in Sydney. He'd support them working as a cop while she studied. At some point they'd marry and start a family. Life would be wonderful.

Only Emily hadn't seen it that way. She'd wanted to explore the world, spread her wings without him. She'd wanted to be free to date other people, to live life on her terms without having to answer to anyone else.

As much as her decision to end things had devastated him, he'd come to appreciate her position. He'd also spread his wings, taken on positions that probably would have taken a toll on their relationship. In letting her go, he'd given them both the space to grow. But the past few days had made it clear he'd never given up hope on a future with her.

She completed him. She was his soul mate. His destiny. Her turning up unexpectedly in Broken had opened the door to a second chance and while the circumstances were less than ideal, he intended to grasp the opportunity and work on convincing her to take another chance on him.

He'd purposefully invited her to his home to avoid the distraction of prying eyes. As he navigated the supermarket aisles, tossing things into his trolley, he mentally ran through his go-to recipes and finally decided on something simple. Steak Diane, accompanied by steamed beans, honeyed carrots and fluffy mashed potato. Best not to go too fancy and mess it up. He was a fairly good cook, but he was also nervous. Much better to wow her with something simple.

She'd mentioned she was returning to Sydney straight after dinner. She had a shift the next day and she also needed to organize some additional leave. Though he felt a pang at the thought of her leaving, he took heart from the implication that she'd be back. He intended to use their dinner to reawaken memories of how good they'd once been together.

The gloves were off. He'd take whatever time he'd been given and work on making it enough. This was a start. And she'd be back. Finding her mother remained his top priority but re-building a relationship with Emily was the key to his future happiness.

Carrying the groceries into his house, he dropped them on the counter and headed for the shower. He had barely ten minutes before she was due to arrive. Luckily, he didn't need to waste time shaving. He'd worn a beard now for more than two years. It had seemed appropriate while working for the DEA. It made him look older, more experienced. At least, that's what his family said. He wondered what Emily thought about it.

Maybe I should just come right out and ask her? Am I brave enough to do that?

It was quite a personal question and one that would be filled with implications. Was she ready to hear he still had strong feelings for her? What if it were too soon? He didn't want to risk frightening her off.

No. Better to take things slowly. Reconnect as friends first. They'd been friends long before they became lovers. This dinner was all about catching up and reminiscing over good times. That would have to be enough. For now. He comforted himself with the knowledge she'd be back. Hopefully this dinner was the first of many more to come.

Chapter Nine

Emily felt more nervous than she'd expected to feel as she pulled into Zac's driveway. She'd already said a tearful farewell to her father with a promise to return as soon as she could. Leo sat in his carrier on the front seat. She picked him up and walked up the short path to Zac's door.

He lived in an upscale part of Broken. The neighborhood comprised of original, freestanding houses that had undergone impressive gentrification, along with a series of newly built apartment complexes and townhouses. The wide leafy streets were complimented by tidy, well-maintained lawns and gardens, contributing to the overall middle class feel of peace and tranquility.

Zac lived in one of the older style homes. Though she could tell it had been recently painted and there were new window trims, some of the original features, including stained glass windows facing the front garden, had been retained lending it their beauty and charm. She knocked on the front door and waited.

It had been so long since they'd had dinner together and apart from the odd burger and fries at the local café as teenagers, they'd never dined alone. Her parents had often invited him over for a meal. Occasionally, she'd been allowed to have dinner with Zac's family. But most of the time, they'd only gotten to hang out at school or in the afternoon, when Zac had football practice.

Inevitably, most of his time was spent on the field, but if she were lucky, her parents sometimes let her go with him afterwards to the café for a milkshake. It was only after she'd turned seventeen and had a driver's license that she'd been able to see him more often outside of school.

Just the thought of those lazy summer afternoons down by the river brought a smile to her face. They'd used those few occasions to explore their physical chemistry. She smiled at the memory of their teenage passion. The urgency, the fumbling, the tenderness. He'd always made her feel special. And she'd loved him.

She'd been surprised when he suggested they eat at his place. Even more surprised when he told her he'd cook. Though she had a distant memory of Zac's mother being a great cook, she couldn't remember him ever expressing an interest in it. Then again, it had been six years since they'd been together. They'd still been teenagers. A lot could change in that time. For her as well as him.

The door opened and Zac filled the opening. He was dressed in jeans and a red polo that picked up the olive tones in his skin. His hair was damp from the shower and curling at the ends. It was longer than how he used to wear it. The beard was also new, but it suited him. Made him look older, more distinguished, sexy. She wondered if it felt as soft as it looked and was immediately annoyed by the direction of her thoughts.

He looked at her and then at Leo and his face broke into a grin. "Welcome to my humble abode, both of you. Please, come in."

He led them past a sitting room with the stained glass and down a long corridor. Her high heels clacked softly against the polished wood floorboards. Framed family photographs lined the walls. He turned and she followed him into a large and airy kitchen. Pots and pans and cooking utensils hung from iron hooks above the gas stove and the mid-century Formica counter.

Like the stained glass windows out front, the room retained many original features, including a pressed metal ceiling and a red brick fireplace where a cheery fire filled the room with warmth. But it had been updated with modern colors, glossy white cabinetry and state of the art stainless steel appliances. The overall feel of the room was warm and cheerful. It felt like a room that was lived in, rather than a showpiece.

"You have a beautiful home," she said as she set Leo's carrier on the floor and let him out.

Zac beamed. "Thank you. I only bought it a few months ago. I'm still adding bits and pieces to the décor and I have a couple more rooms to paint, but it's coming together nicely."

"I thought you'd go for one of those modern places. All chrome and glass."

He shuddered, his expression one of mock-horror. "Oh hell, no. I couldn't imagine living in a showpiece." He looked around him. "I like to feel comfortable and prefer character and charm. Something that has a story to tell. I wonder about the people who've passed through these halls, walked the floorboards, told stories by the fire…"

He grinned, looking abashed. "Sorry. I get a bit carried away. I've always been fascinated by history. I love hearing stories from old timers, people who've spent their whole lives in this town. They can recall anything of significance and they know every man, woman and child. There's a certain connectedness in a small country town. That's one of the reasons why I found my way back here. The city just doesn't have the same feel."

"What were the other reasons?" she asked, curious.

Zac blushed and averted his gaze. Emily frowned.

Surely he didn't come back here for me? I don't even live here anymore…

The possibility intrigued her and also filled her with a level of panic. She didn't want to think about her and Zac together and how good it had been between them. She wanted different things now. She had her own life. In the city. The thought of returning to the quaint little town of Broken and picking up again with Zac… No. They were over and that was for the best.

Isn't it?

She felt a twinge of regret over her decision, and pushed it aside. Zac was a small-town country boy. She preferred the glitz and glamor of the city and though she looked forward to the peace and serenity afforded her in Broken whenever she came to visit, she was always glad to leave, but that didn't mean she couldn't enjoy dinner with an old friend.

"Can I get you something to drink?" Zac asked, filling the awkward silence.

She smiled. "Sure. I'll have a glass of wine if you have it."

"Red or white?"

"White."

"I have a Chardonnay or a Sauvignon Blanc. Which would you prefer?"

"I'll have a Sauvignon Blanc. Thank you."

He winked. "Coming right up."

He moved over to the fridge and pulled out a bottle of wine. "Just so you know, we're having steak for dinner, so you can switch to a red later if you like."

"Thanks, but I have to get on the road right after dinner. One or two glasses will be my limit."

He frowned at her reminder but refrained from commenting. She turned away from him and walked over to an antique kitchen dresser where several framed photographs of his family stood proudly on display. She picked one up and studied the picture.

"That's a picture of the triplets," Zac said, watching her. "It was taken a few years ago."

"So Charlotte and Trace became police officers like you," Emily mused, taking note of the uniform worn by Zac's sister and brother.

"Yes. Trace lives right here in Broken. Charlotte's a homicide detective, based in Cronulla. Although given they're a couple of years older than me and graduated first, I think they like to think they're the ones who inspired *me*."

Emily chuckled, grateful for the change in subject. She looked at the picture again. "And Molly's a paramedic?"

"Yes. She lives in Cronulla too. In fact, she's only a couple of blocks away from Charlotte." He gave her a crooked grin. "What can I say? We're a close family."

Emily smiled softly. "I remember that about you. I was always a bit jealous of your closeness to your brothers and sisters. It was nice. And there were so many of you. No way was anyone going to come between you. How are they?"

Zac shot her a quizzical look. "You really want to know? I thought my family represented the devil to you."

She stared back at him. "I'm still angry at your family, especially the ones who are connected to the mine where Evan worked. No matter what the courts said, I still believe the accident shouldn't have happened. Someone was at fault. My parents received compensation, but no justice."

Her breath came fast, like it always did whenever she thought about what had happened to her brother. Zac looked bewildered and hurt. She felt a pang of regret. This was meant to be a nice dinner between friends. She didn't want to ruin that. With an effort, she breathed deeply and tried to let the pain and anger go.

She managed a strained smile. "I'm sorry. Please, tell me about the rest of your family. I'd love to hear where they all ended up."

Though she didn't know Zac's older brothers very well, she'd gone to school with most of the others. The triplets were only a couple of years older than her. Apart from Zac, there was a Barrington sibling in the year above her and another one in the year below. They'd all been good looking, friendly and popular. Even if you hadn't been friends with them, you knew who they were.

When she and Zac started dating and spending time at each other's house, she'd gotten to know his siblings better. They'd been friendly, kind and welcoming. She frowned suddenly, wondering how some of those same kind, friendly people could be responsible for what had happened to her brother.

"Let's have a drink first."

Zac handed her a glass of wine. She murmured her thanks.

"Here's cheers," he said and clinked his glass with hers.

"Cheers," she said and took a sip.

The wine was crisp and fruity. It slid down her throat much too easily. Leo barked at her feet and looked at her expectantly. She laughed.

"I'm sorry, buddy. This is for grown-ups. I'll see if Zac has something you can eat."

"Of course," Zac said, returning to the kitchen. "What would he like?"

"What do you have?" Emily asked, coming around to stand beside him. She caught a whiff of his cologne and tried not to notice how good it smelled.

"I haven't cooked our steak yet. I could cut off a small piece for him. Do you think he'd like that?"

She grinned. "Are you kidding? He'd love you forever if you did that."

Right on cue, Leo barked. They both laughed, but suddenly the air was charged between them. Emily's breath halted. Her heart thumped. Nerves jumped in her belly. With an effort, she dragged her gaze away from Zac's and, setting aside her wine glass, bent down and picked up her dog. She buried her face against his soft fur and fought for her equilibrium.

She should have known to expect to feel the same instant attraction she'd always felt for Zac. After all, she'd felt it the very first time she'd unexpectedly set eyes on him again, but she wasn't a teenager any longer, giddy and in love. She was a mature twenty-something woman with a life and a career and a future she looked forward to. A future that didn't include Zac. She just needed to keep reminding herself of that.

Drawing in a deep breath, she set Leo back on the floor and reached once again for her wine glass. She took a fortifying sip and made an effort to slow her pulse. Zac passed her a plate containing a few tidbits of fresh steak. She murmured her thanks and once again bent down to Leo.

"Here you go, buddy. Look what Zac has for you. Yes! Doesn't that look good!"

The little dog made short work of the meal and then looked up at her, licking his lips. Emily laughed.

"That's enough now. I already fed you before we left, remember? That was just a little something extra for being such a good boy. Now, go and sit down by the fire, okay?"

Leo trotted off and did as she asked. Emily's heart turned over with love.

"He's a good dog," Zac commented. "Very obedient."

She laughed. "Yes. Although that didn't come without a lot of training. We spent weeks at puppy school."

He chuckled. "You always wanted a dog."

"Yes, but Evan was allergic, so I wasn't allowed to get one."

At the mention of Evan again, Zac's expression sobered. "I'm so sorry about what happened, Emily."

Her chest went momentarily tight, a familiar reaction when it came to Evan and the Barringtons. She drew in a breath and made a deliberate effort to ease the tension inside her. Whatever had happened, it wasn't Zac's fault.

"Thank you," she said. "It was a terrible time for my family, but it was wrong to blame you. You can't be held responsible for something you had nothing to do with."

Relief flooded his face. "Thank you. I appreciate you saying that. But I'm sure my family were just as upset by the accident as yours was."

She sighed quietly. "If it's okay with you, I'd rather not talk about this again."

"Of course," he readily agreed.

"So, tell me what everyone else has been up to," she said, tactfully changing the subject.

While Zac washed and peeled vegetables, he filled Emily in on the whereabouts of the rest of his family. When he got to Vaughan, he paused.

Emily saw the change in Zac's expression. It was like a shadow had passed over his face. She tensed. Vaughan had been connected to the mine.

"Zac? What is it? Did something happen to Vaughan?"

For a horrible instant, a part of her wanted that to be the case. As the Managing Director of Barrington Mining, Vaughan was responsible for overseeing all the mining operations. Though he wasn't on the ground at the mine where Evan had been killed and worked mostly out of an office in the city, she couldn't help but think that if Vaughan had done his job better, Evan might still be alive.

Unaware of her thoughts, Zac sighed. "It's nothing like that. He's fine. At least, I think he is. The thing is, we haven't seen him for months. He took off to Bali, of all places, without a word to anyone. We only recently found out he was there. Poor Mom and Dad. They've been so worried. For weeks we didn't know what had happened to him. We still don't know why he left and why he hasn't tried to contact more of us."

"So no one knows why he took off like that?" Emily asked, her mind spinning.

"Right. He's sent Dad a few emails, but that's it. We hope they're coming from Vaughan. They've been sent from his email address, but everyone knows how easy that would be to fake."

"Do you think he's in trouble?"

Zac scrubbed at his hair. "I don't know. That's the problem. He's told us nothing. Not even to Dad."

"Has anyone gone to Bali to try and find him?"

Zac shook his head. "No. We've been trying to respect his wishes and give him some space."

"But if he's in trouble and not saying anything..."

She had no idea why she was pursuing the questions. Why should she care if he were in trouble? An eye for an eye, right? She immediately felt ashamed, but anger was a powerful thing.

Maybe I should talk about it with someone? Maybe I should look into getting some professional help? After all, Evan is gone and nothing, not even my anger, is going to bring him back...

Zac compressed his lips. "You're right. Maybe it's time I had that discussion with my folks. I'm sure Mom would jump at the chance to go to Bali. It's been driving her crazy not knowing why he's there or for how long. She just wants to know he's safe."

"He works closely with your father at Barrington Mining, doesn't he?"

"Yes. At least, he did before he went MIA."

"So he'd know all about the lawsuit involving Evan?"

Zac stared at her. "What are you saying?"

"Nothing. But things got ugly for a while. Maybe his disappearance had something to do with that."

"But that happened a year ago."

"No. Evan was killed a year ago. The litigation was drawn out for months. We only reached a settlement a couple of months ago."

"Vaughan's been gone nearly four months. He must have left in the middle of it," Zac mused.

"To be fair, the negotiating occurred mainly between the insurance company and the lawyers. I'm not sure which members of your family were giving them instructions, but I'm guessing Vaughan was probably one of them."

Zac sipped from his glass and stared off into the distance, his expression thoughtful. Emily felt a stab of guilt for bringing the court case up again. She'd asked Zac not to talk about it and yet she'd been unable to resist the urge to remind him of what his family had done. Once again, she was overcome with shame. Time for another change of subject.

"So, can I help you with dinner?" she asked.

The steak Diane was delicious and cooked to perfection. Conversation started to flow again and they reminisced about high school days and the fun they'd had growing up in Broken. Emily felt pleasantly nostalgic and had to keep reminding herself about all the reasons she'd left. They'd been important enough to her at the time that she'd left the only boy she'd ever loved. Even worse, she'd ended the tiny life that had been growing inside her, a life she'd been unaware of until after she'd left.

She was five weeks pregnant and in her first month of university, taking the initial steps toward a career she knew she'd love. Life was good, life was fun. Life was a wide-open buffet of choices. The discovery of the baby had broken her heart all over again.

But a baby would have ruined everything and put an end to her hopes and dreams. It would have also put an end to Zac's dreams for his future, or at least it would have put them on hold. They were little more than kids, not ready to raise a child. Based on her circumstances, her future plans and what she knew at the time, she'd made the only decision she thought she could.

She'd once thought breaking up with Zac was the hardest thing she'd had to do. She was wrong. She'd live with the regret for the rest of her life, but at the time she'd thought it was the only sensible course of action. Her father would have demanded they marry. While she knew Zac would have been willing, even happy, to do that, she hadn't wanted to put such a responsibility onto him, taking away his choices. She'd never told Zac and she never intended to do so. What was done was done. It was her decision, her body, her secret.

Resolutely pushing aside her feelings of guilt, she sipped from her wine and tried to concentrate on the here and now. When Zac invited her to have coffee on the back veranda, she eagerly followed, glad for something to distract her from her thoughts. It was only when they stood shoulder to shoulder in the darkness, gazing at the blanket of white diamonds twinkling in the sky that she had second thoughts.

Zac stood so close she could feel his warmth and smell his spicy cologne. If she moved the tiniest bit their arms would brush. It shocked her to realize she wanted to touch him, to feel his skin beneath her fingers. Instead, she took a few steps away from him and drew in a steadying breath.

She returned her attention to the sky. She remembered star gazing when they were young. Lying on their backs on a picnic blanket spread out on the football field, long after the game was over and everyone had gone home. They'd hold hands and make out, hearts pressed together, counting each other's breaths.

Emily's pulse raced. The harder she tried to force the images away, the more the memories bombarded her. The feel of Zac's lips on hers, soft and supple and shy with discovery. He'd been as inexperienced as she was in the art of kissing. They'd learned together and had practiced as often as they could.

She snuck a glance in Zac's direction and found him staring at her. His gaze was heated and intense. Her heart stopped and then kicked into overdrive. Leo wandered around, idly sniffing at several large terracotta pots filled with flowers that decorated the back veranda. Emily tried to focus on her dog, but it was impossible with Zac looking at her like that.

He took a step toward her. His gaze remained locked on hers. She wanted to turn and flee, but her feet stayed where they were. He took another step and her mouth parted of its own volition. Her heart continued to pound. And then Zac's fingers grasped her chin and he turned her face to his. He lowered his head, slowly, slowly and then touched his lips to hers.

Fire and sparks erupted. Memories collided. She felt like she was coming home. He kissed her softly, gently, giving her plenty of time to pull away. But kissing him was like a drug addict taking a hit. Clean for six years and now the drug was back. Flooding her veins, filling her with a need so great it overwhelmed her. Her arms came around his neck and she pulled him close against her.

She was taken aback at the passion that exploded through her, like a molten river of desire. He kissed her with the same fiery passion and she knew he felt it too. Then all of a sudden, it was too much. The power of their feelings frightened her. They hadn't been together for six years. They shouldn't still feel like this. She didn't *want* to feel like this about Zac. Not just because of the pain and suffering the Barrington family had caused hers when Evan had died, but because she had a new life in Sydney, a life she loved, and it didn't include Zac.

Pulling away from him, she stumbled back, putting some distance between them. Her breath came fast, her chest rose and fell as she tried hard to slow her heartbeat. Zac looked equally affected. He also looked confused.

"I'm sorry," she gasped. "I shouldn't have kissed you. I'm sorry. I'm really sorry. It was wrong of me. You and I... We're over, Zac. We're only ever going to be friends."

Chapter Ten

Vaughan Barrington was nervous. No...more than nervous. He felt downright queasy. His palms were sweaty, his stomach was in knots, he felt like he might be sick. And all because he'd decided it was time: time to propose to Ruby Ashworth, the love of his life. He wasn't usually given to spontaneous decisions. His family were the first to give him a hard time about how long it took him to make up his mind.

He was a planner and a thinker. He liked to look at an issue from all angles. Front side, back side, upside down. He'd turn the problem over and over in his mind—sometimes for weeks—before he settled on a solution. Now, in the space of less than four months, he'd dropped out of his life in Sydney and had holed up in Bali with barely a word to his family and now he'd decided to marry.

It was the last that had him so twisted in knots. He'd met Ruby more than a month ago, but he still didn't know a lot about who she was. They'd barely discussed her career or her life in Sydney. Just like they hadn't talked about his. He'd deliberately left her in the dark about who he really was—the adopted son of mining magnate and billionaire, Frank Barrington.

At first, Vaughan had wanted to remain anonymous. An easy enough thing to do in Bali. That was one of the reasons he'd chosen the small tropical island as his escape destination. He wanted the beautiful blonde to like him for himself. He didn't want her perceptions of him colored by who his family was. Especially given recent developments over his biological mother, which threw the whole notion of who he was into disarray. He didn't think wanting Ruby to like him for who he was, was too much to ask.

He'd gotten lucky. Over the weeks since they'd met, he'd fallen deeper and deeper in love. They had a connection that transcended money and status and went to the heart of what really mattered: Two people who were so in sync they could finish each other's sentences. She was his soul mate. Meant to be. A chance meeting, but now he couldn't imagine life without her.

In all his forty years, Vaughan had never felt like this. In fact, he sometimes had to pinch himself to convince himself it was real. Though he'd witnessed his oldest brother, Christopher, fall in love—a miracle if ever there was one—he'd never thought the same thing would happen to him.

For all his adult life, he'd been content to play the field. He dated and flirted with abandon, never hanging around too long for anything too serious to develop or for feelings to get hurt. And that's the way he'd liked it. Footloose and fancy free. That had been Vaughan Barrington.

Then there had been a fatality at one of the family mines. A young guy Vaughan didn't know personally, but who'd gone to school with his younger siblings. A terrible accident. It had shaken him. A young man's life had been tragically cut short. It was a wake up call for Vaughan. Time to take stock of his life. Time to assess his priorities. Time to get serious.

Then came the bombshell about his biological mother. Elizabeth Craigdon, no less. One of the wealthiest matriarchs in Sydney. He still didn't know if her claim to be his mother was true, but why would she lie about such a thing? And why now? After forty years?

That news was the reason he'd fled Sydney. His departure had been inconvenient for his father and the lawyers, with Evan Wilson's lawsuit not yet finalized, but Vaughan felt he had no choice. He had to get away, clear his head. Give himself time to think through Elizabeth's revelations. He'd never intended to meet someone and fall in love. That hadn't been on his radar at all. But now that it had happened, he couldn't be more thrilled.

No doubt his family would laugh themselves silly if they could see him now. Worked up and nervous to the point of being sick over the thought of proposing marriage to the woman he loved.

What am I so afraid of? She's the one. I feel it in my bones.

So what if she didn't know who his family was? He knew very little about hers. That didn't matter. They weren't committing a lifetime to each other's families. It's what they felt for each other that counted.

That's all *that counts...*

"That's all that counts," he repeated aloud.

His fingers closed around the small velvet box in the pocket of his shorts. He was suddenly filled with a sense of calm and serenity and a certainty that this was right. He loved Ruby Ashworth and she loved him. Nothing else mattered. They'd deal with other issues as they arose and they'd deal with them together. Nothing would change the way they felt about each other.

It was time to ask her to be his wife.

Emily tucked a strand of loose hair behind her ear, one that had escaped her ponytail. She adjusted her uniform. It was a few minutes before her afternoon shift was about to start. As much as she hated leaving her father behind in Broken, until they had some clue as to her mother's whereabouts, there was nothing she could do except offer comfort. She'd be more use at work. Besides, being at work would help take her mind off things, and she knew her patients and work colleagues relied on her showing up.

She pasted a smile on her face as she walked into the pediatric ward. No matter what was going on in her personal life, she made it a priority to be cheerful around her patients. Given the battles they were fighting, that's the least she could do for them.

She'd been away three days. A lot could have happened in that time. She prayed none of her patients had deteriorated or worse, on her days off. She was particularly concerned about Izon Fernando. The ten-year-old hadn't been doing so well when she last saw him. His blood results had been all over the place. The doctors had put him on a new drug regime in the hope that it might slow down his cancer, but so far his body hadn't responded in the way everyone had hoped.

After sitting through the handover with her colleagues, the conversation eventually touched on Izon.

"How's he doing?" she asked, bracing herself for bad news.

Her best friend, Jane Radcliffe, slowly shook her head. "It's not looking good. The drugs don't seem to be making any difference. If anything, they might even be making things worse. He's been so sick these past few days. Constantly vomiting. We're doing our best to keep his fluids up, but it's been difficult."

Emily's heart sank. "What are the doctors saying?"

Jane shrugged. "You know. They're remaining hopeful. They've prescribed anti-nausea medication to cope with his vomiting. Poor thing, his throat is raw from all the acid. I've been giving him warm saltwater gargles to help with that. The doctor wants him to continue on the same drug regime for another week and see what happens. We're monitoring his blood work daily."

"And in the meantime, that poor little boy is suffering," Emily mumbled under her breath.

Jane shot her a sympathetic look but refrained from commenting. Emily didn't blame her for staying silent. It wasn't their place as nurses to question doctors' orders who were ultimately in charge. The nursing staff could only keep the patient as comfortable as possible and continue to hope for the best.

As the morning shift gathered their bags and left, Emily collected her patient charts and then headed for Izon's room. Before she'd gone on days off, he'd shared the room with another young boy who'd been discharged the day before. Though Emily was glad for the other boy, she felt for Izon. He'd been in hospital for months. No doubt he longed to go home too.

As she stepped inside, she plastered a big smile on her face. "Hi, buddy! How're you doing? It seems like ages since I saw you last!"

The young boy lying so pale and still in the bed turned his head slowly toward her and managed a weak grin. "Hey, Emily. You're back."

She winked. "You bet. How could I stay away from my favorite patient?"

He grinned again. Izon's mother sat in a chair beside his bed. There was a book open in her lap.

"Nice to see you again Emily," she said with a weary smile.

Having a seriously ill child was hard on everyone, but it was especially difficult for the child's parents. Izon's mother and father took turns to be with him. They lived in the country, several hours' drive from Sydney. They also had two other children. That meant they couldn't both be with Izon. Someone had to stay behind to run the household and take care of the others. Sadly, it was a heartbreaking situation faced by many of her young patients and their families.

"How's our boy been doing?" Emily asked. "Finished that jigsaw yet?"

Izon's mother shook her head sadly. "I'm afraid we haven't been feeling up to that lately. He's been doing it fairly tough."

Emily swallowed the lump in her throat and patted Izon's thin arm comfortingly. "I heard you've been feeling sick. We can give you some medicine to help with that. You let me know when you start to feel nauseous again and I'll get you something to take, okay?"

Izon nodded, his expression resolute. "Okay."

He looked even thinner than he had three days ago. It was worrying, along with the chalky white pallor of his cheeks. She picked up his wrist and checked his pulse. It was weak, but steady. She also checked his temperature, his blood pressure and his respirations. All were on the lower end of normal limits. Still, it was obvious the drugs weren't having the effect everyone had hoped for. Not that she'd tell Izon. He needed to stay positive. She could help him with that.

She perched on the side of his bed. "What would you like to do this afternoon? It's a beautiful day out. Would you like to go outside for a bit?"

He perked up. "Could I?"

She looked across at his mother who gave a small nod. Emily turned back to Izon and grinned. "I don't see why not."

The boy smiled. It lit up his dark eyes which looked enormous in his pale, ravaged face. His simple joy filled Emily's heart. Then his excitement dimmed.

She frowned. "What is it?"

"I... I don't know how far I'm gonna be able to walk."

Emily looked at his mother. "The past couple of days he's barely been able to make it to the bathroom and back without assistance," she explained.

Emily nodded. "That's no problem. I'll fetch a wheelchair. We could tear up the corridors with a set of wheels! Will you be all right with that?" she asked him.

Izon smiled, his enthusiasm returning. "Sounds cool."

Emily held up a finger and rearranged her features into a mock stern look. "Okay, but only if I get to push. If we go racing down the corridors, we don't want to take out some of our less confident patients. They're not all as competent or as strong as you. Deal?"

Izon grinned. "Deal."

She gently high fived him and they both laughed at his struggles to get it right. It felt so good to see a smile on his face. After fetching a wheelchair and carefully helping him to slide onto the seat and covering his leg with a blanket, she released the brakes and with his mother following behind them, headed for the lifts. As they exited the building into the bright afternoon sunshine, Izon lifted his face to the sky.

"That feels so good. It seems like forever since I was outside."

"It certainly is a beautiful day," Emily replied.

They found a spot beneath a shady tree and parked the wheelchair. Emily and Izon's mother sat on a nearby bench. They sat in silence for a while, letting Izon enjoy the outdoors. For a long time, he tilted his head back and stared at the vast blue sky above him.

Then he turned to her and said, "Thanks for bringing me out here, Emily. It's the best thing I've done all week."

Her heart clenched. Though she liked to think her colleagues made time every shift to take their young patients outdoors, she knew that wasn't always possible. With staff shortages, emergency situations developing and all manner of other pressing issues to fill their time, it wasn't all that often they had the opportunity to take their patients out into the sunshine. She was glad she'd made time to do it now.

"That's okay, buddy. I'm glad you're enjoying it. We all need to get out into the sunshine every now and then, right?"

He grinned. "Right."

The tiniest hint of color stained his cheeks. The happiness in his eyes warmed her heart. Silence once again fell between them until Izon broke it with another quiet question. "I'm not getting any better am I, Emily?"

Though she should have been expecting it, his question took her by surprise. She blinked and frantically tried to gather her thoughts. She wasn't sure how much his doctor and his mother had told him. As the silence lengthened, he spoke again.

"I'm not a baby, Emily. I want to know. Please, Emily. Tell me the truth."

Her chest tightened with panic. She hated when her patients reached this point in their treatment. It was never easy to deliver bad news. She tried hard to stay positive for as long as she could. She gazed over his head to his mother who gave her a tear-filled nod. Emily drew in a deep breath and looked at him.

"I'm not sure what you've already been told, buddy. It's true. The new medicine isn't working the way we hoped, but it's early days yet. The doctor wants to keep you on it a bit longer. Sometimes these things take time. I know it makes you feel sick, but if it works to beat the cancer, then that's a good thing, right?"

He gave her a half-shrug, looking far from convinced. "I hate feeling sick all the time. My stomach hurts. My throat's on fire. I feel weak all the time. Sometimes I just want it to end; for the pain to go away."

Tears blurred Emily's vision. She couldn't bear to look at Izon or his mom. She blinked hard in an effort to stem the emotion that threatened to undo her.

"I understand how you might feel like that, buddy." Her voice was nothing more than a hoarse whisper. She cleared her throat and tried again. "We're all here for you. We're fighting as hard as we can. Don't think for a minute we're giving up on you. You're a fighter, but we need you to stay strong. Without you fighting hard, we're like a one-legged turkey. A silly bird going nowhere except in circles."

A tiny smile lifted the side of Izon's lips. Emily closed her eyes against a surge of relief. She hated giving him what might turn out to be false hope, but neither was she ready to concede defeat. She'd fight with everything she had, right to the end. Like she always did.

"Do you believe in God, Emily?"

His question came from nowhere and even though it was posed in an uncertain whisper, she felt the power and responsibility of it all the way to her core. Before she responded, she once again took her cue from his mother. With an effort, she met the other woman's pain-filled eyes. At the sight of the woman's distress, Emily's eyes filled with tears. She couldn't hold back her feelings any longer, but neither would she allow herself to break down. She owed Izon more than that.

With another tearful nod, Izon's mother once again gave silent permission for Emily to speak freely. She drew in a deep breath. She turned and looked Izon in the eye.

"Yes. I believe in God. I don't know if I ever told you, but my father's a pastor in a small town outside of Sydney. I grew up there."

"Did you go to church?"

"Yes. All the time when I was growing up."

"Did you like it?"

"Not always. Sometimes I just wanted to be outside, running around in the sunshine, playing games with my friends. But my parents taught me how to pray and how to leave my troubles at God's feet. Sometimes I let myself down..." She thought of the baby she hadn't given a chance at life and more tears filled her eyes. And her brother...

"Does God forgive you?" Izon asked quietly. "When you let yourself down?"

She looked at him, her vision blurred. "I like to think so."

"Do you ever think about heaven?" he asked, staring up at the sky.

"Sometimes."

"I wonder what it's like?"

Emily drew in another deep breath and eased it out in an effort to regain control of her tumultuous emotions.

"We're told it's the most beautiful place we can imagine. Flowers, sunshine, happiness all the time."

"No one gets sick in heaven, right?"

The hope on his face sent a shard of pain to her heart. She bit her lip against another surge of emotion and nodded. "Right."

Izon stared up at the sky a moment longer, then he looked at her. "I'd like to go back inside now, Emily."

On their way back to the ward, Emily tried her best not to think about the possibility Izon might not make it home. She wanted so much to cling to the thought that the medications would begin to work, but the signs weren't great. She was shocked at how much he'd deteriorated in the three days she'd been away. Though Izon wasn't the first patient she'd lost, he'd spent so much time in hospital these past months, she'd grown closer to him than some of her other patients. He was a beautiful soul who deserved so much more out of life. She couldn't bear to think he might lose his fight.

She thought of her mother and the words of comfort she might offer. The worry over her whereabouts continued to gnaw. She needed to trust Zac that he'd keep looking for her.

Zac...

He was also playing on her mind. Life had become so fraught and complicated in such a short space of time. She thought about the dinner they'd shared the night before. Not only was he a good cook, but he was also good company. They'd easily slipped back into the comfort zone they'd created between them all those years ago. It hadn't felt like six years had passed since they were last in each other's orbit. That wasn't the only thing that hadn't changed.

There was no denying the spark of attraction was still there, burning as brightly as ever, if not brighter. She hadn't expected to feel so drawn to him again. For a long time, she'd dismissed their relationship as nothing more than high school love that could never have matured into something that would last the distance. That was something she'd told herself over and over when she'd made the heart wrenching decision to terminate their baby. Now she wasn't so sure.

Could I see myself with him? Married? Kids? A white picket fence?

The driving force behind her leaving had been her career and her need to make her own mark on the world. She felt like she'd managed to achieve that. She was working in a job she loved. Even on difficult days, she knew she was making a difference. That's what mattered. That's what gave her comfort when things didn't go to plan. Like Izon.

But if she was truthful with herself, she could probably bring that same depth of love and passion to any nursing job. The older she got, the more she thought about what else she wanted out of life. She'd never been against marriage and children. During their teenage romance, Zac had hinted at getting married one day, but she also knew he wanted to pursue a career. Back then the timing hadn't been right for her. Now she wondered if that had begun to change.

Then she thought about her brother. She hadn't expected to ever have tender feelings toward a Barrington again after what had happened to Evan, but it was hard to maintain the rage in the face of her feelings for Zac. Feelings she'd had for a long time. She'd tried to ignore them for six long years, burying herself in work and dating regularly, but from the moment they'd kissed it was obvious those long-dormant feelings were still there.

She remembered their parting last night with a pang. She'd told him they were done, that they would only ever be friends. It had killed her to witness his hurt and disappointment, but she hadn't retracted her words, even when she knew it could never be true. She was kidding herself thinking she could run from the overwhelming connection they'd rekindled. No matter what she told herself, told him, she and Zac could never just be friends. The truth was, she desperately wanted to do more than just kiss him again.

And that was the scariest want of all.

Chapter Eleven

Zac made his way home through the quiet streets of Broken. He'd spent another long shift making calls and chasing anything and everything that might give him a clue as to Lorraine Wilson's whereabouts, but so far all his efforts had come to nothing. It had been two days since Emily had returned to Sydney. Two days when most of his waking moments and all of his dreams had been consumed by her. The feel of her, the taste of her, the touch of her lips on his.

He was in love with her. He'd probably never stopped loving her. He was gutted that she only saw them as friends; that she wasn't willing to admit there was something special between them. It had been there when they were teenagers and the kiss showed him that something special was still there, burning brighter, damn it!

He cursed aloud. Damn the accident that had killed her brother! At least she appeared to be thawing toward him as far as blaming him was concerned, but it was still a point of contention between them. He could only hope the specter of Evan's death wouldn't become an irreconcilable issue. He needed Emily in his life.

No, I need to talk to my father and find out what really happened. That way I might have some answers for Emily. That's the only way I'm going to get her to let this go…

He also needed to find her mother. That would go a long way to redeeming himself in her eyes. He wasn't responsible for either trauma in her life, but he wanted to do everything he could to give her closure. The problem was, the only lead he'd had as to Lorraine's possible whereabouts was Anita Marshall's recollection that she'd seen Joe Sampson outside the Wilson house the day she disappeared. And that, along with his other inquiries, had gone nowhere. Though Joe admitted to being there, he'd denied knowing anything about Lorraine's whereabouts now, or even that she was missing.

And that was the problem. Without something concrete tying Joe to Lorraine's disappearance, he had nothing. It seemed Emily's mother had simply vanished into thin air. Of course that was impossible, but right now he was out of ideas. The one issue he could deal with was finding out more about what had happened at the mine which had been officially determined an accident.

Had Vaughan played any role in that? Is that why he'd been AWOL all these months?

Reaching for his phone, he dialed his father's number.

Emily's feet were sore. She'd been on them all day during another busy evening shift. It had been two days since she'd last seen Zac. Twenty-four hours since her conversation with Izon. Another twenty-four hours that the meds hadn't done their trick. No matter how hard she hoped and prayed, the results weren't good. He'd continued to deteriorate and there didn't seem to be anything they could do about it.

Her rubber-soled shoes were silent as she padded into his dimly lit room. She used her torch to illuminate her way. It was late. Nearly ten. Most of her patients were asleep. Izon was due his medication. She walked quietly up to his bed.

"Is that you, Emily?"

She started at his unexpected question, murmured in sleepy tones. "Izon! I thought you were asleep. How are you feeling?"

"Tired. Sore. I hurt all over. I've had enough."

Her heart clenched. "Oh honey! That makes me so sad to hear. I have something for the pain. Can you sit up and I'll help you take them."

The young boy struggled to a sitting position. He was so small and slight, his body barely made a bump under the bedsheets. It pained her to see him like that. Though he'd been ill when he'd first come into hospital, he'd lost so much weight he was barely recognizable. She hated how the disease continued to ravage his body, taking everything from him.

Swallowing a sigh, she handed him the tablets and then gave him a cup of water. He took them from her, murmured his thanks and swallowed, chasing them down with a small sip. Then he handed the cup back to her. She set it back on his table and perched on the side his bed.

His mother lay on the makeshift bed beside him. It wasn't a bed. More like a fold-out couch that was barely big enough to hold a medium sized child, let alone an adult. She looked cramped and uncomfortable, but from the sound of her soft snores, she'd finally managed to snatch some sleep.

"How's your mom?" Emily asked quietly.

Izon shrugged. "She's trying to be brave for me. I told her tonight not to worry about that. I don't need her to be brave. I know I'm going to die."

Tears immediately sprang to Emily's eyes. She fought against the wave of emotion, not wanting to break down in front of him. She reached for his small hand and squeezed it, too choked up to say anything.

He looked at her with his big dark eyes. "It's all right, Emily. I'm not afraid of dying. I'm going to heaven. And I know it's going to be much better for me there. I'll miss my family and you, of course. Besides, I'll see you all again one day."

Despite her best efforts, her breath hitched on a sob. She pressed a fist against her mouth, trying to hold back her pain. She was beyond words for this brave little fighter.

Izon continued to regard her with a soft, almost dreamy expression on his face. "Don't be sad, Emily. I'm sure I'll be up there having a good time. After all, it's the most beautiful place I can imagine, right?"

She gulped. "R-right. You'll be up there wreaking havoc among God's beautiful gardens. I can see you now, running around with all the other boys and girls, giving God a hard time."

Her voice cracked. She choked back another sob. The tears she'd tried so desperately to hold back spilled over and ran silently down her cheeks. She was overwhelmed with sadness, but she was also overwhelmed by his quiet faith. It was humbling. She'd been a regular church goer right up until she'd left school. But over the years, she'd drifted away. Life had gotten in the way. Including her decision to have an abortion. It was hard to reconcile that with the church teachings that had been drummed into her all her life. It still haunted her.

But there was no turning back time. She'd learned to live with the consequences. But lately she'd been thinking about forgiveness and hoping the loving God of her childhood would forgive her for what she'd done. She'd also started praying again. Firstly, for the safe return of her mother and now she prayed fervently for Izon to get better.

But she only had to look at him to know her prayers weren't being answered. She wanted to rage against that. It was so unfair. She couldn't help but think maybe her prayers for her mother's safe return would remain unanswered too.

Zac sat at his mother's eighteen-seat mahogany dining table with his brother, Lincoln, on one side and his sister, Charlotte, on the other. After hearing that Zac was making the effort to come home for dinner, his mother had phoned around his brothers and sisters and asked them to set aside time to come. Unfortunately, Molly was working and so was Trace, but apart from Vaughan, his other siblings and their better halves had turned up.

Lincoln sat beside his new girlfriend, psychologist Zoe Parker. Wade also had a new girlfriend. Zac had met Alice Coleman and her sons recently at a family barbeque. From the way the two of them kept looking at each other, it was obvious they were very much in love.

Charlotte sat holding the hand of her fiancé, Grayson Thorpe. The two had met during the course of a homicide investigation. In fact, Grayson had been the chief suspect for a while. Love turned up in strange places. Charlotte and Grayson and Trace and Cassie Webster were planning a double engagement party. It was to take place the following month at the Barrington estate. Zac couldn't be happier for them all.

The biggest transformation had come in the form of his oldest brother, Christopher and the woman the family credited with changing his life for the better. Lexi Greenaway was the mother of eight children. Five of them had been legally adopted. The remainder of them were foster children. Extra seats had been brought in so all eight of them could fit around the crowded dinner table.

Lexi had devoted most of her adult life to helping disadvantaged and vulnerable children and now it seemed she would continue to do that with Christopher by her side. The pair were due to marry in the spring.

Christopher was a pin-up boy for the power of love. Seated across from him on the other side of the table, Zac scarcely believed the change in his brother. The man positively glowed with happiness and contentment. Every time he looked at the woman beside him, he smiled with so much tenderness it was almost too intimate to watch. Zac hoped he could feel such emotion for the woman he chose to make his wife. With an effort, he managed to steer clear of thoughts of Emily. He wasn't going there. He was here on a mission.

The only other single Barrington sibling at the table was his youngest sister, Hannah. Feisty, young and independent, Hannah worked as a manager at one of their father's mines. She was making her way in what was traditionally a male world and if the rumors could be believed, she was kicking serious ass. He was proud of her.

As the meal progressed, the food was passed around, plates filled, glasses tinkled and conversation was loud. Zac sighed with contentment. It was always good to be home, surrounded by his noisy, opinionated, exuberant family. Time around the Barrington dinner table had always been like that.

As dinner wound down and the port was passed around, Zac cleared his throat and addressed his father.

"Dad, would I be able to have a private word with you?"

His father, Frank, looked at him with surprise, but nodded amiably. "Of course. Let's go to my office."

Zac took his glass of port with him and followed his father into the richly appointed room that served as his father's home office. Floor-to-ceiling bookshelves lined three of the walls. The other wall was filled with French windows that looked out on the manicured lawns.

Frank took a seat behind his large carved wooden desk and stacked his fingers together. Zac took a seat opposite. Frank looked at Zac expectantly.

"What did you want to talk about?"

Now that the moment was upon him, Zac felt a stab of nerves. Then he got a grip on himself and asked the question.

"What happened to Evan Wilson?"

Frank's thick white eyebrows rose in surprise. "Evan Wilson?"

"Yes. Don't you remember? He was killed at a Barrington mine a year ago."

"Oh, yes. Evan Wilson. Of course I remember. Why would you want to talk about that You already know what happened."

"I thought I did. The courts ruled it an accident, right?"

"That's right."

Zac compressed his lips. "I've heard rumors there might have been something else at play."

Frank sat up straighter. A frown creased his forehead. "What rumors?"

For a moment, Zac thought about keeping Emily out of it, but then he changed his mind. It was only fair his father know. "I ran into Evan's sister. Emily."

Comprehension flooded Frank's face. "Oh. Emily. I see. I'd forgotten the two of you were once sweet on each other."

Zac flushed and was immediately annoyed with himself. He had nothing to hide and nothing to be embarrassed about. So what if he'd once thought Emily would be his wife? So what if she dumped him? So what if he still yearned to be with her? None of that was relevant to the current conversation.

"What happened to Evan?" Zac repeated. His tone left his father in no doubt he wasn't prepared to leave without an answer.

Frank drew in a breath and blew it out on a noisy sigh. "Evan was killed in a tragic accident. At the time, he was employed by a contractor. We investigated it, along with the police and Worksafe, but we never got to the bottom of it."

Zac frowned, his police training kicking in. "How could that be? There must have been witnesses, technical experts, a whole plethora of people who could reconstruct what had happened and arrive at a conclusion."

Frank regarded him steadily. "You'd think so and we spent a lot of money on independent experts. Worksafe investigated the accident for months. The official decision was that it was a tragic accident and nobody was to blame. No charges were laid. Evan's family commenced a wrongful death lawsuit against the company. It dragged on for months because there wasn't sufficient evidence of any negligence on our behalf. For some reason, they didn't sue the contractor. It was finally settled out of court. Case closed."

Something about his father's brusque tone caught Zac's attention. He looked closely at his father.

"Why do I get the impression you weren't convinced it was an accident?" he asked.

Frank grimaced. "No one found any evidence of wrongdoing, which I found quite strange. Evan was driving a brand-new piece of equipment at the time he died. Apparently, he lost control for no apparent reason and crashed into an embankment. He was killed on impact."

"But you don't believe that," Zac guessed.

"I have my suspicions."

Zac sat forward. "What do you think happened?"

Frank took his time in answering. Zac sipped from his port. When his father finally began to speak, Zac was taut with apprehension.

"Evan worked for our then contractor, Joseph Rodriguez. Rodriguez had become disgruntled. I'd threatened to fire him for several safety breaches in the weeks prior to Evan's death and had demanded he clean up his act. He continued to flagrantly breach safety regulations. He was a danger to everyone at the mine. Finally I carried through with my threat and fired him."

"How soon afterwards was Evan killed?"

"The very day I fired Rodriguez."

Zac's eyes widened in surprise. "The same *day?* Talk about a coincidence."

Frank's expression was grim. "That's what I thought. Rodriguez knew the quickest way to get the mine shut down was to cause an accident. An accident resulting in a fatality would see us shut down for weeks, even months, costing us billions."

"What did you do?"

"What could I do? I brought in experts and investigators, the police, and Worksafe. No one could find anything. Rodriguez was smart. He had the wherewithal and the knowledge to pull something like this off without leaving a trail. I couldn't prove anything. But to this very day, I think Rodriguez had something to do with it."

Zac stared at his father in shock. It was the last thing he'd expected. He tried to gather his thoughts.

"What about Vaughan? What role did he play in the litigation?"

"Vaughan had nothing to do with it. He knew about the lawsuit, of course, but I was the one who dealt with the insurance company and their lawyers."

"Are you sure?"

Frank waved his question away. "Of course."

"Then why did he run away?"

Frank sighed quietly. "Is that what you think he's done?"

"Hasn't he?" Zac shot back.

Frank's shoulders slumped. "I don't know what's behind Vaughan's sudden need to take off, but one thing I'm sure of, it had nothing to do with Evan Wilson's death."

Zac took a sip from his drink. "Emily told me Barrington mining fought tooth and nail against paying out any compensation. Is that true?"

Frank nodded. "Sounds about right."

Zac shook his head with confusion. "What the hell, Dad? Why would you do that?"

Frank sat forward and sighed. "You must understand: Evan was employed by Rodriguez. It wasn't our fight. Also, the matter was out of my hands. The insurance company took over the moment I informed them of the accident. Their lawyers don't take instructions from me. If it had been up to me, I would have paid the family whatever they wanted. We live in the same community. I know Evan's parents, and Emily of course. They're fine, upstanding folks. Unfortunately, insurance companies don't work like that. There was a lot of arguing back and forth as to who was liable for Evan's death. Things got messy."

"It still doesn't seem right," Zac said.

Frank nodded. "You're right, son. It isn't, but that's the way things are. I'm just glad the case finally settled and the Wilson family got what they deserved."

"Except what they really wanted was their son back. Or at the very least some justice. Like you, Emily doesn't believe it was an accident."

Frank compressed his lips and averted his gaze. There was nothing more he could say to that.

"Did you even go to see them? The Wilson's? Emily's mother and father? Did you apologize? Offer condolences? Attend the funeral?"

Frank shook his head. "The lawyers advised against it. The insurance company was even more adamant we stay away.

They didn't want anything we might have said or done to be taken as an acknowledgement of our guilt."

And that was that.

Lexi Greenaway settled the last of her children into their child seats and secured the seatbelts. Then she pulled closed the sliding door of the minibus which their large family required. Christopher sat behind the wheel with the engine running. Hot air poured out of the air-conditioning vents, taking the chill off the winter air. Lexi climbed in beside him and smiled.

"Whew! What a night! It's been awhile since we had a Barrington family dinner like that."

Christopher glanced at her with a grin. "They just keep getting bigger. Watch out for when some of my brothers and sisters tie the knot and start breeding. Mom and Dad are going to need a bigger table and probably a bigger house!"

Lexi laughed. "At least a bigger table. We managed to squeeze twenty people around a table built for less. No mean feat."

Christopher chuckled. Putting the bus into gear, he pulled out onto the road and then reached for her hand, threading their fingers together. Lexi sighed with contentment. She couldn't believe how quickly her life had turned around. From despairing over being evicted onto the street, to finding the love of her life. Things couldn't get any sweeter. And now she'd also managed to reconnect with her mother after so many years.

"There's something I haven't told you," she said quietly.

Christopher glanced at her in surprise and a little concern. "Okay."

"I put in a freedom of information request to get access to my foster home file," she said.

"Wow. When did you do that?"

"The same day I reunited with my mother."

"Okay."

"It might sound crazy, but now I have my mother back in my life, I want to find out all I can about my family. That includes my maternal grandmother. For so many years I knew nothing about my family. Only that they didn't love me enough to keep me and raise me themselves. It hurt too much to even think about that. You've given me the courage to finally go looking."

Christopher shot her a concerned look. "Are you sure you're up for that? You might not like what you find."

"That's true," she conceded, "but I couldn't use that as an excuse for not finally discovering the truth."

Once again, he expressed surprise. "You've already found something?"

She half-turned in her seat to face him. "Yes. I needed to know what happened. Why I was given up. My mom's filled in some of the gaps, but I needed more. I wanted to find out about the brooch. The one given to me by my grandmother. When did she leave that with me? Why did she leave me in foster care? Why didn't she take me home with her? She obviously knew where I was. Didn't she want me? I was her granddaughter! And yet she left me that beautiful brooch. It didn't add up."

"And you discovered…?"

Lexi drew in a deep breath and carefully eased it out. Her emotions were running high these days and she needed to maintain control.

"There was a letter from my grandmother in my file. It was dated back to when I was five."

Christopher's eyes were wide with shock. "Wow. That's two years after you were put into foster care."

Lexi nodded sadly. "Yes."

"What did she say?"

Once again, Lexi blew out her breath on a quiet sigh. "She told me the brooch had been given to her by her mother and she wanted me to have it. She expressed her regret that we'd never get to know each other, and said it was now too late."

Lexi's voice cracked with emotion. Tears burned in her eyes. She turned to Christopher, feeling stricken. "I was five years old! How could she say it was too late?"

"Oh, honey. I hate that you're having these wounds torn open all over again. Are you sure you want to do this?"

She pushed aside her sadness. "It's too late for that. I've already read the letter through. I know everything she said."

"What else did she say?" Christopher asked softly.

"She wrote how my grandfather died a year after my mother ran away. Apparently, he died of a broken heart."

"But your mother's parents were the ones who threw her out," Christopher protested.

Lexi nodded, feeling grim. "Exactly. What's even worse, is that my grandmother came to see me in the foster home and *then left me there.*"

That was the hardest part to accept. That her grandmother had been fully aware of Lexi's circumstances and had done nothing to help her. She'd left her a valuable brooch. Big deal. Jewels didn't make up for the loss of a family's love. A love she'd wanted desperately. Even now, it was hard to comprehend her grandmother's actions.

"I'm sorry, honey. At least you now know how you came to have the brooch," Christopher said quietly.

Lexi's hands tightened into fists. She wished she'd never set eyes on the thing. Now she saw it for what it was. It was a guilt gift. She wanted no part of it. As soon as she could, she'd pawn it and donate the money to a charity that supported abandoned kids. Though she would continue a relationship with her mother, she was done with the family she'd never had. Her family was here. With Christopher and their kids. They were all the family she needed.

Chapter Twelve

The sun hung low in the sky when Zac switched on the ignition of his police cruiser and reversed out of the station parking lot. Another day was almost done. He scrubbed at his eyes. He was tired. It had been another long and pointless day of pounding the streets, door knocking with other officers, asking questions, talking to anyone and everyone about Lorraine Wilson and trying to work out where she was. The last thing on his list to do that day was to check in on Emily's father.

He hadn't spoken to Bob since that day in his office. Seeing as how Bob hadn't contacted him, Zac could only assume the man hadn't heard from his wife. It was now eight days since Lorraine had disappeared and there was still nothing to indicate her whereabouts.

CCTV footage of the bus and train stations had revealed nothing. Zac had searched through hours of footage. Lorraine wasn't in any of the frames. He could only conclude she hadn't left Broken on public transport. That left the help of a friend or a stranger to give her a lift out of town, but Zac couldn't see

Lorraine hitchhiking and none of her friends knew anything about her leaving. He'd also checked her bank account. The last activity was a transaction at the local supermarket the morning she was last seen. She didn't own a credit card.

It was becoming more and more clear that it was either a very well-planned secret escape from Broken or she might have met with foul play. The latter seemed the only reasonable explanation. As much as Zac didn't want to contemplate the possibility, the more time that passed without hearing from her or seeing some other evidence she was still alive, the more he had to accept the search for Emily's mother might not end well.

A hard ball of dread centered in his gut at the thought. His mind rebelled against the idea, especially coming so soon after the tragedy of Evan's death, but he had to be realistic. If this was anyone else's mother and his judgement wasn't clouded by his feelings for Emily, he would have already come to that conclusion. And he'd had that very same conversation with Trace earlier that afternoon.

Trace had stopped by Zac's desk to inquire about the progress on the missing person case. Zac had filled him in. Trace had looked resigned when Zac suggested they start searching the surrounding bushland for a body. As much as he didn't want to accept it, in his gut he knew he couldn't discount the possibility Lorraine had been abducted or murdered. Especially with the likes of a violent, drug addicted, repeat offender like Joe Sampson in the area.

With a weary sigh, Zac made the turn into the driveway that led to the rectory and pulled the cruiser to a halt. He climbed out and made his way up the concrete path to the front door and knocked. He tried not to remember the last time he'd been there and Emily had answered the door. Or how she'd told him after kissing him senseless that they would only ever be friends...

He heard the sound of shuffling footsteps on the other side of the door. A few moments later, Bob stood there before him, looking pale and gaunt.

"Hi, Bob. Do you mind if I come in?"

The man mumbled something under his breath and turned away. Zac followed him down the hallway and into the living room. The place was a mess. Dirty plates were stacked high in the sink. Food scraps covered the counter, along with an opened bottle of milk and a box of cereal. The bin overflowed with rubbish. There was an odor of rotting food in the air. Emily had only been gone a few days, but it was obvious Bob wasn't coping with the absence of his wife.

"How are you doing, Bob?" Zac asked gently.

The man scrubbed at the stubble on his chin and shrugged. "How do you think?"

"I take it you haven't heard from Lorraine?"

"Course I haven't heard from her!" Bob snapped. "Don't you think I would have called you?"

"You're right. I'm sorry. I want you to know, we're doing everything we can to find her. I've been talking to anyone I can find. Someone must have seen something. Someone must know where she is. I'm not giving up on her, Bob. We'll find her and bring her home."

Bob merely threw himself into a well-worn armchair and sighed. Feeling helpless, Zac took the seat opposite him.

"Have you heard from Emily?" he asked.

Bob nodded and sighed again. "Yes. She called a little while ago to ask how I was. Wanted to know if I'd heard anything."

Zac felt again the weight of responsibility, along with the accompanying disappointment that he didn't have anything to offer.

"Are you sure there's nothing you remember that might help pinpoint where Lorraine went? Anything at all, no matter how inconsequential. You never know what might lead to something important."

Bob stared down at the carpet and shook his head. "I've wracked my brain. I keep thinking about the last time we were together... I can't think of anything."

"Have you ever heard of a man by the name of Joe Sampson?"

Bob frowned. "I don't think so. Should I know him?"

"He's a friend of your wife's. She met him at the soup kitchen. She was trying to help him get into rehab. She told him the church might cover the costs. Did Lorraine ever mention him to you?"

At the mention of Joe Sampson's name, Bob Wilson went cold with fear. Even worse, he'd just lied to the detective. Again. The truth was, he didn't know the drifter, but he certainly knew who he was. The last time he'd seen him was right outside his house the very afternoon Lorraine had gone missing. He couldn't be certain what Sampson had overheard, but Bob was sure the man had heard something. Why else had he taken off like that?

The young Barrington boy was persistent; trying so hard to find Lorraine. Too hard. Bob was scared he'd eventually stumble on the truth. The thing was, Bob had never meant to kill her. Things had gotten out of control. He hadn't meant to cover it up either. He'd panicked. Now he was stuck with living a lie. It was slowly killing him.

He wasn't cut out for deception. He was a pastor, sworn to uphold God's truth! Ever since he'd started down this path, he'd felt his soul slowly slipping away until he felt like a hollowed-out shell. For the past eight days, he'd been merely existing, going through the motions in a daze. All along he mourned the loss of his wife, the woman he'd loved for most of his life.

Now he felt an impending sense of doom. Zac Barrington wasn't the type of man to give up. He'd been just as persistent in achieving his goals when he'd been young. Good at school and excelling on the sporting field, Bob had been proud to watch the boy grow up into a fine young man. He'd been proud at the thought of his only daughter marrying such a man.

But that hadn't happened and that was fine. Emily had the right to choose her own path, including who she shared her life with. If that man wasn't Zac, then Bob respected her decision. But that prior knowledge of the young Barrington boy meant that Bob knew it was only a matter of time before Zac stumbled upon the truth. Bob needed to give him a distraction, point the finger away from himself. The realization of what he was about to do filled him with shame, but he had no choice. Someone had to take the fall.

He shifted in his chair and frowned, as if the thought had only just occurred to him.

"Actually, Zac. Now that I think about it, there *is* something I remember from that day. It was your mention of Joe Sampson that made me think of it. Yes. Joe Sampson. I remember him now. Lorraine spoke to me about him. She really wants to help him."

He grimaced. "You remember how she is. She's always seen the good in people. That's my Lorraine. After she mentioned him, I checked into his background, made a few discreet inquires. He seems to have a long history of drug abuse that often results in violence. He's done time in jail. That's why I was a little alarmed when I saw him outside my house the afternoon Lorraine disappeared."

Zac visibly started. "You saw him outside your house?"

"Yes. I'm not sure what he was doing there. I was in my office. I happened to get up and look out the window and I saw him standing near the front gate."

"How did you know it was him?"

"It was an educated guess. Lorraine had told me he was…a drifter down on his luck and he'd been living pretty rough. The man I saw fit that description. Besides, who else could it have been? We don't get many visitors like that around here. If anything, they come to the church office."

"Did you say anything to him?"

"No. But I was concerned he was there. I was also worried he might be high on drugs and dangerous. I wondered if he'd come there to confront Lorraine about getting him into rehab. I hadn't yet decided about that, but Lorraine had told me he'd been bugging her about that. I was relieved when he left without a confrontation."

Zac sat up straighter in his seat. "Lorraine had a notation in her diary. She was meant to meet with Joe that day. At three o'clock."

"Three. Yes, it was probably about that time I saw him."

"He said she was supposed to meet him at the soup kitchen, but she didn't show. That's why he turned up at your house. At least, that's what he said."

"I know nothing about any meeting, but Lorraine had mentioned more than once how persistent Joe had become," he lied. "Though she hadn't made him any promises, he seemed to have gotten it into his head that we would pay for his treatment."

"Was Lorraine afraid of him?" Zac asked.

Bob paused and pretended to think for awhile. "Yes. I think she was," he lied again. "She didn't say anything, but I could tell she was concerned. The way she looked when she mentioned his name... She wanted to help him, but she was also wary of what he was capable of, especially when he was high."

Bob cleared his throat and looked directly at Zac, playing his trump card. "I don't know what was going on in Joe's head or why he turned up outside my house. All I know is my wife's gone missing and he might very well have been the last person to see her. And someone like that..." Bob gave an exaggerated shudder. "No doubt you know more about his past than I do... You must know what he's capable of..."

Zac's expression turned serious. "Someone else saw him outside your house. I spoke to Joe about it. While he acknowledge he was here, he denied any wrongdoing. It looks like he and I need to have another chat."

Zac stood and held out his hand. "Thanks for your time, Bob. I really appreciate it. This might just be the breakthrough we've been looking for."

Bob shook the outstretched hand and nodded. "No worries, son. Anything to help you find my wife. I just want her home, safe and sound."

Zac turned to leave. Bob breathed out a sigh of relief. But then Zac turned back to face him. He was frowning.

"Why didn't you tell me about Sampson hanging around your house when we first spoke? You obviously knew he was potentially dangerous."

Bob thought fast. At the same time, he tried to keep his expression blank. "I wasn't thinking straight back then.

I'd forgotten about him. I only just remembered when you mentioned his name."

Zac nodded. Though he appeared to have accepted Bob's explanation, the detective's expression remained troubled. Bob rearranged his face into a pitiful look. Zac patted his shoulder.

"Take care, Bob. If I hear anything, I'll be in touch."

Zac jumped back in the cruiser and spun the tires on his way out of the rectory driveway. Night had settled in and the streetlights softly illuminated the road in front of him, but he couldn't go home. Not before speaking with Sampson again. The news that Bob had also seen Joe outside his house that day supported Anita Marshall's recollection and knowing now how persistent Joe had become about having the church cover his rehab costs put his visit in a much more sinister light.

What had *he been doing there? Had he come back sometime later and confronted Lorraine? Had he hurt her? Why hadn't Bob told me earlier that he'd seen Joe there?*

The questions circled Zac's head, filling him with tension. He radioed the station and let them know his location. He wasn't afraid of Joe Sampson, but there were protocols to follow and they were all about keeping him safe. He got that.

He pulled up in the visitor's parking lot at the Lazy B Caravan Park and once again found his way to Joe's mobile home. He banged on the door. A moment later, the door opened and Joe stood there looking confused, but sober.

"Detective. What are you doin' here again? Have you found Miss Lorraine?"

"We need to talk."

Joe's tone turned belligerent. "We've already talked. I told you everythin' I know."

"No, Joe. I don't think you did. Now, you'd better come clean in a big hurry or else you and I are going to have an issue. You don't want any issues with me, do you Joe?"

Zac gave him a hard look. The man turned away and spat on the ground near Zac's feet.

Zac refused to be cowed. "Why did you go to Lorraine's house that day, Joe?"

"I already told you. I went there to find her. I needed to speak with her, to show her I was sober."

"But you weren't sober, were you Joe? You were as high as a kite that afternoon."

"No! Fuck you! You don't know anythin'."

"Then tell me Joe. Explain to me what went on that afternoon. And this time, I want the truth."

"I wasn't high. I'd been clean for three days. Ever since the Friday when I'd promised Miss Lorraine I'd get off the drugs. But it wasn't easy. I wanted to talk to her. We were supposed to meet at the soup kitchen, but she didn't show." He sent Zac a baleful look. "I've already told you all this. Why are you wastin' my time?"

"Because you're still not telling me the truth. You went there to confront Lorraine, didn't you? You went there to demand she give you money for your rehab."

"No! You're wrong. I went there to talk to her and to check to see if she was okay."

Zac glared at him, fighting impatience. "Why wouldn't she be okay, Joe?"

Joe averted his gaze and started to fidget. "No reason."

Zac's cop instincts went on alert. "What is it, Joe? What aren't you telling me?"

"Nothin'! I don't fuckin' know anythin'. Leave me alone!"

Zac moved closer. "Joe. A woman's gone missing. Apparently she was your friend. She was trying to help you. The least you can do is help me find her."

A long moment later, Joe's shoulders slumped on a sigh. "Miss Lorraine told me she and her husband had been havin' a few problems at home. They'd lost a son last year. They'd taken it hard. It had caused some...issues."

Zac stilled, silently kicking himself that he hadn't delved deeper with Bob or Emily on what effect Evan's death had had on all of them. "What kind of problems?"

Joe shrugged. "I don't know. Miss Lorraine wasn't specific. I didn't push. But when she didn't turn up like she'd promised, I went to her house to make sure she was okay. That's when I heard them."

Once again, Zac tensed. "Heard them? Who?"

"*Them.* Miss Lorraine and her husband. The pastor."

Zac's gut clenched. His heart began to thump. "What do you mean you heard them?"

"I heard them shoutin'."

"As in arguing?"

"Yes."

"Where were you?"

"Outside the house."

"And Lorraine and her husband were inside?"

"Yes."

"Are you sure?"

"Yes."

"What time was this?"

"A bit after three."

Zac frowned. "Bob Wilson told me he was in his office from about two. It's in the building attached to the church. It's separate from the residence. Are you sure it was him?"

"Yes. I saw him through the front window of the house. I'd opened the gate and had moved closer toward the house. I was goin' to knock on the front door and see if Miss Lorraine was home. That's when I heard them fightin'."

"What did they say?'

"I couldn't make out all the words, but they were both angry. Yellin' at each other. Then I heard someone cry out."

Zac stared at him. "You heard someone cry out?"

"Yes."

"What did you do?"

Joe scrubbed at his face and averted his gaze. "I didn't know what to do. I was scared. I'm on parole. Any violation of my conditions and my ass is back in jail. I froze for a moment or two, then I turned and left. I was back outside the gate when some woman walked by with two dogs. I can't remember whether she spoke to me. The dogs were yappin'. I was frozen there on the spot, still in shock. I was worried about Miss Lorraine, but I didn't want to get involved. The woman walked off. After a bit, I left."

Zac looked at him, incredulous. "Why didn't you tell me this before?"

"I was scared, damn you! I didn't know Miss Lorraine had gone missin' until you told me. Then all I could think about was the argument and that I shouldn't have been there. I had no right to be in her yard. I was trespassin'. I don't want to go back to jail."

Zac felt like he'd been sucker punched. His thoughts were racing a mile a minute, trying to make sense of what he'd heard.

Is Joe telling the truth? Why didn't Bob tell me about the argument? Why did he say he was in his office all afternoon?

With a deep feeling of disquiet, Zac thanked Joe for his time, climbed into his police cruiser and headed back toward the rectory. He needed to have another chat with Bob. Something was awry...

His phone rang. He checked the screen.

Trace.

Good. The very person he needed to talk to. Maybe Trace would be able to make some sense of what Joe had said. Zac answered the call.

"Good timing, bro. We need to talk."

"It will have to wait."

The grimness in Trace's tone made Zac go cold. "What is it?"

"Some campers have found the body of a woman buried in a shallow grave on the edge of the forest."

Zac's gut filled with dread. "Lorraine?"

"Could be."

With his heart pounding, Zac did a U-turn and headed out of town. The whole time he prayed Trace was wrong. He couldn't bear the thought of telling Emily she'd lost another beloved family member. Sometimes life wasn't fair.

Chapter Thirteen

Zac drove out to the crime scene with dread weighing down his very soul. Though he clung to the hope that the body wasn't that of Lorraine Wilson, after taking one look at his brother's face, he knew his hopes had been dashed.

"It's her, isn't it?"

Trace nodded, his face grave. "Yep. We'll ask Bob to formally identify her, but I'm almost certain it's Lorraine. The cold weather's slowed down decomposition. She's in pretty good shape, considering."

Zac's gut clenched on an agony of pain and dread. Lorraine Wilson had been a good woman and her life had been cruelly ended.

"Do we know how she died?" he asked.

"No," Trace replied. "There's no blood or other trauma readily visible on the body. We'll have to wait and see what the coroner has to say."

Zac looked around him. The crime scene was surrounded by lighting plants that flooded the area with light. A swarm of forensic personnel, other police officers and morgue staff crowded around, busy doing their jobs. He looked at Trace. "Who found her?"

"Those two."

Trace indicated a young couple who stood off to one side.

"They were looking for firewood," Trace added. "Stumbled across her. They could see part of a foot where scavengers had begun to dig up the grave. That's when they called the police."

"Have you found anything else?"

"Yes. We've had a stroke of luck. The sandy soil has retained a clear set of tire tracks leading up to the grave and another set leading away. I've spoken to the campers. They left their vehicle a distance from here. We can only assume the tire tracks belong to our killer, or at the very least, the person who buried her. The forensics team is in the process of taking plaster imprints now. They'll be sent to the lab."

Trace paused. He shot Zac a quick glance. Zac frowned. "What is it?"

"The body was wrapped in a blue floral bedsheet."

"Okay."

"There's more. There were rosary beads in her hands."

Zac's gut clenched. In all his years as a cop, he'd never heard of such a thing. It was strange. And very personal. It seemed whoever had killed Lorraine Wilson had known her well. His thoughts went straight to Bob. With an effort, he pushed them away. He needed to keep an open mind and see where the evidence led them. He braced himself to give the sad news to Emily.

Emily tied her hair back into its customary ponytail and swiped some tinted lip gloss over her lips. She was rostered on a morning shift and was due on the ward by seven. If she didn't leave soon, she'd be late. Leo was asleep on her bed. He'd woken earlier and she'd taken him outside and had filled his dish with food. He'd eaten his fill and had then made himself comfortable on her bed.

Now she stared at her reflection in the bathroom mirror. There were dark circles under her eyes and her skin was pale. She hadn't been sleeping well since the discovery about her mother. On top of that, she was worried about Izon. She wondered what sort of night he'd had and sent up a silent prayer that he was doing all right. Then her thoughts shifted back to her mother.

She'd spoken to her father yesterday. He had nothing new to share. He'd spoken only briefly in a dull monotone. People reacted to traumatic situations differently. Some became incoherent with distress. Others shut down. Her father's reaction wasn't unusual, but she was almost as concerned for him as she was about her mother.

The worry for her mother had become a constant, dull ache. Emily yearned to know something definite, even if that meant her mother had up and left without a word to anyone and needed some time on her own. Though that would have been shocking, at least they'd know where and how she was.

The sound of her phone ringing sent her hurrying down the hall to the kitchen where her phone was on the charger. She unplugged it and checked the screen.

Zac.

Her stomach dropped and then her heart skipped a beat. With her chest tight, she drew in a deep breath and answered the call.

"Hello?"

"Emily. It's Zac. I'm afraid I have bad news. It's about your mother."

A buzzing sound started in her ears. She barely heard the rest of what he said. Snatches of words and phrases. A garble of sounds. Her mother was dead. Found buried in the bush.

Dead. Dead. Dead.

All she could hear was her mother's voice when she called to tell her about Evan. It was happening all over again. This time, her mother had been murdered, but the outcome was still the same.

Dead. Dead. Dead.

"Emily? Are you still there?"

She heard the concern in Zac's voice but she was beyond responding. Not an ounce of strength to reassure him. As he continued to speak into her ear, she slowly slid to the floor. On a howl of pain and disbelief, she dropped the phone and collapsed into a ball of shock and grief. She buried her face in her hands and sobbed.

It was a long time later, when the sound of her phone ringing again dragged her out of the dark place she'd fallen into. She scrambled around on the floor and finally located her phone. The number was unfamiliar. In a daze, she answered the call.

"Hello?"

"Emily? It's Jane. I'm calling from work to check that you're okay. You were rostered on this morning."

Emily managed to stutter out an explanation. Jane was shocked and sympathetic and offered words of comfort and then reassured her to take all the time she needed. Jane would alert HR about the sudden death in the family and smooth things over. She knew Emily had been planning on taking some leave anyway.

Emily sagged against the wall with relief. She didn't feel up to talking to anyone at the moment, let alone an anonymous HR employee who had the power to refuse or grant her leave. Thanking Jane for everything, she ended the call and stared blindly in front of her. She needed to call her father. No doubt he'd already been told the awful news. She couldn't imagine his devastation and shock.

As if sensing her distress, Leo appeared in the kitchen and began licking her face. She grabbed him and hugged him close, taking comfort in his warmth and softness. He whined softly and continued to lick at her tears. She could almost hear his silent words of comfort.

Two hours later, with Leo beside her in his carrier and a suitcase in the back, she drove into Broken. Feeling completely numb, she arrived at her childhood home. She had no recollection of the trip, operating solely on autopilot. She collected Leo and her suitcase and climbed up the familiar front steps. She opened the front door and fell into the arms of her father, sobbing.

The pale, early morning sunshine struggled to cut through the heavy clouds that gathered threateningly on the horizon. A fittingly dismal beginning to what was an altogether dismal day. Zac reversed out of his driveway and headed toward the morgue. Halfway down the street, he leaned over to turn up the heat on the cruiser's air-conditioner.

Trace had asked him to meet outside the Lidcombe morgue where Lorraine Wilson had been taken to be autopsied. She'd been formally identified by her husband. He'd heard on the grapevine that Emily was back in town. She must have left shortly after his phone call.

He didn't think he'd ever forget the sound of her pain. He wanted to go over to her place and offer comfort, but her mother was his priority. They needed to get clues as soon as possible. Poor Emily. First Evan, now her mom.

An hour later, he pulled into the carpark outside the Lidcombe morgue. He walked into the reception area and found Trace waiting for him. Trace looked as grim as Zac felt.

"Hey," Trace said.

Zac inclined his head. "Hey."

"Thanks for coming."

"No worries."

"You spoke to Emily?"

"Yep.

"How did she take the news?"

Zac grimaced. "About as well as you'd expect. I'm not sure how much of the conversation she took in. I've never felt more helpless, listening to her pain on the other end of the phone and not being able to comfort her."

With that, they signed in and collected their badges from the woman who sat behind the reception desk before making their way through the corridors to the autopsy room. Zac was relieved to see Doctor Samantha Wolfe standing beside the steel gurney where the body of Lorraine Wilson had been laid out. Samantha was the chief forensic pathologist and was well known for both her exceptional skills and professionalism.

"Doctor Wolfe," Zac greeted her. "It's good to see you again, albeit in grim circumstances."

She smiled slightly and nodded. "You, too." She looked from him to Trace and back again. "You boys just keep on getting more good looking. No doubt I'll get into trouble for making such a remark, but what the heck? I might be heading toward forty, but I'm not blind."

Zac blushed. Trace merely grinned. He'd known Samantha much longer than Zac and the two of them had a healthy, professional relationship. Trace was actually good friends with Samantha's husband, fellow detective, Rohan Coleridge.

After pulling on protective clothing, including masks and gloves, Zac and Trace watched while Samantha conducted the autopsy. She took x-rays, drew blood, collected tissue samples and eventually made the Y incision down the front of the woman's chest. As she worked, Samantha kept up a running commentary, explaining her findings as she went. By the end of it, Samantha had determined Lorraine Wilson had died from manual strangulation, but she'd also been struck against the temple with a blunt object pre-mortem.

She directed their attention to a large bruise that had formed on the back of the woman's head. There was also a large gash where the skin had been broken. A decent amount of blood was matted in her hair. Zac's gut clenched at the thought of Emily's poor mother dying amidst so much violence.

"The blow might have been hard enough to render the victim unconscious, but it didn't kill her. There would be no bruise if that were the case," Samantha said.

She cut the victim's fingernails and collected the clippings into a sterile bag. "I'll send them to the lab and have them tested for foreign matter, especially skin cells. Although it's my guess the victim was struck from behind, it's always possible she put up a fight before she died."

Zac had already filled Trace in on what he'd been told by Joe Sampson. Though neither of them had voiced their concerns aloud, Zac knew they were now seriously uneasy when it came to Emily's father. If what Joe Sampson had said was true, Bob had some explaining to do. Coupled with the strange finding of the rosary beads, Zac's gut was telling him Emily's father knew more about what had happened than he was saying. As much as Zac dreaded being a witness to Emily's reaction when they arrived to interview her father, it was time to shake his tree.

After thanking Samantha for her time, they headed back out to the carpark.

"Where to?" Zac asked.

"We need to talk to Bob Wilson."

The grimness in Trace's expression told Zac his brother took no more joy over the prospect than he did, but it needed to be done.

"I'll organize a warrant to search his house," Trace added as he climbed into his unmarked vehicle.

Zac wanted to object, but he knew his brother was right. More often than not, the murderer was someone close to the victim. With the addition of the account given by Joe Sampson and the presence of the rosary beads, which had obviously been put there by the killer, it was an extremely personal killing which made it necessary to rule the pastor out.

"You might want to include the church office in that warrant," he muttered and climbed into his cruiser. With a heavy heart, he took the exit back to Broken.

Emily continued to walk around her parents' home in a daze. In an attempt to distract herself, she began cleaning up. Dirty dishes, left-over food wrappers, spills and other messes. She'd been there for a couple of hours already, but still couldn't shake the feeling that somehow none of this was real. Any moment, Zac would arrive and tell her there had been a mistake. That it was some other woman they'd discovered buried in the forest. But the longer time went on and there was no phone call, she was forced to slowly accept the truth.

Her father was in just as much shock as she was. He'd barely stirred from his armchair and stared blindly at the wall. Her efforts to engage him in the briefest of conversations had resulted in nothing more than a dull stare. She was worried about him and for the last hour had considered whether to call his doctor.

The sound of a knock on the front door interrupted her thoughts. With a sigh, she wiped her hands on the tea towel and headed down the hallway. Zac and Trace stood on the other side of the door. They wore matching grim expressions. Zac looked particularly distressed. Her heart plummeted.

"Emily. We're so sorry," Zac said.

She bit her lip against a surge of emotion and managed a nod. "Thank you."

"We're here on official business," Trace said.

He passed her a folded piece of paper. She turned it over in her hands. "What's this?"

"A search warrant," Trace replied.

Emily felt like she'd been kicked in the stomach. She stared at Zac in confusion. "A search warrant? What on earth for?"

Zac flushed and looked away. Trace supplied the answer. "We're investigating the murder of your mother. We have a reasonable suspicion she died in this house."

If she'd been shocked before, that was nothing like the utter horror and disbelief that ricocheted through her after Trace's announcement.

She gasped. "I beg your pardon?"

Before she could say anything else, Trace pushed past her, followed by Zac. Crime scene technicians in overalls with the word "Forensics" written in large letters across their backs stepped in behind them. A few other officers carrying cameras and other equipment she couldn't identify moved inside the house.

Emily watched in shock and disbelief as the officers went around examining every nook and cranny of the house. Opening drawers, moving furniture, checking under the seats of the couch. Leo went crazy, barking and snapping at anyone who came close. At one point, Trace approached her father and asked him to provide them with a sample of his DNA. Despite Emily's loud protest, her father agreed.

"I have nothing to hide," he said, as he swabbed his mouth and handed the stick back to Trace.

Emily looked on in silence. She'd never been so shocked, nor so furious. She glared at Zac at every opportunity as he went about the business of destroying her life, unable to believe he could do this to her family. Finally, her patience snapped. As Zac bent low and started scraping at a stain on the carpet, she screamed at him.

"For heaven's sake! You can't be serious! There's no way my father did this! You're wasting time while the real killer is still out there. You're turning my father's life upside down. He's a well-respected member of this community! What the hell!"

Zac continued to ignore her, which only sent her fury skyrocketing. She grabbed his arm, forcing him to look at her.

"This is Evan's case all over again! The high and mighty Barringtons throwing their weight around, treading on anyone in their path. I won't stand for it! Not again! I'll sue you for defamation! I'll take you for everything you have and I'll bring the Broken Police Station down too."

Zac continued to regard her calmly. He said nothing in his defense. Somehow that made it worse. She glared at him, her breath coming fast.

"I won't forgive you for this, Zac Barrington!"

Zac heard the anger and pain in Emily's voice and wished there was something he could do or say to take away the devastation that wreaked havoc on her face. Her eyes were red and swollen. Tears had dried on her cheeks. Her ponytail had come loose and her hair hung in haphazard skeins. But it was the shock, the disbelief, the utter *fury* that burned in her blue eyes that was the most difficult to take.

He knew how much she was hurting and how shocked she must feel. Coming so soon after the discovery of her mother's body, now the police were combing through their lives, looking for evidence that might point to her father being the killer. No one wanted to think someone they loved could be capable of this.

It was beyond comprehension, especially when the man in question was the local pastor and her dad. No wonder she looked at Zac as if he'd cut out her heart. Or maybe she wanted to cut out his? It killed him to know that their burgeoning relationship had been set back again, perhaps forever.

Bob sat in his armchair looking dazed and confused. When Trace explained the point of the search warrant, he'd spluttered angrily, shouting at them that they were wrong. But for the past fifteen minutes, he'd sat silent. Tears ran down his cheeks.

It pained Zac to see him like that, but he was there to do his job. He was there because some things weren't sitting well. If there was a chance Lorraine had been murdered by her husband, as heinous as that was, they owed it to her to seek the truth and get justice for her. If that meant Emily would hate him for the rest of his life, then there was nothing he could do about that.

The forensics team moved toward the bedrooms, accompanied by the police photographer. Emily let out another cry of frustration and anger, as if finally coming to the end of her tether. With her eyes blazing, she strode over to where her father sat. Taking him by the arm, she pulled him to his feet.

"Come on, Dad. We're leaving."

She turned and glared at Zac. "Do you have a problem with that?"

He held her gaze steadily, refusing to feel guilty about doing his job. He deliberately kept his voice even. "You can leave the house, but don't go leaving town."

Chapter Fourteen

Bob Wilson climbed awkwardly into the passenger seat of his daughter's car. He felt sick and was shaking with fear. He couldn't believe they'd found Lorraine's body. It had taken him hours to dig her grave. Okay, so he wasn't as strong as he used to be and his shoulder had begun to ache not long after he'd started digging and hadn't let up until he stopped, but he thought he'd dug deep enough that she'd never be found again. Apart from that, he didn't like the thought of her being dug up by scavengers. That kind of desecration wasn't right.

But now the game was up. It was only a matter of time before the police realized he was the culprit. Though he'd cleaned up as best he could, who knew what kind of evidence he'd left behind? He'd been in such a panic. It wouldn't matter that he'd never meant to kill her. Things had gotten out of control.

But perhaps this was for the best. In fact, in some peculiar way, he felt a strange sense of relief. He'd been in hell ever since it had happened. Every time he closed his eyes, all he could see was Lorraine's expression of shock and fear as he'd squeezed the life out of her.

He shot a look sideways toward his daughter. Her face was taut with anger and grief. A wave of agony washed over him. He couldn't bear the thought of her finding out. And when she did, she'd never forgive him. Now he was going to jail. His life was as good as over.

With Emily and her father out of the house, Zac concentrated on doing his job without her glare boring a hole into his back. The stain he'd found on the carpet in the living room had turned out to be coffee. Now he took the time to examine the stairwell that led down to the basement garage.

The lighting in the stairwell was dim. He switched on his torch and trained the powerful beam across the wooden treads. A dark, smudged stain appeared in his vision. He bent low and took a photo of it on his phone and then blew the picture up with his fingers.

Calling out to one of the technicians, he waited while someone joined him on the stairs. Pointing out the stain, Zac waited while the technician withdrew a testing kit and applied it to the mark on the stairs. Before their eyes, the swab stick turned blue, indicating the presence of blood. Zac's heart sank.

Of course, there was no proof yet it was human blood, nor that it belonged to Lorraine, but still...

Zac continued carefully down the stairs. He spied a couple more spots of blood, each one on a different step. Like something had been dripping... He followed the path to where Bob's car was parked. There were more blood-like stains on the concrete floor of the garage, close to the rear of Bob's car. Once again, the technician did his thing and confirmed the additional stains also tested positive for blood. Casts would need to be taken of the car tires.

With his stomach tight with dread, Zac went back upstairs. It gave him no joy to report his findings to Trace. Within moments, the mood changed. The house was declared a crime scene.

Hours later, Emily still seethed with fury. She'd returned to the house with her father to find the place looking like it had been ravaged by a cyclone. Cupboards had been left open, gaping. Furniture had been moved, upturned. Even the bed linens were missing.

She'd also had to run the gauntlet of nosy reporters. She couldn't believe news had gotten out so quickly. Thank God there were only a handful of them, but having cameras and microphones shoved in their faces had been infuriating. It had been all she could do to get her father safely inside.

This was ridiculous! The very notion her father was responsible for her mother's death was laughable and yet, it seemed that was the turn the investigation had taken. For some reason, they were fixated on him, not even trying to look for anyone else. According to the neighbors, the police had been at the house all day. They'd also searched her father's office. She had no idea what they were looking for or why they were targeting him like that. It infuriated her that the Barrington brothers, and Zac in particular—who knew her parents well—could think for even a moment that her father could be the killer.

She'd heard rumors the police had found blood droplets in the basement. Big deal. They could have been there for years, come from anybody. There was no guarantee they were even blood stains. No one could tell that for sure by just looking and they definitely couldn't tell who or what they'd come from. There would need to be a proper forensic analysis and that kind of thing took time. In the meantime, waiting for justice to clear her father, their lives had been turned into a nightmare.

She was still disgusted and appalled that Zac could even contemplate her father could be responsible. It was so wrong. Such a slap in the face. An insult she'd never get over. She couldn't believe she'd let herself have tender feelings for him again. What a joke! She'd been right the first time. The Barringtons were a law unto themselves. They didn't care who they trampled or whose lives they destroyed. As long as they got what they wanted. She was done with them once and for all.

Zac's head ached almost as much as his heart. After a long and tiring day, he'd arrived home to an empty house and had immediately started drinking. He was three beers in and had a light buzz, trying to do his best to block out Emily's harsh words.

The TV was on mute. Images flickered on the screen, but Zac had already tuned out. The story about Emily's mother had made it to the six o'clock news. He wasn't sure how word had leaked out. Then again, Broken was a small community. The police storming the local pastor's house with a search warrant within hours of the discovery of a body was sure to get attention.

The town was already swarming with media. He hated that Emily would be forced to endure the cameras and the endless questions from reporters. This wasn't her fault. She was grieving and in shock after the news of her mother's death. Having to deal with a media mob, and one with bloodlust, was the last thing she needed. Not that there was anything he could do to fix it. Besides, she wouldn't accept his help even if there was something he could do.

He took another gulp of beer. The ringing of his phone made him frown. He dragged himself off the couch and walked over to the kitchen counter where he'd left it.

Trace.

Drawing in a deep breath, he answered the call. "What's up?"

"Samantha put a rush on the lab tests. DNA's confirmed it's Lorraine. No surprises there. Bob's car has been impounded. They've found traces of blood in the back of it. Also a single hair. We're waiting to hear if any of the physical evidence belongs to Lorraine."

Zac's gut somersaulted with dread. "What else?"

"I had a call back about the tire impressions left at the gravesite. They match the tread on Bob's car. The bedsheet we confiscated off Bob's bed is a match for the one our victim was wrapped in. We're yet to make a definite link to the rosary beads, but we did find a similar set in Bob's office. I'm in the process of preparing an arrest warrant..."

Zac felt numb. Even without formal confirmation, he knew they had their man. Bob Wilson had murdered his wife. Whether he'd done it himself or in concert with someone else was still unknown, but Zac felt with an awful certainty that Bob, with his bare hands, had squeezed the life out of his wife. He felt sick at the thought of telling Emily. How many times had she told him her parents loved each other deeply and hadn't had a cross word in thirty years? Though he was only the messenger, he knew she wouldn't see it that way. It would only give her one more reason to hate him.

Emily couldn't sleep. It was late. Her father had retired hours earlier. She'd straightened his bedroom and had made up the bed with fresh sheets. She'd bid him goodnight outside his door and then left him alone.

He'd barely spoken a word since their return. Every question she put to him was either ignored or responded to in monosyllables. Though she had no appetite, for her father's sake she'd heated up a tin of tomato soup and had toasted some bread. At her insistence, her father had taken a couple of mouthfuls, but had then pushed the bowl away.

For what felt like the hundredth time, she turned over in her bed. The house was still and quiet. She wondered if her father had fallen asleep. How he could sleep with their lives in turmoil she didn't know, but a part of her hoped he had. He needed his rest. This had been as rough on him as it had been on her. Neither of them had been given time to process the fact her mother had been murdered, let alone that the police somehow thought her father was responsible. She half-expected them to return and drag him away in handcuffs. A shiver of foreboding ran down her spine.

Her thoughts kept returning to the blood that was rumored to have been found in the basement. Her mind kept turning over something else: That first night when she'd learned her mother was missing, her father had told her his initial thoughts had been that her mother had gone to the shops. But her father hadn't come in until after dinner and they both knew her mother didn't like to walk anywhere at night. It wasn't feasible that she'd be at the shops. That's if they were even open that late at night...

So why had he said that?

She didn't want to think her father could be capable of murdering her mother—murdering *anyone*, for that matter. The idea was preposterous. But the police seemed certain he had something to do with it. They'd combed the house from top to bottom, removing bags of evidence. That they'd even taken the bedsheets and had impounded her father's car filled her with dread. She felt guilty for even thinking he might have had something to do with it, but the growing niggle in the back of her mind refused to be still. She had to know the truth. She'd never get any peace until she'd had it out with him.

With a weary sigh, she pushed off the blankets and climbed out of bed. The wooden floorboards were cold beneath her feet. She switched on the lamp that stood on the bedside table and reached for her robe. Leo whined quietly in the darkness from where he was curled up at the end of her bed.

"It's okay, little guy. Go back to sleep. I'll be right back."

She tiptoed out of the room. She stood in indecision outside her father's door. *Should I knock?* The decision was taken out of her hand when the door to his room opened and he stood there in the darkness, staring at her.

Her heart skipped a beat. She put a hand on her chest to still its flight. "Oh, Dad! You gave me a fright."

"I couldn't sleep," he said. The utter sadness and resignation in his expression pierced her heart.

Emily sighed. "Oh, Daddy. I still can't believe she's gone." She paused and then added, "I can't sleep either. Would you care for some hot chocolate? It might help us both relax."

"Sure," her father mumbled.

He followed her down the hallway to the kitchen. She switched on lights as she went. Dispensing with the darkness made her feel a little better and helped to dissipate the ghost of her mother that she felt in every corner of the room. Earlier, she'd tried to remove the signs of the police search and had set rooms back to right. She filled the kettle and set it to boil and then reached for two mugs.

"We haven't had a chance to really talk about what happened," she said quietly as she handed him a cup of hot cocoa and went to sit at the kitchen table.

Her father wrapped his hands around the mug as if to warm them. He bent his head low and sipped. The silence lengthened between them.

"Daddy? I know how difficult this is, but we have to talk about it. Mom was murdered! The police have been here! They..." She stopped, unable to bring herself to utter the words, but then she remembered her earlier resolve to have this discussion and get everything out in the open so they could begin to grieve properly, and she continued.

"The police think you might have had something to do with it."

There. I've said it. I feel awful, but at least I've addressed the elephant in the room...

Her fingernails dug into her palms as she waited for his response. He was silent and unmoving for so long she wasn't sure if he would respond. When he did, she was shocked beyond all comprehension and belatedly, desperately wished she'd never said a word.

"The police are right. I'm responsible for your mother's death."

Emily was speechless, completely numb with shock. Her mind went blank, unable to grasp the import of what he'd said. She'd heard the words, but surely he didn't mean... No, of course he didn't mean that. Before she could formulate a reply, he spoke again.

"I didn't mean to do it. It was an accident. We got into an argument. It was terrible. We were both shouting. She was crying. My whole world was disintegrating..."

Emily's chest was so tight she felt like she was suffocating. She sucked in a breath. The air barely made it to her lungs. Finally, she found her voice. "Oh my God! Dad! What are you saying?"

He looked up at her with an expression so filled with sadness and remorse, it snatched her breath away again.

"I'm sorry, Em. I'm so sorry."

He bent his head. His shoulders shook from the force of his sobs. Emily felt a stirring of anger. Realization washed over her, drenching her in a fresh wave of disbelief and shock.

"Dad! Nooo! Nooo!"

My father killed my mother... Oh God. He just confessed. What now? What do I do? It's too much...

"I need you to understand," her father implored her through his tears. "I didn't mean to kill her. Things got out of hand."

Emily stared at him. She couldn't imagine what had happened between her parents for things to end with one of them killing the other. She felt like running from the room with her hands over her ears, screaming her distress, but it seemed her father had an urge to try and make her understand.

He started talking again. She wanted to stop him. There was nothing he could say that would make this all right. But her mind was in turmoil, her thoughts scattered and confused. The roaring in her ears almost made it impossible to hear. She didn't have the strength to stop him. And so she sat there like a robot and let him speak.

"You know how hard it's been since Evan's death. We all took it hard. Especially your mother. She buried a part of herself the day we buried Evan. A light went out inside her and no matter what I said or did, there was nothing I could do to reignite it.

"She withdrew into herself. Oh, from the outside she was much the same person, but on the inside... When we were alone... She wouldn't let me touch her. Love her. We hadn't been intimate since Evan died."

Emily stared at him. She didn't want to know these details and then wanted to protest that was no reason to end her mother's life, but it seemed any response right then was beyond her.

"Lorraine was no longer interested in sex," her father continued. "I loved her too much to force her. I tried all I could to get her out of her doldrums, to get past her grief, but she clung to it. It was almost as if grieving for Evan was the most important thing she could do to honor his memory."

Emily shook her head, bewildered. She'd noticed her mother's withdrawal after Evan's death, but that was natural. The woman had lost her son! And then for things to be dragged on through the courts... It had been a terrible time for them all. There's no way she'd blame her mother for losing interest in sex.

As if he read her mind, her father spoke again. "Of course, I didn't blame your mother. She was dealing with so much. I lost myself in my pastoral work. She just got lost. On the surface, she kept up her charity work and volunteering at the soup kitchen. She cooked and cleaned and did the shopping. But it was like watching someone on auto pilot. She wasn't really there."

He sighed and scrubbed a hand over his stubbled cheeks. "I tried to get her to see a therapist, but she wouldn't have that. She didn't want anyone to know how much she was struggling to cope. Not even you. She put on a brave face during your infrequent visits. When you left, she'd return right back to the place where she'd been. Dull, disinterested, merely going through the motions... It's been that way ever since Evan died..."

His voice drifted off. Emily tried to get a handle on her tumultuous thoughts. All she could focus on was that she should have seen past the brave face her mother had shown her and gotten her some help.

Why didn't I see it? Why didn't I see she wasn't coping? I was too caught up in my own grief and then the anger over the lawsuit...

Now it was too late. The guilt was overwhelming.

"I'm not proud of what happened next," her father said quietly. "It shames me to admit I turned to online sites to get my satisfaction."

Emily stared at him in shock. An ugly stain of shame colored his cheeks.

"What are you saying, Dad?"

"I have a porn addiction," he said brokenly. "I never meant for that to happen. Going online...searching for girls... It was meant to be a way for me to relax, blow off steam, connect in a sexual way with another human being. I didn't think of it as cheating. I'd never cheat on your mom. I still loved her with everything I had. But I needed some release, some intimacy, even if it was only through a computer screen."

Big fat tears rolled down his cheeks. "But it got out of control. I became addicted. What started out as the occasional online hook-up turned into nightly feasts. I ran up huge debts on my credit card."

His shoulders once again began to shake as he dissolved into sobs. Emily tried to remain dispassionate, but it wasn't easy. This was her father and he was devastated.

"How did Mom find out?"

Her father's sobs quieted. "She got a visit from a debt collector. He knocked on the front door. She was in the middle of preparing dinner. I was in my office. I had no idea until she called me and asked me to come home for a minute. I walked in and she hit me with it."

He shook his head slowly back and forth, as if remembering. "She told me about the debt collector and then asked how it could be that we owed so much money. We've always lived modestly, as you know."

"What about the money from Evan's settlement? Why didn't you use some of that to pay off your debts?"

Her father looked away. "Your mother and I agreed not to use that money. We set it aside in a trust for you." He gazed at Emily. "The thing is, I never expected your mother to find out about the money I owed."

"What did you say when she confronted you?"

"I told her the truth. I confessed to my porn addiction. Your mother was understandably shocked and hurt. And then she got angry. We got into a terrible argument. She came at me with her fists, pummeling me in the chest, the head, anywhere she could reach. She was sobbing, screaming at me. She was hysterical.

"I needed to quieten her down. I didn't want the neighbors hearing her rant. So I picked up a marble paperweight and struck her across the head to shut her up."

Emily gasped. She stared at him in horror, paralyzed with shock.

Her father's gaze was fixed to the table. "She fell to the floor and just lay there. I thought she was dead. I nearly had a heart attack. I'd wanted to quieten her down, not end her life. But then I realized she was still breathing. I'd only knocked her out.

"I was filled with relief, then I started remembering what she'd said. She'd accused me of some awful things. I'd never seen her so enraged. She'd threatened to tell you and the whole world, my parishioners. I'd be a laughingstock, run out of town, never able to hold my head up in public again.

"That's when something came over me. I'm sure it was the devil. He saw my suffering and whispered a suggestion. The next thing I knew, I had my hands around her throat."

Once again, Emily stared at him in horror. She pushed a fist against her mouth in an effort to hold back the pain and devastation and shock. Who was this man who sat before her, calmly confessing to killing her mom? It was so shocking, so terrifying, so unbelievable.

"Afterwards, I wrapped her in a bedsheet I took off our bed. It was her favorite. The blue floral one. I carried her downstairs into the basement and put her in my car. After the evening prayer meeting, I returned home and drove out of town. I dug a grave and buried her. I thought it was deep enough. The last thing I did was kiss her goodbye and put rosary beads in her hands."

Emily stared at him, aghast. "What?" She gasped.

Her father's gaze was steady and calm. "I had to make sure she was ready to meet her maker."

The shocks just kept coming. Emily's mind spun. She pushed back from her chair and stood, dazed and confused. She couldn't focus on anything. Everything she'd heard collided in her head. The noise in her ears was deafening.

I need to call Zac... I need to tell him. I need...

She thought about the awful things she said to him and cried aloud in shame. He'd been right all along. They were her parents and yet she hadn't seen it. Had refused to contemplate the possibility for even a millisecond. When all along, the answer was staring her in the face. The face of her father.

Stumbling from the room, she made it back to her bedroom before she collapsed onto the bed. Leo whined and moved closer to lick her face. Sobs wracked her body, leaving her completely drained. It was a long time later that she found the strength to call Zac and tell him what her father had said.

Chapter Fifteen

Zac and Trace were already on their way over to arrest Emily's father when her call came in. They arrived at the rectory and put Bob Wilson in handcuffs. He went without a fight. With his head hung low and his shoulders slumped forward, it was obvious he was a broken man. Emily stood nearby, watching everything in silence. Her face was frighteningly pale, her eyes wide with shock. She answered Zac's brief questions with even briefer responses. He could see what an effort even that much cost her.

He yearned to go to her, to take her in his arms and give her comfort. To stroke her hair, to whisper reassurances, to hold her close. But he could do none of those things. He was there on official business. To arrest her father. To destroy her life. At least, he was sure that's the way she saw it. No matter that her father had confessed and that she'd been the one to call the police. No doubt this would also be the Barrington family's fault.

Maybe I'm doing her a disservice? Maybe she won't be like that?

But the baleful glares she shot his way when she summoned up the strength told him differently. He could only hope once the shock had subsided and common sense was allowed back in, she'd see this for what it was.

As he led Bob away in handcuffs, Zac glanced behind him to where Emily stood. Her arms were tightly folded across her chest. Her face held a forbidding expression, frozen with anger and grief. She looked right through him, as if he weren't there. She didn't acknowledge their departure.

With a weary sigh, Zac turned away, taking Bob with him. He helped the man into the back of the police cruiser and followed Trace back to the police station to conduct the official record of interview. It was going to be a long night.

Emily wandered around her childhood home like a ghost. Lights blazed from every room, but she was still numb and cold with shock. Though it had been more than three hours since the police had taken her father away, she still couldn't bring herself to process everything that had happened.

Her father's confession kept reverberating in her ears and though a part of her wished he'd kept quiet, once she knew, she'd done the only thing she could and had called the police. Called Zac. The man whose life was intricately woven into the fabric of hers. She wanted to rage at him. She'd felt the same way when Evan died.

The Barringtons had been involved in that tragedy too. And though it hadn't been fair to blame Zac, that hadn't stopped her from feeling bitter and angry toward him and everything that had gone down. Now it was happening all over again. Another member of her family had been tragically killed and lo and behold, the Barringtons were there again.

Okay, so they were there as representatives of the police and she'd been the one to summon them, but that didn't make things any easier to accept. Nor did it dilute her anger. She wasn't too far gone to admit her reaction toward Zac and his brother was grossly unfair and if she were in a better state of mind, she'd feel ashamed. But right now, with her mother in the morgue and her father recently taken away in handcuffs, she wasn't feeling the least bit charitable toward the Barringtons or anyone else.

With a sigh, she padded into the kitchen and filled the kettle and set it to boil. The first golden rays of early morning light were visible outside the window. Another day was dawning and this one promised to be just as bad as the last. No doubt the media vultures would return at full throttle as soon as news of the arrest leaked out. She felt exhausted at the thought of doing what had to be done.

As if sensing her despondency, Leo sniffed around her ankles and licked her bare toes. She still hadn't found her slippers and her feet were cold. She bent down to collect him and drew him into her arms. Burying her face against his soft fur, she closed her eyes and sighed again.

The sound of her phone ringing stirred her from her funk. She set Leo on the floor and walked over to the kitchen counter. She checked the screen. It was an unfamiliar number.

What if it's a reporter, wanting to get a scoop?

The last thing she needed was to be hounded for details about what had happened through the night. The phone continued to ring and eventually went through to voicemail. A few moments later there was a beep, indicating a message. Curious, Emily dialed into her voicemail and listened. It was a message from her friend and work colleague, Jane Radcliffe.

"Hi, Emily. Can you give me a call please?"

Grateful for the distraction and relieved that the caller hadn't been a reporter like she'd suspected, Emily dialed Jane's number.

"Emily. Thanks for calling me back."

Emily frowned at Jane's somber tone. "That's okay. What's going on?"

There was a pause. "It's about Izon."

Emily's heart plummeted. An ice-cold lump of dread hardened in her stomach. "What about Izon?" she forced herself to ask.

"I'm sorry, Emily. I'm afraid... He didn't make it through the night."

As if from a great distance, Emily heard Jane continue to speak, but the words were incomprehensible. Her ears filled with noise. She heard the sound of her heart breaking. Frozen with pain and disbelief, she slid to the floor and sobbed.

She didn't know how much time had passed, but when she next became aware of her surroundings, the sun blazed through the kitchen window, illuminating a picture-perfect blue sky. Leo whined at her feet. No doubt he needed to be taken outside. She groaned aloud.

"You could use the doggy door you know," she muttered.

Dragging herself off the floor, she walked blindly down the hallway and opened the back door. Leo bolted outside and onto the lawn.

Her thoughts were consumed with Izon. This wasn't the first time she'd lost a young patient, but Izon had been special. And coming so close on the heels of her family tragedy, news of his death seemed too much to bear. She'd always thought of herself as a strong person, but now she felt weighted down and abandoned.

She thought briefly of Zac and then shelved the surge of yearning. No matter how much she might long for his strong arms to close around her, he wasn't her boyfriend, or her lover or even a friend. He was someone she'd known a long time ago and who'd once made her heart smile. Now she was on her own.

With resolve firming up inside her, she took Leo back inside and filled his food and water bowls. Once he was settled back on his bed in the living room, she picked up her keys and handbag and let herself outside. Her parents had never been drinkers and they'd never kept alcohol in the house, but right now she needed a drink to take the edge off the shock and pain. She didn't care that it was barely midday or that she'd have to run the gauntlet of reporters and cameramen that had already returned to her front lawn. She needed something to relieve the pain.

As Zac waited at an intersection for an oncoming car, he scrubbed at his beard and rolled his shoulders in an effort to ease the tension that had kept his muscles taut the past few hours. After a mammoth record of interview with Bob, they finally had the full picture of what had happened to Lorraine. It was sad and tragic, but it also left Zac angry that someone who purported to love her had callously and selfishly taken her life for his own gain. And that's what it came down to.

No matter Bob's tearful pleas that he hadn't meant to kill his wife or that the devil had forced him to squeeze the life out of her and then bury her in the forest, Zac didn't believe it for an instant. Bob Wilson had shown himself to be the epitome of selfish ugliness. He'd murdered his wife because he didn't want to lose his standing in the community or his job steering his parishioners along the lofty path of morality. It was enough to turn anyone away from the Church for good.

No, that wasn't fair. It wasn't God or the Church that had made Bob do what he'd done. That had been Bob alone and he alone would bear the consequences. With all that he'd confessed on record, there was no way he could enter anything other than a guilty plea. Then again, a decent defense lawyer might put up an argument of insanity... He hoped Emily would be spared the stress and embarrassment of a trial. She had enough to bear. God knows how she was holding up.

He'd wanted to call her, to go to her, to offer comfort, but because of his involvement in the case, he'd held off. No matter how he felt personally, he had to do his job. The last thing he wanted was to be accused of interfering with the legal process because of his personal relationship with the defendant's daughter. Cynical laughter bubbled up inside him. *What relationship?* She was wary at best and would now well and truly hate him.

She'd taken one knock after the other. It would devastate the strongest of people. And while he'd only been doing his job, he suspected he was damned simply by association.

It pained him to concede he was likely royally screwed when it came to trying to rekindle their relationship. Well, that and the fact she'd told him they'd only ever be friends. He tried not to think about that. In fact, he knew there was no way she could have kissed a friend like that.

The heat, the need, the passion... He hadn't been mistaken about that. It's what gave him hope that things between them weren't over and that there was more, much more between them than just friendship. *Stupid, so stupid...*

Trace had given him the rest of the day off. He could go over to Emily's right now. Test the waters. See how she was. And he would. But right now, as much as he wanted to put his arm around her and offer her comfort, he also needed to eat. He'd skipped breakfast and lunch in favor of sitting in on Bob's interview and now his stomach rumbled. He'd phoned the Café on Main ahead of time and ordered a hamburger with the works and fries. He'd also added a chocolate milkshake. Food that oozed calories and gave him visions of heart attacks, but he was too hungry to care. He'd think about his arteries another day.

After pulling into the parking lot outside the building, he strode into the café. John Lahood stood behind the mint-green Formica counter. He hadn't been the same since his son had been charged with murder and no one could blame him.

The murder of a fourteen-year-old schoolboy a couple of months ago had rocked the town. Things like that didn't happen in Broken. Now they had a second murder to deal with. The townspeople would rightly be concerned. Zac and the other officers would have to ramp up their efforts and work overtime to reassure the people of Broken that they were safe.

One thing the police had in their favor was that both perpetrators had been caught. Though shocking and tragic, both recent murders had been committed by people who'd had personal grievances against their victims. That didn't make things any less tragic, but at least the townsfolk could take comfort from the fact there wasn't some random serial murderer on the loose.

Zac paid for his meal and thanked John. He took the food to the very last booth. It was *their* booth. His and Emily's. Just being there brought back so many happy memories, but they were also tinged with sadness and that ever-present, tantalizing blip of hope. When he'd brought her there recently, he could tell she was also remembering the times they'd sat in that very booth, talking, laughing, eating, making out. It had been such an innocent, joyous time. Their whole lives had stretched out before them. The possibilities were endless. Though he knew she had ambitions and wanted a career, he'd never imagined she'd strike out on her own in the city.

He kept telling himself he had to grasp whatever opportunities presented themselves, give it all that he had and hope for the best. That was his plan with Emily. He wasn't buying her "just friends" act. Once they'd been as close as two people could be. The strength of such feelings just didn't go away. But he wouldn't kid himself that it would be easy. Circumstances and recent events dictated otherwise.

He knew she was angry and he was well and truly in the firing line. But if he didn't try, he'd always wonder and he didn't want to die with regrets. She'd always been the most important person in his world. A dream for the future he couldn't let go of. He'd give it one last shot.

Finishing the last of his hamburger and with a renewed sense of purpose, Zac waved farewell to John Lahood and headed out the door. He climbed into the police cruiser and put the car into gear. He turned in the direction of Emily's house. He'd barely gone a block when he spied her car parked outside one of the local bars. He frowned. It was early afternoon. Not exactly drinking time. Then again, she'd had a rough time of it lately. And if she was inside having a drink, who was he to judge?

Coming to a decision, he swung the cruiser into the parking lot and pulled up beside Emily's car. He climbed out and walked into the bar. The interior was dark and intimate, even at that hour of the day. Country music played from a jukebox somewhere in the back. The place was nearly empty. It didn't take him long to spot her seated at the bar.

Her head was down, her shoulders slumped. She looked so lonely and dejected. His heart clenched with compassion. If only he could take away her pain... He'd gladly bear it for her. If only things worked that way.

So far, he'd lived a blessed life. No one close to him had died or even fallen seriously ill. Until Vaughan's disappearing act, he hadn't been troubled by too much. He didn't take that peace of mind for granted and valued his family's health and prosperity, but it made him acutely aware of how much some others suffered. People like Emily.

She was made from sterner stuff, but how much was one person expected to bear? The tragic death of her brother, her mother murdered, her father in jail... Her entire family destroyed. No wonder if she'd turned to alcohol.

She had a glass of what looked like whiskey in front of her. As he watched, she reached for the glass, held it to her lips and tipped it back in one smooth motion. She swallowed and set the empty glass back down on the bar and then caught the bartender's attention and ordered another. Zac slid onto the stool beside her.

Her eyes widened with surprise and recognition. "What are you doing here?"

Her speech was slightly slurred. He wondered how long she'd been there and how many she'd had. "I could ask the same thing of you."

Her lips twisted into a grimace. "Don't judge me. I have my reasons."

He held his hands up in a sign of surrender. "Hey. No judgement here. I know what you've been through."

The bartender arrived with her drink. She thanked him and handed over some bills before Zac could reach for his wallet. Then she took a large gulp of the liquor. Sighing wearily, she spoke again.

"You don't know the half of it."

Her expression was so wretched, he immediately felt alarmed. He wondered what else had happened to make her feel so desolate.

"What is it?" he asked softly.

She looked at him again. Tears filled her eyes. His gut clenched. His fists tightened.

"I lost a patient last night."

He immediately understood her distress. "Oh, Em."

He fought the urge to close the distance between them and pull her into his arms. All he wanted was to offer her comfort and wipe away her tears. But she looked so tense, so fragile, like she might break into a million pieces if he made a move.

So even though it was difficult, he stayed where he was and satisfied himself with giving her a long gaze filled with all the emotion he felt inside. She stared back at him, her eyes wide with pain. He saw her swallow and then fresh tears overflowed her eyes. It was as if the dam gates had finally been breached.

Words tumbled out of her. She told him about a little boy called Izon. How he'd battled cancer for years. The long months he'd spent in hospital, on her ward. The doctors had tried everything, but in the end, Izon had lost his battle. The worst thing was, she hadn't been there in his final moments.

"I'm so sorry, Em. I can't imagine what you're going through," he whispered, his voice hoarse.

And then he couldn't sit by a moment longer without offering her comfort. He stood and gently framing her shoulders with his hands, he lifted her to her feet and folded her into his arms. She went willingly, surrendering with a soft, defeated sigh.

He held her tightly, stroking her back and murmuring words of comfort into her hair. She clung to him, her head pressed against his chest. Tears slid down her cheeks. He held her all the while, letting her cry out her grief. After a long moment, her sobs quieted and she pulled out of his arms.

"I-I'm sorry," she hiccupped. "I didn't mean to fall apart."

"Hey, it's okay," he whispered. Tenderly, he tucked a loose strand of hair behind her ear. "You can fall apart on me anytime."

She offered him a wobbly smile and turned back to the bar. She finished her drink and ordered another. He could tell from how unsteady she was on her feet that she already had quite a few under her belt, but he wouldn't be the one to urge her to ease up. After all she'd endured, she could get as drunk as she wanted.

In that spirit, he also ordered a drink. His shift was over. What the heck. But while Emily threw back neat scotches, he sipped on a beer. She finished another three drinks before she turned to him and would have toppled over if he hadn't reached out and steadied her in time. She half-fell against him and then laughed uproariously. He couldn't help but smile.

He'd never seen her drunk. Though they'd both turned eighteen in their final year of school, they hadn't gone out drinking. As Emily's parents were both non-drinkers, it hadn't been on their radar. Besides, they'd had plenty of fun that didn't involve hanging out at bars on a Saturday night. But he was pleased now to see she didn't get mean or nasty or abusive when she was drinking. Some people did.

"Have you had anything to eat?" he asked as he helped her back on her stool.

She shook her head. "Not since last night."

He looked at her, aghast. "Last night?"

She gave him a look. He got it. So much had happened since then. No doubt eating had been the last thing on her mind.

"How about I take you home and fix you a sandwich?"

She frowned. "I don't think there's much in the fridge. Could we go to your place?"

He smiled. "Sure."

"But first, I need to check on Leo."

"Sure."

Zac finished his beer and she did the same with her drink. Getting to his feet, he held out his arm toward her. She shot him a grateful look and reached out. She held onto him with a death grip. He negotiated their way across the bar and out the front door, ignoring the curious looks they were getting from the locals. He could hear whispered comments about her family. Emily suddenly straightened her spine but continued to cling to his arm. He slipped his arm around her shoulders and pulled her close. She sighed quietly.

As he led her to his cruiser, he tried not to think how good she felt against him. She fit neatly under his chin, like she had back in high school. They'd been made for each other. He'd thought that from the moment he'd seen her, all those years ago. But could he convince her? Again.

Chapter Sixteen

Emily didn't want to let go of Zac's arm. The firm muscles beneath her fingers, the reassuring strength of his chest made her feel safe and secure and protected, like nothing awful would ever happen to her again. But when they reached his car and he pulled open the door, she had no choice but to release him and haul herself inside.

Her head spun from the sudden movement. She gasped and reached out to steady herself. Zac looked at her with concern.

"Are you all right?"

"Yes," she managed. "Just a little dizzy."

Zac shot her a knowing look and closed her door and went around to the driver's side. He climbed in behind the wheel and started the ignition. They rode in silence. Emily's head had begun to thump. She tried to remember how many drinks she'd had but gave up.

They arrived outside her parents' home a few minutes later. Most of the reporters and news vans had packed up and left. The story was as good as over. While Zac shielded her from a lone cameraman, they hurried inside. Leo met them with an exuberant round of barking at the door.

"It's okay, buddy. Settle down. I'm home now."

She bent down and picked him up and buried her face against his soft fur. He licked at her face with wild enthusiasm. She giggled. It felt odd to be giggling after everything she'd been through, but the alcohol combined with a wriggling, jiggling, loving Leo in her arms tipped her over the edge.

She looked over at Zac. He stood watching them in silence. A tender smile played around his lips. She'd forgotten how handsome he was. How masculine. Especially with the beard. It framed his strong jaw and gave him a mature, confident look. Or maybe that was just the man he'd become—strong, confident, commanding.

He'd always been her rock.

She'd railed at him for thinking the worst of her father when all along, he'd been right. If he hadn't pursued that line of questioning, they might never have found her mother's killer. Though it devastated her to know that killer was her father, it would have been far worse never knowing, going through life forever wondering who'd taken her mother's life, where they were, whether they'd killed again...

It wasn't Zac's fault that he and his family had been caught up in some of the worst moments of her life. Her fury at his family over Evan's death and now Zac's investigation of her mother's had given her something to cling to; something to give her strength in railing against the unfairness of life.

She thought of poor Izon and the other children she'd lost in the fight against disease and death. So much loss... She'd been furious at the hand she'd been dealt with. She'd been furious at Zac, when none of this had been his fault. She'd said some awful things. Things she was now ashamed of. She owed him an apology.

Drawing in a deep breath, she lifted her head and stared at him. "I'm sorry."

His eyes flared with surprise and then slowly with admiration. "It's not necessary, but thank you."

"I was out of line," she said. "You were only doing your job. As it turned out, you were right." She grimaced.

His gaze remained steady on hers. There was no criticism or judgement in his eyes. "That gives me no satisfaction."

She closed her eyes briefly and nodded. "I know."

A fresh wave of pain went through her. All of a sudden, the emptiness of a house that had once been filled with love and gentle laughter closed in on her. Her mother was dead. Never again would Emily hear her voice, kiss her goodbye, talk to her, seek advice. There was now a gaping black hole that could never be filled. And every time she thought about her mother, she thought about her father who'd taken her mother's life. On top of that, was Izon's death. It was too much.

As if sensing her precarious hold on her emotions, Zac stepped forward and folded her in his embrace. Leo was caught between them. He yelped and squirmed to get free. Chuckling, Zac moved away from her. When he did, she felt lost. Panic rose inside her. She couldn't stay in the house where her father had so callously ended her mother's life.

"Do you think I could stay with you tonight?" she asked, trying to tamp down her panic.

Zac blinked in surprise. "Of course. If that's what you want."

"It's just that... I can't bear the thought of being here tonight. Not after everything that's happened... I just need some time away from here to come to terms with it." She sent him a pleading look. "Am I making any sense?"

Zac reached out and cradled her cheek against his palm. The touch was so tender and gentle, her heart lurched.

"Of course you are. But there's no need to explain or try to justify your feelings. I understand. Come home with me. I'll make up the spare room. Bring Leo. Let me fix you something to eat. Then you can rest."

Her stomach took that opportunity to growl. They both heard it.

"See? Your stomach agrees," Zac said.

She offered a brief smile. "You're right."

"I make a mean toasted cheese sandwich," he teased.

She smiled. "That sounds wonderful. It'll also help me sober up. My head's spinning."

He chuckled. "No doubt you'll have a doozy of a hangover tomorrow. I can probably help with that too."

They smiled at one another. It felt good. It felt comfortable. It felt like old times.

"I just need to grab a few things for Leo and I. Are you sure you don't mind if he comes along?"

"No, of course not. I love dogs. And besides, you'd only worry about him."

Warmth flowed through Emily at his admission. With all that had happened, with the increasing emotional toll her job was taking, she stood there wondering why it was she'd left him in the first place. Something about a desire to spread her wings. She'd have to contemplate that later. But right at that moment, she'd had too much to drink to do anything more than wonder.

Dragging her gaze from his, she pointed toward Leo's bed, his food bowl and his toys and asked Zac to assist her while she went to bedroom. She grabbed her overnight bag off her bed. In her rush to return after being told of her mother's death and then grieving with her father, she hadn't had time to unpack.

She looked around the room in despair. Her happy childhood memories had been obliterated by the cruel and selfish actions of her father. Right now, she never wanted to return to her childhood home again.

She steadied herself with a deep breath. She still felt a little dizzy, but she was also hungry. A toasted sandwich was just what she needed. She just hoped she'd be able to keep it down.

Making her way back to the living room, she found Zac waiting for her. He had Leo in his arms. Her heart lurched again. She was done remembering and questioning her decisions. Tonight, she just wanted to be; to forget her heartaches and troubles. She was exhausted. Everything else could wait.

Zac showed Emily and Leo to the spare room and then went in search of linens. He found a clean set of sheets, a pillowcase and a towel in the linen closet and brought them back to her. Together, they made up the bed. Leo spent the time searching the perimeter of the room, sniffing in every corner. Finally, as if satisfied, he plopped down on his bed.

Zac handed Emily the towel. She sent him a grateful look. "Thanks."

"The shower's down the hall." He hadn't wanted to say anything, but she looked like hell. Her hair was a mess. There were purple shadows under her eyes. Her clothes looked like they'd been tossed on in the dark. Permeating all of that was an air of hopelessness that he yearned to erase.

There was nothing he could do about her family situation, or the boy who'd lost his battle with cancer, but that didn't mean he didn't want to do something to remove the sadness from her beautiful eyes and make her laugh again.

"I'll go and fix you something to eat."

He left the room and quietly closed the door behind him. Pulling the sandwich maker out of the cupboard, he set about fixing a toasted cheese sandwich. By the time it was done, he'd also made a fresh pot of coffee. He'd arranged both on a tray, ready to take it into Emily, when she appeared in the open doorway. She looked marginally better with wet hair and fresh clothes but was still way too pale for his liking. Leo padded at her feet.

"How are you feeling?" he asked.

"A little better. I have a headache. I guess I shouldn't complain. All self-inflicted, but I just needed to obliterate me for a while."

He went to the cupboard above the fridge without comment and pulled down his box of over-the-counter medications. He found some paracetamol and handed them to her, along with a glass of water.

"Here."

She shot him another grateful look. "Thanks."

After tossing down the painkillers, she picked up the toasted sandwich and took a small bite.

"*Mm*. This is good. Thank you."

"No worries. How do you take your coffee?"

"White with one."

He poured coffee into two mugs and fixed it the way she wanted. She took a sip and sighed.

"Oh, that's good. Thank you."

"No worries," he said again. "And please stop thanking me. I'm happy to help you out. That's what friends do, right?"

She looked at him with an inscrutable expression for such a long time he almost groaned. *What does it mean? Is she ready to admit I mean more to her than a friend, or is that just wishful thinking?*

Now wasn't the time for deep conversations, especially about something as important as that. No, best to leave that for another time, when she was sober at least. As much as he wanted to know where he stood with her, she was in no shape for such an emotionally demanding conversation. Instead, he'd be her friend.

By the time she'd finished most of her sandwich and all of her coffee, she looked like she could hardly keep her eyes open. Zac wasn't sure at what time the night before she'd found out what her father had done, but she'd called him early in the morning. Right now, she looked dead on her feet.

Though it was only mid-afternoon, he insisted she go to bed. It seemed natural to take her by the hand and lead her back to the spare room bed. As he went to release her hand, she tightened her hold on his fingers. He stared down at their joined hands.

"Do you mind staying for a bit? At least until I fall asleep? I don't want to be alone right now. It hurts too much."

Her voice was a husky whisper that rasped against his soul. Her eyes shone with sadness and vulnerability. He couldn't have refused her request if he'd tried. Instead, he followed her into the room. She lay down on the bed and pulled him down beside her. His heart thumped overtime at her nearness, but he forced himself to remain detached. What she needed right now was a friend.

Lying fully clothed on top of the bed, Zac took her in his arms and held her. She rested her head against his chest and closed her eyes on a weary sigh.

"My head feels funny," she murmured against his shirt.

He smiled and pressed a tender kiss against her forehead. "*Shh.* Go to sleep. Let the medicine do its thing."

He moved slightly to get more comfortable. Her arm immediately tightened across his chest. "You're not leaving, are you? Everyone I love keeps leaving me," she whispered hoarsely.

The fear in her eyes filled him with compassion and love. He pressed another kiss against her forehead. "I'm not going anywhere. I said I'd stay and I will. Now, close your eyes and go to sleep."

Zac continued to hold Emily close long after she'd fallen asleep, loving the feel of her in his arms, loving her. He'd never stopped loving her. But he'd put another obstacle in the path of any future they might have. He was responsible for putting her father in jail, and while she'd recognized he was only doing his job, he feared it might be too big a hurdle to overcome. The Barringtons continued to be front and center during the most painful moments of her life.

He sighed quietly and stroked her soft hair off her face. He couldn't bear to think about all that right now. All he could hope was that it wouldn't destroy her, or any chance the two of them might have of working things out.

Emily woke to the sound of someone talking. She opened her eyes. Bright sunlight leaked in from between the gaps in the curtains. Morning had arrived. She looked around at the unfamiliar room. It took her a moment to get her bearings, then everything came back in a rush.

I'm at Zac's house... I'm in his spare room...

She looked down at herself. She was still dressed in the sweatpants and T-shirt she'd pulled on after her shower yesterday. She couldn't believe she'd slept through. She'd been exhausted. Both mentally and physically. Her body had done what it could to heal and gather strength for the trials that lay ahead.

The murmur of a male voice continued. She listened harder and realized it was Zac. She wondered who he was talking to. And then she heard Leo bark. She smiled. Zac was talking to her dog. Her heart rolled over. Snippets of conversation from the day before came back to her, as well as the feeling of safety and contentment she'd felt falling asleep in Zac's arms. He could have taken advantage of her, but he hadn't. He'd been supportive, kind and honorable. He'd been her friend.

A friend. Is that really what I want from him? Friendship?

Everything inside her seemed to rebel at that idea. Despite all the anger and pain and loss, she'd recognized in recent days that she was still in love with him. She'd left Broken six years ago to forge her own path without the restrictions that came with being in a relationship. She'd been too immature to appreciate the depth of their feelings for each other or the special connection they had. That kind of thing didn't come by every day. She knew that now.

Though she'd dated plenty in university and later, she hadn't found anyone who understood her like Zac did. Not only that, he'd cared for her deeply. She'd seen that same caring in him recently and she'd taken heart.

Is he still in love with me?

A surge of yearning took her by surprise. She'd spent years trying to fulfil her destiny, make her mark on the world, alone, when all along, she could have been making her mark and sharing the highs and lows with her soul mate, right here in Broken, or anywhere else. Hindsight was all well and good. At the time, it had been the best decision for her to make.

But now she was ready to explore new possibilities. She realized now that while she'd been seeking new horizons, Zac had stayed constant in his love for her. It wasn't just because she was now alone in the world, though that had opened her eyes to her feelings. She'd seen it in his face, through his actions.

The revelation felt surreal, like an elusive secret that had finally been revealed. She wanted to turn it over, wonder at it, examine it from all angles, but she also needed to speak with Zac, to make sure she hadn't misinterpreted the signals. She knew she was still in love with him. The question was, did he feel the same?

What if he doesn't think of me like that anymore? What if he doesn't love me? What if he's happy being friends?

As the questions circled around in her head, she made a sound of disgust in the back of her throat.

This is ridiculous! Yesterday I didn't even know I felt like this. Now I'm worried Zac won't want to start dating me again...

The only thing to do was to be brave. Lay it all out on the line. Be honest about the way she felt about him... And see where things would go from here.

Chapter
Seventeen

Zac had let Leo out to do his business then filled his food bowl with dog food. He'd cooked and eaten breakfast and had placed a plate of bacon and eggs in the oven for Emily. He'd arranged with Trace to collect Emily's car and leave it at his place. He'd also called into work and told them he was taking a mental health day. Something told him Emily needed him more than anyone else right now.

He'd checked in on her a while ago and had been pleased to see she was still sleeping. Every now and then she'd frown and whimper in her sleep and his heart would clench. Not for the first time, he wished he could take away her pain.

As hard as it had been to leave her side last night, it had been even harder to stay there and watch her sleep. He'd been overcome with emotions—love, tenderness, need. All he'd wanted to do was wake her with a kiss and make love to her.

Then he'd forced himself to remember the last time they'd kissed, she'd told him they would only ever be friends and he'd pulled back, literally and figuratively. He couldn't allow himself to fall any deeper in love with her. Not until he'd had a frank discussion with her about how he felt. If, after he'd laid open his heart, she still insisted on friendship and nothing more, he'd accept that and try to move on. It might take him forever to get over his broken heart, but he'd finally take the advice of his brothers and sisters and erase Emily Wilson from his life once and for all.

As if his thoughts had conjured her up, she appeared in the open doorway looking adorably mussed. Her hair which was usually groomed to within an inch of its life (at least in the old days), was every which way. Her clothes were rumpled. She had a crease on her face from the pillow. Still, the tentative smile on her face set his heart thumping.

"Good morning," he said, his voice suddenly hoarse.

"Good morning." She met his eyes briefly, then averted her gaze.

He frowned, confused. If he didn't know any better, he'd think she was feeling shy. He hurried to assure her.

"Last night... We didn't do anything, Em. You asked me to stay with you and I did for a while, but nothing happened. I swear."

Her cheeks turned crimson. He cursed under his breath.

Did I read her all wrong?

"I know it didn't," she said. "That's what I wanted to talk to you about."

And then she looked at him and the heat in her eyes stole his breath. His heart stopped in its tracks and then started hammering.

"What is it?" He couldn't believe how normal he sounded.

"Yesterday… Last night… You were so wonderful. So kind and caring. So compassionate." She gave a disparaging laugh. "I didn't deserve it and I was a mess. I'd had way too much to drink. I barely remember arriving here, let alone stopping by my place to collect Leo." And then she frowned. "We did stop by my parents' place, didn't we?"

He smiled tenderly. "Yes. We did. How do you think we ended up with this little guy?"

He bent and picked up Leo who'd been sitting by his feet. No doubt it had more to do with Zac feeding the dog bits of bacon off his plate than an immediate bonding, but he wouldn't tell Emily that. From her melting expression, she loved the fact he and her dog were getting along.

She smiled. "I thought so, but it's all a little hazy. My fault for drinking too much."

"Hey, cut yourself some slack. You had a lot going on. You still have a lot going on."

"You're right. That's why this is so crazy."

"What is?"

Once again, she looked at him. The intensity in her gaze sent blood rushing to his cock. He willed the rush of desire away. There was no knowing what she was about to say. Best not anticipate anything or he could be setting himself up for disappointment. Drawing in a deep, calming breath, he asked her again.

"What's so crazy, Em?"

"You and I. Us. Even waking up to the mess of my life, it's all I can think about."

She moved closer. He caught the sweet scent of her perfume. It had driven him crazy last night, just like it was doing now.

"What... What are you thinking?" he rasped.

She reached up and framed his face in her hands. "I've realized I'm still in love with you, Zac Barrington. What do you think about that?"

Zac felt like he'd taken a punch to the stomach. He could scarcely believe what he'd heard. Any minute, he expected to wake up and discover this had all been a dream.

Uncertainty flooded Emily's face. "Zac? Say something. Please."

Zac shook his head slowly from side to side, still trying to comprehend it. "You're in love with me?"

A tentative smile played around her lips. "Yes. It took me a while to see it, but it was staring me in the face all the time. All these years I've been searching for something and it was right here all this time. It's taken a few tragedies of mammoth proportions for me to realize it, but hey... Better late than never, right?"

The vulnerability in her expression tugged at his heart. He wanted to whoop with joy, pump the air, shout his happiness out loud. Instead, he took her in his arms and kissed her with all the love and passion in his heart. Her arms came up around his neck and she matched him kiss for kiss. Leo barked excitedly around their feet.

They broke apart, laughing and gasping for breath. "Looks like Leo approves," Zac said.

Emily's expression was luminous. "Does this mean you love me too?"

He sobered. "I've never stopped loving you, Em. You broke my heart the day you said goodbye, but I was also happy for you. I knew I needed to let you go. You wanted to spread your wings and you wanted to do it alone. As hard as it was, I understood that." He gave her a wry grin. "I didn't like it, but I understood it. I kept repeating a saying my mother had quoted to me not long after we broke up."

She tilted her head, curious. "What was that?"

"It goes something like this: If you love someone, set them free. If they come back to you, they're yours. If they don't, they never were."

"Yes. I've heard that before. It's beautiful," she breathed.

"And true. You wanted to explore the world, find yourself. If I'd tried to hold onto you, hold you back, you would have ended up resenting me. I had to take the chance you'd come back. That if we were meant to be, things would eventually work out."

She kissed him softly on the lips. "And they have."

"And they have," he repeated against her lips.

Passion ignited. By unspoken consent, she let him take her hand and lead her down the hallway to his room. Leo followed behind them.

"Sorry, buddy." Zac closed the door on him.

Emily smiled. "Oh, poor Leo!"

"I'm sure he'll be fine. I've waited so long for this moment. I want you all to myself."

Without waiting for her response, Zac drew her back in his arms and kissed her over and over again. It had been so long since they'd been together; since he'd had the right to call her his. He explored the familiar texture of her lips, dipped inside her mouth for a taste. She tasted of toothpaste. That reminded him she hadn't eaten breakfast.

"You must be hungry," he murmured between kisses.

"Yes. Hungry for you."

Her words sent a shaft of desire arcing through him. It settled in his groin. He pressed his erection against her and felt another surge of desire when she pressed herself against him. They kissed until they were breathless. Then Zac bent and picked her up and carried her to his bed.

The bed was neatly made. He'd picked up his dirty clothes and had put them in the laundry hamper. The room was as tidy as he could want it. Not that he'd done that with Emily in mind. He always made his bed whenever he left it. It was second nature. He wasn't a neat freak, but he liked a tidy house. Nothing wrong with that.

Then Emily sat up and pulled the T-shirt over her head. She wore a plain white cotton bra beneath it. Her breasts spilled over the top, full and tempting. Before he had a chance to move, she shimmied out of her sweatpants.

His breath caught in his throat. The skimpy cotton underwear barely covered the necessities. She was just as beautiful as he remembered. And then she looked embarrassed and he realized he was staring. She made a move to cover herself, but he gently reached for her hands.

"Please don't. You're so beautiful. You take my breath away."

She smiled uncertainly. "I don't look the same as I did at eighteen."

"No. You look even better."

She reached up toward him and started to loosen the buttons on his shirt. Once they were undone, she spread the shirt wide. She placed her warm palms against his chest. His heart jumped.

"You're beautiful too," she whispered.

She undressed him slowly, taking the time to press kisses on each inch of skin she exposed. By the time they were both naked, he was rock-hard and on fire. Though he hadn't been celibate during their time apart, neither had he been promiscuous. He could count the number of women he'd slept with on one hand. None of them had moved him like Emily. None of them had stolen his heart.

That's why he'd never been in another serious relationship. His heart had always belonged to Emily. It wasn't fair to anyone else for him to pretend otherwise, though he'd been sorely tempted once, when he'd been desperately trying to erase her memory.

Chloe had been the complete opposite to Emily, both physically and emotionally. She was a fiery redhead, with a temper to match. She'd kept him on his toes, and she'd also been fun and playful and that was attractive to him when he'd been trying to exorcise a memory. But in the end, he'd known it would go nowhere. She was a great girl, but she wasn't Emily. And that was that.

Now the woman of his dreams was back in his arms and she'd put herself there willingly.

She still loves me! How good is that? After everything... She still loves me...

The words echoed in Zac's head like a joyous mantra. He'd never given up hope of hearing those words from her mouth again, but some days it had been hard to justify, and he'd cursed himself for a fool. With each year that had passed without a word from her, he'd lost a little more hope. Now he was glad he'd kept the faith and hadn't hooked up with someone else or married for the sake of it. Sometimes miracles happened and dreams came true.

Making his way down her body, he loved her with his mouth. He kissed his way across her collarbone, down her sternum, skimmed over her ribs. His hand closed around one soft breast, while his mouth opened over a nipple. He licked and suckled. She gasped and arched beneath him.

Though their lovemaking back in high school had been sweet and innocent and beautiful, neither of them had been experienced. They did what felt good and made it up as they went. Now they were older, with more experience between them, but there was a wonderful familiarity that reminded him that this was his Emily, the beautiful girl and now woman who'd forever be the keeper of his heart.

Kissing his way down her belly, he finally buried his face against her mound. She made a sound of surprise. During their brief sexual encounters in high school, he'd never engaged in oral sex. It wasn't that he didn't enjoy the idea. There just hadn't been enough time.

They'd come together secretly, in the back of his car, or on a blanket on the riverbank. Each time, they'd been overcome with guilt. They both knew what Emily's parents would have thought. And so, though they hadn't been able to refrain from expressing their love by having sex, there was always a kind of sad relief afterwards that they'd gotten away with it.

That was one of the reasons why Zac had been looking forward to graduating. He'd planned to propose to Emily right away and then they could move in together. Their parents might have preferred they wait until after they were married, but they were eighteen. They could do what they wanted.

Only, it hadn't worked out like that.

Refusing to dwell on the past, Zac focused firmly on the present and the feast of the senses before him. He explored Emily's sweet flesh with his mouth. He stroked her with his tongue, slowly, rhythmically until she gasped again and buried her fingers in his hair, digging her nails into his skin. He listened to her breathy murmurs of encouragement and kept up the pressure of his tongue. And then she was there, at the precipice.

She cried out aloud and gripped his head, pulling at his hair until it hurt. But he didn't care. All he wanted was to please the woman he loved. She climaxed in a shudder of gasps and fast breaths. Slowly, he slid his body up hers, loving the feel of her silky softness beneath him. She stared up at him, her eyes wide with wonder and delight.

"Zac... That was... So intense."

Her words filled him with pride and contentment. And then he captured her mouth with his in another deep and passionate kiss. The fire continued to build inside him. His cock was like molten steel. But he wanted to savor this moment, to make it last forever. He refused to be rushed. For once, they could take all the time they liked.

As if sensing this, Emily pushed him onto his back and straddled him. She shot him a cheeky look. "My turn."

First, she nuzzled his ear. They'd always been sensitive. It pleased him that she remembered that. She moved to his neck and stroked his skin with her tongue, licking, tasting, sucking. Then she kissed her way down his chest.

Just as he'd done, she paused to pay attention to his nipples. She tweaked them with her fingers and then suckled them in her mouth. The combination of warmth and moisture on his sensitive skin sent another rush of blood to his cock.

Her hands caressed his pectorals, squeezing and shaping the muscles. She dragged her fingers through his chest hair, scraping him with her nails. All the time, he held himself still and prayed he wouldn't disgrace himself.

As she moved lower, his belly twitched when her lips skimmed over his six pack. And then she took hold of his cock and squeezed and he nearly came off the bed.

"Oh, God. Em..."

She merely smiled and stroked him, rhythmically and with firm pressure, just like he'd stroked her. Then she bent her head and took him in her mouth. Once again, the combination of heat and moisture sent his heart rate skyrocketing. With clenched fists, he withstood the sensual onslaught as she sucked him for all she was worth. It was only when he arrived at the point where he was seconds away from exploding, that he moved and dislodged himself from her questing lips.

"Enough," he gasped, his voice hoarse with need.

"But..."

"Enough," he repeated. "I want to come inside you." With that, he leaned across the bed and pulled a condom out of his bedside drawer. She watched while he sheathed himself. When they were younger, they didn't always use protection. They'd been willing to take the risk. And though he'd love to have babies with her, he was older and more responsible now. Marriage and babies were for another conversation.

Emily watched Zac pull on a condom and was reminded of the past. Times when they hadn't been so careful. She veered away from taking her thoughts down that path. Then Zac positioned himself between her open legs and all thoughts but the need to have him inside her, disappeared. He probed her entrance. With one quick thrust of his hips, he was inside her. Thick and hard, stretching her wide, she gasped from the impact.

It felt so good to have him in her arms again, loving her as she'd loved him. There was something so wonderful about making love to a man who adored you and who you adored right back. It couldn't be compared to the frantic couplings she'd engaged in with men in university—sometimes with men she'd known for less than a month. She realized now she'd been trying to get over Zac and had used other men for that purpose. It was only years later, when she'd matured, that she saw it for what it was.

Now he was here, in her arms. They were in his bed! A luxury they'd never enjoyed in their youth. As he moved inside her, strong and sure, she'd never felt safer or more protected. Or more loved.

As another wave of desire washed over her, she clung to his strong shoulders and met his thrusting hips. Her breath came faster, her chest went tight. The rhythmic stroking built a new fire deep inside her core. From the strain evident on Zac's face, she could tell he was also close. She urged him on with quiet encouragement and then she was at the precipice again.

This time, Zac was with her and they cried out together as they plummeted over the other side.

Wave after wave of pleasure washed over her. She clung to him, breathless and spent. He collapsed against her and sighed. Emotions overwhelmed her. For the first time, they'd climaxed together.

Chapter Eighteen

An hour later, after showering together, which had resulted in them making love again, Zac finally convinced Emily to eat. He pulled out the plate of food he'd kept warm in the oven and made her some fresh buttered toast to go with it. While she ate, he sat across from her at the breakfast nook and drank coffee. He couldn't keep the goofy grin off his face.

He'd dreamed of this moment for so long, the two of them together and in love, that he had to stop from pinching himself to make sure this was real. He was happy beyond belief, but he also wanted to make sure this wasn't a one-off. She'd suffered some terrible shocks. It was possible she was still reacting to the trauma, using him as a means to distract herself from the pain.

He could understand such behavior, but it would devastate him just the same if that's all this was. Though even thinking about putting that question to her filled him with apprehension, he had to take his courage with both hands and ask it.

"Is it too early to ask where this is going?"

She blinked in surprise and finished swallowing the food in her mouth before responding. Those extra few seconds of waiting were agonizing.

"What do you mean?"

He bit back a groan. "Em, you're killing me. I love you. You love me. I want you in my life. Forever. Does that terrify you?"

She looked at him with so much love and tenderness, some of his nervousness dissipated. She reached across the table for his hand.

"Zac. The thought of walking away from you, from us, again—*that's* what terrifies me."

Joy exploded in his heart. "So... You're okay with dating me? After all that's happened.?"

She nodded. "I'm more than okay with dating you."

"Yes!" He pumped the air with his fist.

Emily laughed. "Don't forget I live in Sydney. This dating thing isn't going to be easy."

"It just means we'll have to have sleepovers." He winked.

"Sounds like a good plan," she quipped.

They shared another laugh and then Zac slowly sobered. "I'm really sorry for the pain my family inadvertently caused. I want you to know, I talked to my father about Evan's accident. I'm not sure if you know, but your brother was employed by a contractor by the name of Joseph Rodriguez. He wasn't employed by Barrington Mining. Though we were involved in the lawsuit, it was the contractor who was ultimately liable for his death. I'm so sorry for the prolonged settlement negotiations, but we had nothing to do with that."

Emily stared at him, her eyes wide with comprehension and finally, resignation. "Thank you for telling me that. I didn't know. My father gave me the impression that your family were front and center in that awful time. I'm not sure if he made a genuine mistake about who was liable or not, but that's what he told me. Though I'd reached the point where I no longer blamed you for anything, I'm relieved to hear it wasn't the Barringtons who fought so hard against Evan's compensation."

Zac stood and moved closer. He framed her face with his hands and planted a kiss on her lips.

"I love you, Emily Wilson."

She smiled softly. "I love you too, Zac Barrington." And then her smile slowly faded. "This would be so perfect if my father hadn't..."

Her voice cracked with emotion. Zac's heart clenched. He drew her to her feet and held her close. The tension in her body told him how close she was to breaking down.

"It's going to be okay, Em. I'm not going to pretend things aren't going to be darn tough for the next while, but we'll get through it together. I'll be here for you every step of the way."

She swiped at her eyes and then looked up at him. "Th-thank you. That means a great deal to me. When I think about everything I'm going to have to deal with... I feel overwhelmed."

"Most people would. Cut yourself some slack. You've had your world turned upside down on a number of occasions. So many shocks. So much pain." He stared at her, hoping to make her see. "But you don't have to face things alone now. I'm here. And I intend to stay for however long you'll have me."

Once again, she leaned in toward his chest. She tightened her arms around his waist and clung to him for long moments. Finally, they eased apart.

"What happens now?" she asked.

"You mean with your father?"

"Yes."

"He'll be taken before the court today for a bail hearing. There's not much chance he'll be successful. He provided an extensive confession. Along with the forensic evidence, there's a high probability he'll be found guilty if the case goes to trial. If bail is refused, he'll remain in custody until his next court appearance, which might be three or four weeks down the road, or until his lawyer files a successful bail application with the Supreme Court, whichever comes first."

She regarded him steadily, her eyes dark with concern. "What if the Supreme Court bail application's not successful?"

Zac owed her the truth. "Then he'll stay in jail until his trial date."

"When will that be?"

"It's hard to say. At least six to eight months away."

She gasped. "Six to eight *months*?"

"The court dockets are full. It could be longer."

Emily shook her head slowly back and forth. Zac could tell she was trying to come to terms with the fact her father might be in prison for that long before he went to trial. Though he was loathe to do it, he needed her to understand if her father pleaded guilty or was found guilty by a jury, he'd be spending a lot more time than that behind bars.

"We have a strong case against him, Em. He confessed. Not only to you, but to us. It's all on record. Plus there's a lot of forensic evidence that points to him. I hate to say it, but it's very likely he'll be in jail for a long time."

"How long?" she rasped.

"Twenty, twenty-five years."

She gasped again and went pale but remained silent. Zac could tell she was trying to process what he'd said. She had to know being found guilty of murder would come with a significant period of incarceration but knowing that and being faced with the reality that it was her *father* who'd be doing the time were completely different.

"Can I see him?" she asked quietly.

"Of course. I'll call Trace and see where he's being held. There's a chance he might have been taken over to the courthouse already."

She merely nodded. It was obvious her mind had moved on. He hated that this hung over what should have been one of the happiest days of their lives, but there was nothing he could do about it. All he could do was support Emily through it the best way he could. Moving away, he pulled out his phone and called Trace.

Emily dreaded the thought of seeing her father again, but at the same time, she couldn't bear to think it might be twenty years or more before he was a free man. He'd murdered her mother in order to protect his reputation and she'd struggle to forgive him for that, but he was still her father. The only father she had. The only family she had left.

No. That wasn't true. She had Zac. He was now her family. She was so thrilled to have him back in her life. She glanced at the man beside her. His focus was on the road in front of them. His quiet air of confidence and strength filled her with hope. She'd get through this. With Zac by her side, she could get through anything.

Her father was still in the holding cells at the Broken Police Station. Zac escorted her inside and she waited in the reception area while he went and cleared things with his colleagues. She looked around at the plain gray walls and nondescript furniture and remembered being there only a little over a week ago with her father. Back then she was there to file a missing person report. She still had hope they'd find her mother safe and sound. Her father had given a convincing performance of bewilderment for her and the police. She'd believed his every word.

How little she'd known him... How could she have spent the first eighteen years of her life in his company and still not know when he was lying? She felt weighed down by the knowledge.

Just then, a side door opened and Zac reappeared. She couldn't help remembering the first time she'd seen him again, standing in exactly the same position. She'd been worried about her mother and furious at the Barringtons. They'd both come a long way since then. So much had happened in such a short time. Some of it good, some of it ugly. All of it heartbreaking.

"Are you ready?" Zac asked quietly.

Drawing in a deep breath, she nodded and got to her feet.

"He's been taken to an interview room. There's a Perspex partition between you, but you can see and hear each other well enough."

"Will he be handcuffed?" she asked.

"No. I asked them not to do that."

She gave him a grateful look. "Thank you."

He merely shrugged and opened a door off a short corridor. It led into a small room that contained a single chair. On the other side of the partition sat her father. She gasped at the sight of him. Though it had only been yesterday morning that she'd last seen him, he seemed to have aged a decade. He was unshaven, unkempt and was dressed in the same clothes he'd been arrested in. But it was his defeated and desolate expression that got to her the most.

She didn't want to feel sorry for him. No one had forced him to squeeze the life out of his wife and to leave his daughter motherless. He was sitting in jail for what he'd done. He had no one to blame but himself. Still, it was hard to see him like that. Broken.

"Hi, Dad."

He looked up at her with bleary, red eyes. "Emily. You came."

"Yes."

The anger she'd been trying to hold at bay raised its head. She glared at him. "Why, Dad? *Why?*"

"You already know why."

"No, Dad. All I know is that you wanted to protect your reputation as a fine and upstanding citizen of this town. A pastor, no less. That's not a reason. That's a spineless admission that you murdered my mother for your own selfish gain."

Her father looked distressed. "No! Emily! Please don't say that."

"What do you want me to say, Dad? It's true. You didn't have to kill her. You said yourself the blow to her head only knocked her out. I might have understood it if you'd stopped there. I would have still been appalled that you'd struck her, but I know people do things in the heat of the moment. But after that, you made a conscious decision to end her life because otherwise *your* life would have gotten difficult. That's the truth, Dad. Isn't it?"

He hung his head. Shame washed over his cheeks, turning them crimson. It gave her no comfort when he eventually heaved a sigh and nodded. "You're right."

She wanted to rail at him, scream her anger and distress. He'd robbed her of her mother for his own selfish reasons. But nothing would bring her mother back and her father was already going to spend at least the next two decades in jail. There was no point being there any longer.

She pushed away from the partition and stood. Her father looked up at her in surprise.

"You're leaving?"

"Yes, Dad."

"But you only just got here. Do you know how hard it is being in here with no one to talk to? No one who cares?"

"No, Dad. I don't. But no doubt you'll adjust. You're going to have a long time to get used to being on your own."

"Will you come back and visit soon?"

She thought about her answer. Her first response was to tell him he could rot in hell for all she cared. But another part of her mourned the loss of her father. Her mother was lost to her forever. So was her brother. At least her dad was still alive. No matter what he'd done and how devastated she felt, nothing would change that. Staying angry and bitter at him would only eat her up inside. Somehow, she had to find the strength and courage to forgive him. But not today.

"I don't know," she said non-committedly. "We'll see."

Her father's eyes flared with hope. No doubt it was better than he'd expected.

"Goodbye, Dad."

"Goodbye, Emily. I love you."

Tears burned behind her eyes. She turned and stumbled away, unable to say the words back. She didn't know if she'd ever be able to say those words to him again and right now, she hated him for that.

The next week was the hardest of Emily's life. Not only did she attend Izon's funeral, she also buried her mom. She couldn't have gotten through any of that without Zac. He helped her make the funeral arrangements. He sat by her side and held her hand. First at the celebration of Izon's short life and a few days later, at her mother's service. Both services were terribly sad for different reasons and Emily struggled not to fall apart.

At least Izon was now free from pain and hopefully having a great time in heaven. She smiled softly at the thought. As for her mother, Emily found it hard to cling to anything positive at all. Lorraine Wilson had been a wonderful woman with so much love and caring and compassion for those around her. She'd touched so many lives. The huge number of people who turned up to her funeral and spoke about how she'd helped them was testament to that.

There wasn't a dry eye in the church when Joe Sampson spoke to the crowd gathered there. In a shy and halting tone, he spoke about how for the first time in his life, he'd been treated like a person, like someone who mattered. She'd been instrumental in helping him to get clean and sober. He was proud to say he'd been that way since the last time they'd spoken.

She'd been a tireless supporter of many charities and had given endless hours of her time as a volunteer. Though Emily was aware her mother had always believed in giving back to her community, even she was surprised at the extent of her mother's involvement in good causes. It was obvious she'd been loved and admired by the people of Broken. She hadn't deserved to die. The fact her death had come about at the hands of someone she'd once loved and trusted only made it harder to bear.

There was also fear and bewilderment in many of the Broken townspeople. This was the second murder in only a couple of months to have rocked the town. It was no surprise people had begun to lock their doors at night, something that had never happened in all the years Emily had lived there. Their feeling of insecurity was just another thing her father had been responsible for.

"Hey. How are you holding up?"

Zac's gentle question interrupted Emily's musings. She'd found a quiet corner away from the crowd that had gathered for her mother's wake and had taken refuge in a strong cup of coffee. Now she looked at him and managed a tired smile.

"It's been a tough week."

Zac moved closer and put an arm around her shoulders. He pressed a kiss against her hair. "You'll get through this. You're stronger than you think."

She gave him a grateful smile. Setting her coffee mug aside, she put her arms around his waist and held him tight. She didn't know how she would have managed to get through it without him. He was her rock. A mountain of strength. And they loved each other.

For so long, she'd gone through life on her own. She had her parents, but her day-to-day battles she'd fought all alone. Now she didn't have to do that anymore. Knowing that was a nice feeling.

Tipping her chin upwards with his fingers, Zac bent his head and kissed her softly on the lips.

"I love you," he whispered.

Despite the sad day, her heart swelled with tenderness. "I love you too."

They kissed again. Emily loved the feeling of safety and security she felt whenever she was in his arms. She couldn't believe she'd voluntarily walked away from this. Still, she was a different woman from the teenager she'd been then. She'd established a career, made her mark on the world. And though she loved her job and wanted to continue, she didn't feel the same amount of drive. Her career was no longer the most important thing in her life and that was a good thing. Careers couldn't keep her company and dry away her tears. Careers couldn't make her feel warm and safe at night. She was just grateful Zac still loved her.

He smoothed back the hair from her forehead. "I'm so proud of you. Through all of this, you've been amazing."

"I couldn't have done it without you," she said quietly.

Their lips met in another gentle, tender kiss before slowly pulling apart. Zac gave her a crooked smile.

"I know the timing's not great with your father in jail and everything that's been going on, but I want to re-introduce you to my family. I want to let them know we're together and this time it's for keeps."

"Are you sure that's a good idea so soon? I can only imagine how they took the break-up."

"You're right. My sisters took it especially hard. I think Hannah pasted your picture on the back of the door to her bedroom and threw darts at it."

Emily gasped. "She didn't!"

Zac chuckled. "Okay, maybe I'm exaggerating, but only a little."

"Oh no! They hate me!"

He pulled her close again. "No. They don't hate you. How could they? They know how much I've pined after you. I've lost count of the number of times they've told me I need to move on. Lucky for both of us I didn't."

"You're right. I'm the luckiest girl in the world."

They shared another tender kiss. "My family will see how happy we are and they'll love you as much as I do. You're the strongest, bravest, most amazing woman I know. How could they not?"

Chapter Nineteen

It had been three weeks since Emily had buried her mother. She'd spent most of that time back at work in Sydney. As much as she wanted to stay with Zac, they hadn't made any definite plans about the future and for now her life was in Sydney. Besides, she needed the distraction of work to keep her from falling apart.

She wasn't sure how a long-distance relationship would work. So far, their rosters hadn't lined up. When Zac was on days' off, she was at work and vice versa. It had been tricky for both of them, but they'd spent hours talking on the phone and both were confident things would get easier in the future.

What that future looked like they hadn't yet ascertained. They were still in the early days of their relationship. Though both of them had careers that were geographically mobile, it wasn't as simple as that. Transfers took time and they hadn't yet talked about who would relocate. But right now, Emily was happy to take each day as it came. Starting with reuniting with Zac's family.

The joint engagement party of Charlotte and Grayson and Trace and Cassie would start in less than an hour. It was being held at the Barrington estate, outside of Broken. Emily hoped the storm that had threatened all day would hold off long enough for them to get through the celebrations. She'd never organized anything so extravagant as an engagement party, but she could well imagine the amount of time, planning and sheer hard work that had gone into it beforehand. It would be a shame for those plans to be put into disarray because of the weather. Still, there was no controlling that.

She'd arrived from Sydney earlier that afternoon and had gotten dressed at Zac's house. She planned on spending the night there before returning to Sydney the next day. Right now, she was putting on the final touches to her makeup.

She looked at her reflection in the mirror. Though she was pleased with the scarlet-colored, strapless evening dress that hugged her curves and displayed her trim figure to advantage, she was also nervous about seeing all the Barringtons again. Evan's death at the mine lay between them, along with the awful situation surrounding her mother's tragic death.

Then there was the fact she'd broken Zac's heart all those years ago. They were a close-knit family. She was sure they all knew and had naturally taken their brother's side. If the same thing had happened to her sibling, she would have done the same. Though Zac assured her they wouldn't hold a grudge, she wasn't so sure.

She had one thing going for her at least. She and Zac were back together and very much in love. She was determined to make him happy. Hopefully that counted for something.

Zac appeared in the doorway of the bathroom. He gave her a slow once-over, followed by an appreciative whistle. "You look beautiful."

She blushed at the heat in his eyes. Though they'd explored every inch of each other's bodies over the preceding three weeks, things still felt new.

"You look good too," she said.

He wore a tuxedo and had paired it with a crisp white dress shirt. His broad shoulders filled out the jacket like it had been made for him, and maybe it had. Though Zac didn't parade his family's wealth, the fact was, the Barringtons were among the richest families in Australia. Frank Barrington had made his money from mining and that industry continued to fill the family coffers. It was a testament to Zac's parents that they'd raised such grounded children.

"Are you nearly ready?" Zac asked.

"Yes." She drew in a deep breath in an effort to settle another wave of nerves.

"Relax. They're going to love you," Zac reassured her.

"I hope you're right."

They caught a cab to the party. Though Emily had been to the Barrington home before, its grandeur still had the power to take her aback. Tall stone pillars and high black wrought iron gates announced the entrance to the Barrington Estate. A long, paved driveway wound upwards through mature

Moreton Bay figs that looked like they'd been there for a century at least. Then the house came into view.

An impressive, Hamptons style mansion, it stood high and proud on the top of the hill overlooking the lush valley below. Manicured lawns and gardens made the house look even more inviting and grand. The place blazed with lights, filling Emily with a rush of excitement. She looked at Zac.

"Are you sure Trace and Charlotte won't mind me turning up at their engagement party?"

"Of course not. I already told them you were coming. They were surprised we were back together again, but they wished us well. Trace knows what you've been through recently. If anything, he was pleased you have someone looking out for you."

She closed her eyes against a wave of sad memories. Zac immediately looked concerned. He squeezed her hand.

"I'm sorry, Em. I didn't mean to dredge all that up again."

She sighed. "It's okay. It'll take time to put it behind me. Every day I get a little better, but then something happens and I'm right back there again. I'm sorry."

"Don't be sorry," Zac replied forcefully. "You have nothing to be sorry about. You had nothing to do with any of this." His expression filled with concern. "We don't have to go out tonight. If you'd rather stay in, that's fine with me. We can turn the cab around right now."

"But it's Trace and Charlotte's engagement party! They're your siblings! You can't miss an occasion as special and important as that."

Zac's gaze remained steady on hers. "But you're special and important too. More important than an engagement party."

Warmth flooded Emily's veins. She reached up and cupped his cheek. The soft bristles of his beard tickled her skin.

"I love you for saying that," she whispered.

"I mean it," he said simply.

"I know you do. But I'm fine. I promise."

Just then, a jagged shard of lightning lit up the sky, quickly followed by a loud crack of thunder. Emily jumped in her seat.

"Are you sure?" Zac's face continued to reflect his concern.

She patted him tenderly on the cheek. "I'm sure. Now, let's go and party."

The cab dropped them off at the front of the house. Right on cue, the storm that had been threatening all day erupted. Without warning, rain started bucketing down. She and Zac made a run for it, but by the time they'd ascended the wide stone steps and hurried into the foyer, they were soaked.

Emily pushed the wet hair out of her eyes and laughed. "I can't believe I wasted an hour on my hair. I must look like a drenched rat."

Zac kissed her nose. "You look beautiful."

She smiled. "Thank you, but that's easy for you to say. You don't look any different."

And it was true. His short hair merely glistened with moisture, like he'd just stepped out of the shower. If anything, he looked even sexier. He pulled off his suit jacket and gave it a brisk shake before pulling it on again.

"Let's go inside and warm up," he suggested.

With his arm around her waist, he guided her through the house. It looked much like it had when she was a teenager. They passed room after room. Each room was beautifully appointed, yet somehow, they still managed to look comfortable, homey, inviting. Like this was a family home meant to be lived in. They perfectly reflected the Frank and Evelyn Barrington of her memories. Genuine, kind-hearted, non-judgmental people who welcomed others from all walks of life into their home.

The sudden downpour had forced the partygoers indoors. Through a set of double French doors, she could see tables decorated with lavish flower arrangements and tall candles stood abandoned on the lawn as the guests crowded under the covered patio at the rear of the house. From the amount of laughter, conversation and the tinkling of glassware Emily could hear, the unexpected storm hadn't dampened anyone's spirits.

The first Barringtons they ran into were Zac's sisters, Hannah and Molly. They looked from Zac to Emily and smiled.

"Zac! Emily! How lovely to see you again," Hannah said.

Emily smiled. "Thank you." She self-consciously touched her wet hair. "Sorry, Zac and I were caught in the downpour."

"Oh no!" Molly cried. "Come with me and I'll get you dry."

Before she knew what was happening, Molly and Hannah flanked her and linking their arms with hers, marched her off to another part of the house. Emily glanced over her shoulder toward Zac, feeling helpless. He merely shrugged and laughed.

"I'll catch up with you soon," he called to her departing back.

"We didn't know what to think when Zac told us the two of you were dating again," Hannah admitted as she led Emily into a sumptuously appointed bathroom.

Emily's nervousness increased. Hannah was a year younger than Emily. She'd always been full of life, fearless and ambitious. It hadn't come as a surprise to Emily when Zac told her Hannah was making a mark in the traditionally male-dominated mining world.

"I hope you're not upset," Emily said lightly. "Zac told me you didn't take the break-up well."

Hannah's eyes widened. "I can't believe he told you about that! Hey, I was seventeen. You'd broken my brother's heart. What did you expect?"

Emily nodded. "You're right. I would have done the same."

"That's all in the past," Molly said, before Hannah could respond. "It's true. Zac was so upset after you dumped him. He mooned around for a year at least. Then his career took off in the police force and he appeared to have gotten over you. But he never brought a girl home and as far as we know, he never had a girlfriend. We'd tease him about that and how the best thing he could do was move on and forget about you." She slowly shook her head. "But he couldn't. No matter that you were a world away from him and living your own life, he always held a torch for you. He never gave up hope."

Emily swallowed past the lump in her throat. She could tell from Molly's tone that she wasn't blaming Emily for Zac's devotion. If anything, it sounded like Molly found the whole thing romantic. Zac had told Emily that Molly was a paramedic in the busy and popular beachside suburb of Cronulla. No doubt she was involved in plenty of traumatic situations, like Emily. Emily had nothing but admiration for first responders.

Hannah handed her a thick white towel. Emily thanked her and started drying her hair. She looked in the mirror. The intricate braiding she'd done less than an hour earlier was now a soggy mess. She'd have to do it over. She sighed.

"Don't worry. I'm sure you'll have it looking fabulous in no time," Hannah said. "You were always a whizz at doing hair."

Molly agreed. "Hell, yeah. I was two years ahead of you in school and even I knew about your perfect hair." She bent and dug around in a cupboard and pulled out a hairdryer. "Here. This might help."

Emily laughed and took the hairdryer from her. Setting it aside, she began loosening the tangles in her hair. The women stood by and watched.

"How did you get so good at doing hair?" Molly asked.

"I used to watch videos that showed women doing different hairstyles," Emily confessed. "I spent hours perfecting each style. I didn't want to be a hairdresser. I just liked playing around with hair."

"Well, I used to be incredibly jealous," Hannah announced. "I was lucky to go to school with a ponytail, or maybe a couple of plaits. You'd show up looking like you'd just stepped off some Hollywood movie set. You put the rest of us to shame."

Emily felt bad. "I never meant to make you feel inadequate. Creating different hairstyles was just something I liked to do. These days I rarely get time to do more than a ponytail myself."

"Zac said you're a nurse," Molly said.

"Yes. I work at the Sydney Harbour Hospital."

"That's a fair commute from Broken," Hannah said astutely.

Emily nodded. "You're right. Zac and I have a lot to work out. In the meantime, we're just enjoying each other's company."

All of a sudden, Hannah's expression turned fierce. "Just make sure you don't go breaking his heart again. None of us want to see that. It was bad enough the first time. You'll bring the wrath of the entire Barrington clan down on your head if you do that."

Emily bristled. "I love Zac with all my heart. I have no intention of hurting him again."

Hannah's expression relaxed into a smile. "Good. Then we'll be fine."

Emily gave Hannah a pointed look. "Zac told me you work at one of the Barrington mines. Did my brother die at your mine site, Hannah?"

Hannah turned pale. She averted her gaze. "I'm so sorry about that, Emily. I wasn't on duty the day Evan died, but yes, sadly it happened at my mine site."

At the devastation on Hannah's face, Emily took pity on her. After all, she'd already accepted the accident and ensuing legal battle wasn't the responsibility of the Barringtons.

"It's all right, Hannah. I'm not mad. Not anymore. Zac filled me in on the facts."

Hannah's face flooded with relief. "Oh, thank God!"

Deciding to put it all out there, Emily addressed the other elephant in the room. "I assume you heard about my mother?"

Both women nodded, their expressions somber. "We're so sorry Emily," Molly said.

"We can't imagine what you've been through," Hannah said.

"If there's anything we can do," Molly added. "If you need someone to talk to…"

Their identical genuine expressions of concern warmed Emily through. She'd never had a sister, but she now wondered if this was what sisterly love and support felt like.

"Thank you," she managed, her voice hoarse. "That means a lot."

Suddenly, she found herself in the middle of a group hug. Amid much laughter and a barrage of questions, Emily re-braided her hair and coiled it around her face in an intricate pattern that looked way more difficult to achieve than it was. Zac's sisters stood by and watched, their eyes wide with curiosity and admiration. She also toweled off her limbs and hoped her dress would soon dry. Once she was done, they hurried her back out to the party and delivered her to Zac's side.

His face lit up at the sight of her. Warmth spread through her veins. He looked at her like she was the only one in the room. It was nice to feel so special.

"There you are! I thought I was going to have to send out a search party," he teased. "Especially when you were kidnapped by my sisters. I wasn't sure what they had in mind."

Hannah poked her tongue out at him. "We took perfectly good care of her, didn't we Emily?"

"Yes, you did."

"We just wanted her to look her best," Molly said. "Don't take offense, Emily, but you were looking a bit...bedraggled. Now you look fabulous."

"She always looks fabulous to me," Zac said and pulled Emily in close beside him for a kiss.

Molly rolled her eyes. Hannah made a mock gagging sound. Emily turned to them and smiled.

"Thank you, girls. I appreciate you having my back. Despite what your brother thinks, a woman likes to look her best."

"See, Zac!" Hannah crowed.

Zac merely shook his head and smiled. "Brat."

The rain continued to pour down, but it didn't dampen anyone's spirits. Zac and Emily did the rounds of the crowd. Zac proudly introduced her as his girlfriend to everyone they met. It made Emily feel good inside. Not for the first time, she wondered why she'd been so determined to keep her distance from him.

They found Charlotte and her fiancé, Grayson, canoodling beside the makeshift bar. Zac made the introductions. Charlotte's eyes widened with recognition.

"I remember you from high school," she said.

"Yes."

"I was a couple years above you, but weren't you the girl with the perfect hair?"

Emily blushed and nodded. "That's me. I didn't realize my hair had such an impact."

"Oh, honey. No one could pull off a hairstyle like you could. We were so jealous. I tried a few times with my own hair, but eventually gave up. A ponytail was about as technical as I got."

Emily laughed. "Well, you've certainly achieved in other areas. Zac tells me you're a homicide detective."

"Yes. What can I say? Some days are diamonds, some days are gold."

Emily laughed again. "Well, thank you for being willing to put your life on the line to keep us safe."

Charlotte's expression grew serious. "Thank you. That's a very nice thing to say."

"Hey! What have I been telling you?" Zac protested. "Why do you think I'm so in love with her?"

They all laughed. Looking from Charlotte to Grayson, Emily said, "Speaking about love, congratulations on your engagement."

"Thank you," Grayson said.

He looked ultra-handsome with his wheat-colored hair, striking green eyes and charcoal-gray designer suit that fit him perfectly. Zac had told her he was a lawyer. He had an air of confidence and authority about him that drew people's regard. Emily could see why Charlotte was so taken with him.

She and Zac kept moving through the crowd until they came upon Trace and his fiancée, Cassie. The women needed no introduction. Emily and Cassie Webster had been in the same class in school. Cassie looked stunning in a sparkling black sheath that hugged her enviable figure. With her striking auburn hair, green eyes, and pale ivory skin, she was so beautiful, Emily immediately felt inadequate, but Cassie quickly put her at ease.

"Emily! It's so lovely to see you again! Gosh, I haven't seen you since high school."

Emily smiled. "You're right. That seems like a lifetime ago. So much has happened."

Cassie nodded, her expression turning solemn. "I heard about your mother. I'm so sorry."

Emily bit her lip against a rush of emotion. Of course people would talk about her mother. No doubt they'd be talking about it for years to come. But Cassie had also suffered recent loss. She knew exactly how it felt.

"Thank you. I'm sorry about your brother too. Poor Oscar. That was so…"

"Shocking? Unimaginable? Horrific? Yes, all of those. Still, I'm trying hard to remember the good times. Oscar was the best brother a girl could want. I want to honor his memory by doing something wonderful with my life. Starting now."

She glanced at Trace. He gave her the most tender look, Emily's heart clenched. She was so pleased something good had come out of Cassie's tragedy.

"I'm so happy for you both," she said. "Congratulations."

"Thank you," Trace said, smiling and drawing his fiancée close. "We're happy for Zac, too. It seems he was right to hold out for you after all."

Emily flushed. She had to accept that Zac's siblings would remind her every now and then of how she'd been the one to leave—and how she'd broken his heart in the process. She just hoped she'd have the time to prove to them how much she loved him now and reassure them she never intended to leave.

"Has anyone heard from Vaughan lately?" Zac asked his brother.

"I don't think so."

"It would be good to see him again. I miss him," Zac said.

"We all do," Trace replied.

"Let's hope he's dealt with whatever it was that drove him to Bali. We want him home."

"Yeah. I thought he might be tempted to return for the engagement party, but apparently not," Trace said.

"Maybe he'll make it back in time for Christopher's wedding," Zac said.

"That's not until the spring," Trace said. "Let's hope he comes home before that."

"I guess he'll do whatever he likes. There's nothing we can do about it."

Trace looked resigned. "Yep. You're right about that."

Chapter Twenty

When the rain eased and finally stopped, some of the partygoers made their way back onto the lawn. The band began playing again. People hit the dance floor which had been thoroughly mopped and were soon dancing up a storm. Zac found his parents standing together on the edge of the garden, watching with matching indulgent expressions as Lexi's six youngest children tore around the yard, playing and shouting and having fun.

"Mom. Dad. How're you doing?"

"Zac! It's good to see you," his mother said, turning to kiss him on the cheek.

Emily stood nervously beside him. He gave her hand a reassuring squeeze. "Mom. Dad. You remember Emily Wilson?"

"Of course," his father said. "How're you doing, Emily?"

"I'm fine thanks, Mr Barrington."

Zac's father waved away her words. "Please, call me Frank."

Zac's mother eyed Emily. "So, you're back in Broken," she stated, her tone curiously flat.

Emily flushed. Zac tensed. "We're back together again, Mom. We're in love."

"I see," his mother continued in that same flat tone.

Emily's flush deepened. "I'm sorry for what happened before when we were younger. I... I had to get away from Broken, find my way..."

His mother nodded. "Of course. I understand that. I admire anyone with the courage to leave their hometown behind them and forge their own path, but I haven't forgotten how you broke my son's heart."

"Mom..." Zac's tone was a mixture of warning and embarrassment.

His mother merely held up a hand. "It's all right, Zac. I'm not going to apologize for caring deeply about you." She turned her attention back to Emily. "I've always liked you, Emily and I know you've recently suffered some shocks. First your brother. Now losing your mother that way... It's devastating and you have my deepest sympathies. But I also care about my son. I haven't forgotten how badly he took your break-up. I just want to make sure you're not going to do that again."

Zac's face flamed. First his sisters, now his mom. Could this get any more embarrassing? Suddenly, he wished they hadn't come. But he knew his family. It wouldn't have made any difference to them if he'd brought Emily home a month after they'd reunited or a year down the track, his family would still voice their concerns and warn Emily of dire consequences if she dared to break his heart again.

Not that he thought that would happen. They were happier than they'd ever been. Six years ago, they'd been kids. They'd loved completely, without restraint, but they'd also known nothing about the world. Now they were older. They had a better idea of who they were, what they wanted and who they wanted to share their lives with. For him, that hadn't changed. Emily had always held his heart. But she'd taken a bit more time to arrive at the same conclusion. Now that she had, there was nothing that could keep them apart.

Emily maintained eye contact with his mother. Zac admired her courage. Evelyn Barrington in full-on protective mode was scary. Still, Zac couldn't blame her for being concerned. She was a mother hen protecting her chicks. She did it out of love.

"I can't change history," Emily said quietly. "All I can do is try and shape the future. I love your son with all my heart. I never set out to hurt him, but sometimes we hurt the people we love. I didn't leave because I'd stopped loving him. To the contrary. I did it to protect our love."

His mother frowned. "What do you mean?"

"I knew if I didn't leave, I'd end up resenting Zac and I didn't want that to happen. I was eighteen. I had the world at my feet. I wanted to explore it, see what was out there. That was the only way I could appreciate what I had."

"But Zac could have moved on, found someone else to love," his mother said.

Emily nodded. "You're right. That weighed on my mind for a long time. But that was a risk I was prepared to take. I needed to do this for myself. To find out who I was. I think I'm a better person for having done that." She drew in a deep breath and continued, holding his mother's gaze. "And I truly believed, if we were meant to be together, we'd find our way back to each other some day. I'm over the moon I was right."

His mother's expression softened. She turned to Zac and smiled. "You have my blessing, son. I wish you both well."

Zac breathed a sigh of relief. "Thank you, Mom. That means a lot to me." He glanced at Emily. "To both of us."

"He's right," Emily said. "Thank you for your vote of confidence. Your support is very important to us."

Zac's father cleared his throat. "I'm glad to see you looking so happy, son. Welcome back, Emily."

His father enveloped Emily in a hug. Zac hugged his mother and then drew Emily close and breathed a silent sigh of relief.

"Uncle Zac! Uncle Zac! Come play with us!"

Everyone turned to look at Lexi's children who were galloping all over the grass. Someone had produced a football and they were passing it around between them. Zac grinned and looked at Emily.

"Go," she urged. "I can see how keen you are to play with them."

"You don't mind?"

"Of course not. Go and show them a few of your skills."

Needing no further encouragement, Zac shrugged out of his jacket and handed it to Emily. He jogged over to the kids.

"Okay, whose side am I on?"

"Mine! Mine!"

"Mine!"

Zac held up his hands in a sign of surrender. "Whoa! I can't be on both sides. How about we get Christopher to join us?"

"Yes! Let's get Christopher!" They cheered.

"You were the captain of Broken High's football team weren't you, Uncle Zac?" one of the boys asked.

"I sure was. We won three years in a row."

"Three years! That's cool!"

"Yeah, it was pretty cool. How about one of you go and get Christopher? Then we can play."

Two of the children bolted away. Zac watched as they ran over to Christopher who stood near the bar with his fiancée, Lexi. Zac couldn't hear what was said, but a few moments later, Christopher shrugged, handed his drink to Lexi and started heading toward them, the two kids jumping around with excitement beside him.

Zac's gaze moved over to Emily who stood on the sidelines nearby. A soft smile played around her lips, but there was also a glitter of tears. Zac frowned. *Tears?*

Let's hope they're happy ones...

Emily watched Zac playing football with Lexi's kids. They were laughing and shouting and running about, having a marvelous time. Zac kept calling out encouragement to one child after another, warming her heart.

He'll make such a great father...

She thought back to the Main Street Café incident when he'd taken the time to speak with the young family. The mother had been struggling. Zac's actions had distracted the kids enough that the tension had been broken and the family could get on with enjoying their meal. He'd been so great with those kids, too. He'd been able to communicate on their level and he'd truly seemed to care.

Unwittingly, her hand strayed to her flat stomach. She remembered the baby that had never been. Never been given a chance at life. A baby Zac didn't even know had existed. She realized her thinking about that had changed.

I need to tell him. I owe him that. It's the right thing to do... But will he ever forgive me?

A cold, hard lump of dread centered in her stomach. For a long time, she'd kept it from him, but things had changed. They were now back together, hopefully for the rest of their lives. The decision she'd made six years ago hadn't been easy. She'd thought about it nearly every day since. She couldn't deny it left her feeling sad. Those feelings wouldn't go away just because she was back with Zac. In fact, the guilt she felt over her decision might very well make those feelings worse.

And if she didn't tell him, what about when it came time for them to have other children? How would that make her feel? Would it bring up all that emotional upheaval again? How would she explain that to Zac? He'd surely notice.

No. The right thing to do was to tell him, even if that meant losing him again. To explain the reasoning behind her decision and hope he loved her enough to understand...and forgive.

Unable to stand there another moment and watch the happy scene before her, she turned and stumbled away, needing to be alone to gather her thoughts...and her courage.

Zac called a halt to the friendly game of football by pleading with the kids for a break. They were still climbing all over him when he made his way to the makeshift bar and asked for a drink. He looked to Christopher for help, but his half-brother merely laughed. Promising the children he'd spend more time with them later, Zac finally got free of them and went off in search of Emily.

He was thrilled his family had embraced her again. Even more pleasing was the blessing from his mother. He was extremely close to both his parents and their approval was important. He wasn't sure it would be a deal breaker if they didn't like her, but it would certainly have made things difficult.

He found Emily sipping a glass of white wine in a far corner of the garden. The dim lighting made it hard to gauge her frame of mind, but she looked a little sad and apprehensive.

"Hey," he said softly, coming up to her and leaning in for a kiss.

"Hey."

"What's happening?"

"Not much."

Her tone held no inflection. Neither was there any animation in her face. He felt a frisson of concern.

"Is everything all right?"

His question was met with silence. She took a sip from her wine and then quietly spoke. "Being around your parents... It brought everything back. My mother... My father..."

Her voice cracked. "He's going to spend the next twenty years or so behind bars! I know that's what he deserves, but it still hurts. I can't help thinking about all the things he's going to miss. My wedding, the birth of my kids. So many life events..."

Zac's mind snagged on one thing. It was something they hadn't talked about. "You want kids?"

"Of course. I've always wanted kids. Don't you?"

He laughed, overjoyed. "Of course! As many as you want."

Zac waited for the same jubilation to appear on Emily's face. When she remained quiet and somber, he frowned. Another frisson of unease went through him.

"Em? What is it? What's going on?"

She blew out her breath on a heavy sigh. Her shoulders slumped. She bowed her head.

"Emily? You're starting to freak me out. Talk to me. Please. What's going on?"

And then her head came up and she looked him straight in the eye. "Six years ago, I had an abortion."

He gasped. If she'd told him she was the kingpin of the mafia and currently on the run from the police, he couldn't have been more shocked.

"You *what?*"

"I had an abortion when I was eighteen. It was a couple of months after graduation. I didn't know I was pregnant until after I'd left for university. It must have happened that last time... When we hadn't been so careful about using protection..."

Her voice faded away. He still couldn't get his mind around what she'd said. "An abortion? What? Why?" He gasped.

She gave him a helpless look. "We'd already broken up, Zac. I was about to start the next chapter of my life. I was eighteen. I wasn't ready to be a mother."

Zac could hardly believe what he was hearing. A loud buzzing sound started in his ears. He stared at Emily. It was like looking at a stranger.

"Why didn't you tell me beforehand? How could you make that kind of decision without even letting me know?"

"Because you would have tried to convince me to keep it!" she cried.

His chest was so tight with hurt and anger and shock and disbelief, he thought he might have a heart attack right there and then. There was so much he wanted to say to her, but he couldn't get the words out. He was also shocked and angry and he didn't want to say something he might later come to regret. So he spun on his heel without another word and left.

Too late, he remembered he'd come in a taxi. He'd stopped drinking a few hours earlier, so he wasn't over the limit, but he didn't have any wheels. Then he spied Hannah's BMW. No doubt the keys were still in it. Nobody locked their cars this far out of town.

Hannah lived in the Hunter Valley, about three hours' drive north of Sydney. There was no way she'd be going anywhere tonight. No doubt she'd spend the night at the family home, like she usually did when she visited. He pulled out his phone and sent her a courtesy text.

Have borrowed your car. Will return it in the morning. Zac x

He was already climbing behind the wheel when Hannah sent him a thumbs up in response. Switching on the ignition and putting the car into gear, he left the party with a squeal of tires and headed down the drive. He had no clear destination in mind. His only thought was to get away from there, away from Emily before he said something that couldn't be taken back.

He felt side-swiped, flummoxed, taken completely unawares. Never in his wildest dreams could he have guessed she'd been harboring such a secret. They'd never talked about marriage and kids in high school, but he thought they were on the same page when it came to their future. In his mind, it stretched out before them as one long, lazy, wonderful time of togetherness when they could see each other every day, sleep in the same bed. He'd imagined waking up every day with a smile on his face.

It was only when she dropped the bombshell that she was leaving that he realized they had very different ideas about their future. He couldn't wait to share his with her. She couldn't picture him in hers. It had been devastating.

Despite all that, they'd parted as friends. Zac had set aside his hurt and disappointment and had wished her all the best. He hadn't seen her for six years. Never could he have imagined that in that time she'd made a decision to abort his baby. It was inconceivable that she wouldn't have come to him beforehand. That she wouldn't give him the chance to put forward his case. It had been his baby too. He bit back a howl of distress.

Making the turn onto the main road, he drove aimlessly through the night. Every time he thought about the decision Emily had made without him, he got angry and upset all over again. He wished Vaughan were there. He'd always been close to his older brother. Adopted by his parents when Vaughan was eleven, Vaughan was sixteen when Zac was born. By the time he began turning to him for advice, Vaughan was a grown man, already experienced in the ways of the world and, more importantly, about women.

But Vaughan had gone AWOL and nobody knew when he might return. Zac didn't even know how to contact him. He wasn't answering his phone and emails were sporadic. There was no guarantee he was even regularly checking them. That meant Zac would have to work through this crisis with Emily on his own.

The thought made him sigh. He scrubbed at his face. He couldn't believe how one conversation could turn his whole world upside down. He'd gone from the highest of highs to floundering in the darkness in a matter of moments.

As the traffic started to get heavier around him, he realized he was on the outskirts of Sydney. He wasn't far from Craigdon Manor. In fact, if memory served him right, the place was right up ahead.

The Craigdons were another wealthy family well-known among Sydney's elite. They were also slightly related. Zac's half-brother, Christopher, was a Craigdon. His biological father had been none other than Henry Craigdon, the patriarch of the family. Though Henry had never recognized Christopher as his son, that didn't change the fact.

Over the years, his mother had occasionally made mention of the Craigdons. Zac had met some of Christopher's half-brothers and sisters at a recent family function. No doubt they'd be in attendance at the upcoming wedding. One Craigdon in particular had gotten his attention.

Callum Craigdon was the oldest of the Craigdon offspring, not counting Christopher. He'd been destined for the priesthood until life intervened and he took another direction. Now he was happily married with kids. Go figure.

Still, Zac had been given the opportunity to spend time with Callum and he'd found the guy easy to talk to and full of good advice. A bit like Vaughan. Coming to a sudden decision, Zac made a turn and headed up the paved driveway.

Erected *circa* 1927, Craigdon Manor displayed all the hallmarks of its impressive Art Deco architectural period, including rounded corners and stylized geometric detailing. The three-story house was set across an expansive six hectares, with stately grounds that incorporated a full-size tennis court, golf course and a number of large outbuildings. There was no doubt it was a grand place.

Right now, most of the house was in darkness. It was late, but not too late. Ten at the most. The last time he'd heard, Callum and his wife were living at his family home while they waited for the renovations on their own house to be completed. Zac hoped that was still the case. He could do with someone to talk to. Callum was a good listener. He was just the person Zac needed to pour out his heart.

Chapter Twenty-One

Callum Craigdon was startled awake by the sound of the doorbell. He'd fallen asleep downstairs in front of the fire. The book he'd been reading still lay in his lap. Grace had retired upstairs an hour earlier. Callum had been intending to join her as soon as he finished the chapter he'd been on.

His first thought was that there was something wrong. That something had happened to his mother or Archie who wasn't quite back to full health since he'd been rescued from a house fire. The two of them were currently away on holiday, exploring North Queensland and the Great Barrier Reef.

The doorbell sounded again. Blinking away the residual effects of sleep, he tugged his robe around him and headed to the entryway. He pulled open the door and frowned. Zac Barrington stood on the front step, looking a little worse for wear.

"Callum. It's Zac Barrington. Do you remember me?"

Callum nodded. "Of course. You're Christopher's brother."

"That's right. I was... I was wondering if I could come in. I know this is weird seeing as we barely know each other, but I really need to talk to someone."

Callum raised a single eyebrow. Having Christopher's half-brother turn up this time of night on his doorstep was strange, but who was he to turn him away? The guy looked desperate.

"Sure." He stepped back to allow Zac to enter.

Callum led them into his late father's den where he'd taken to spending his alone time. His father had been a hard man to love, a man with many flaws and just as many secrets, but no one was perfect and Callum preferred to remember his father for his better qualities, rather than focusing on the negatives. When he was alone in his father's den, he felt closer to him. Felt like his father was finally at peace. That was a good thing. For all of them.

"Can I get you a drink?" Callum asked, cracking open a can of Coke.

"No thank you."

Zac roamed restlessly around the den, picking up pictures and ornaments one after the other and setting them down again. It was obvious he had something weighty on his mind. Callum returned to his armchair and took a sip of his drink.

"What would you like to talk about?"

Zac sighed like he had the weight of the world on his shoulders. And perhaps he did. Callum waited patiently for the other man to speak. The silence dragged between them. Callum had learned not to rush this kind of thing. It often took time for someone to find the courage to speak their truth. He was more than willing to wait. His patience was finally rewarded when Zac spoke.

"I just found out the woman I've loved for most of my life had an abortion when she was eighteen."

Callum barely reacted. "I see."

"We were together at the time. Dating. Boyfriend and girlfriend. I thought we'd get engaged right out of high school, but she had other plans. Now I've discovered that included aborting our baby."

Zac's voice cracked with emotion. Callum could see how deeply affected he was by the news. Not that Callum blamed him. It would have been difficult news for anyone.

"What are you more upset about? The fact she had an abortion, or that she didn't discuss it with you first?"

"Both!" Zac cried. "I would never have wanted her to have an abortion. Okay, so we were only eighteen, but so what? We could have made it work. We loved each other so much. I would have gotten a job. Done whatever I had to. And we both had supportive families. It wasn't like we were facing life on the streets..." He stopped as if he couldn't go on.

"Do you think that's why she didn't tell you about it? Because she thought you'd be against the idea of an abortion?"

"Yes! That's exactly why she didn't tell me! She admitted as much tonight."

"And how did that make you feel?"

Zac rounded on him, eyes blazing. "How do you think it made me feel? I felt angrier than I've ever felt in my life. Furious. Hurt. Filled with disbelief. How could she have done this to me? To our baby?"

Callum nodded. His voice remained calm. "You're right. It's a lot to take in. I can understand why you feel so distressed. You feel like you were cheated of something. Like you were left out of an important decision you had the right to help make."

Zac scrubbed at his hair and continued to pace. "Yes! That's exactly it! I accept I would have tried to talk her out of it, but I would have also respected her decision. The thing is, she never gave me a chance. She never told me."

Callum regarded him somberly. "This happened a long time ago. Why do you think she told you now?"

Zac paused. Callum could tell from his expression of surprise and confusion Zac hadn't given any thought to that. He drew in a deep breath and shook his head, feeling helpless.

"I don't know. I don't know why she chose to tell me now. After all this time."

"Are you together now?"

"Yes! We finally reconciled. After six years apart, we're finally back together."

"Do you think that's why she's found the courage to tell you? Because you're now a couple again and she wants to wipe the slate clean?"

"I don't know," Zac said thoughtfully. Some of the tension left his body. He threw himself down in the armchair that stood adjacent to Callum's.

"It can't have been easy for her, carrying around that secret all these years. She must have known how upset you'd be."

"Too right."

"And yet she found the courage to tell you. Knowing you wouldn't react well. Knowing that this might very well result in the end of your new relationship. She sounds like a very brave woman."

"How can you say that? She aborted my baby without my knowledge!"

"Do you know why?"

"She said she wasn't ready to be a mother. She had grand plans for her future. A future that didn't involve me."

"I see."

"Do you? Because I don't. I don't see at all. How could she have done something like that and not told me?"

Callum took a sip of his drink and then set it aside. "The decision to abort a baby is never taken lightly. I don't know your girl, but I imagine she agonized over it for a long time. She wouldn't be human if she didn't. The fact she made the decision to go through with it is something she'll have to live with for the rest of her life. Whether it was the right or wrong decision isn't for us to decide. It isn't our place to judge her. We leave that to a much higher power."

"So you think I should just forget about it? That I shouldn't be making such a big deal about this?" Zac cried.

"No, Zac. That's not what I'm saying," Callum said firmly. "You have a right to be upset. The baby was as much yours as hers. You had a right to be consulted. The fact she didn't has led to this, but that still doesn't change the fact it's not our place to judge."

"But I'm so angry..." Zac sounded helpless.

Callum regarded him steadily. "Tell me, Zac. Do you love this woman?"

"Yes! Of course I do! I've loved her most of my life!"

"Then you must forgive her. That's what love is."

"But—"

Callum held up his hand, cutting off Zac's response. "I know. It won't be easy. Forgiveness never is. But none of us is perfect. We might have been made in God's image, but we're beset with human frailties. We go through life doing the best we can. That's all we can strive for. When we make mistakes, we pray the people who love us will forgive us. That's the only hope we have."

He looked directly into Zac's eyes. "If you truly love this woman like you say you do, you'll find it in your heart to forgive her, no matter how angry or hurt you feel, or what reasons she had for making her decision. Like I said, that's what love is."

Zac left Craigdon Manor dazed and confused, but the white-hot fury he'd been consumed with earlier had left him. He climbed into Hannah's BMW and started back down the drive at a much steadier pace, his head full of what Callum had said. As angry and upset as he'd been, one thing kept circling in his mind: He loved Emily with every fiber of his being. He couldn't remember a time when he hadn't loved her. But what did that mean? Did that mean he was willing to put her before everything else, even his own feelings?

He now conceded that she'd made what must have been an incredibly difficult decision. She'd been raised in a Christian home. There was no way she wouldn't have agonized over what to do, then and afterwards. She'd said she'd thought about it nearly every day since. This wasn't something she'd decided on the spur of the moment. It'd had lasting consequences for her.

And what about when Callum had asked why she'd chosen to tell him now? He hadn't thought about that. The truth was, she could have taken that secret to her grave. He would never have been the wiser. Instead, she chose to tell him. He suspected it was because she didn't want there to be secrets between them. That was no way to start their future. If that were the case, he admired her for having the courage to speak up now, but he needed to hear her reasons; he needed to know the why.

The longer he drove through the dark, quiet streets, the more his anger receded. The thought of Emily having an abortion still upset him, but he was slowly beginning to understand why she might have felt that only she could make that decision. Nothing was going to change the fact he loved her or that he still wanted her in his life. Like Callum said, no one was perfect. One day he might be the one who made a mistake. It might be *him* seeking forgiveness. How would he feel if the woman who purported to love him refused to give that to him?

Drawing in a deep breath, he eased it out, along with a lot of his tension. He rolled his neck and shoulders. He wouldn't feel better until he'd spoken to Emily and cleared the air with her. Only then could they move forward.

"Siri. Call Emily."

Emily's eyes were red and swollen and still her chest was tight with unshed tears. She'd fled the party right after Zac had stormed out and had caught an Uber back to the city. It had taken ninety minutes and had cost a fortune, but she didn't care. She couldn't bear to stay at the Barrington home a moment longer, surrounded by his loving family, celebrating such a joyous occasion as the coming together of people who loved each other enough to commit the rest of their lives to each other.

She'd known she was taking a risk telling Zac about the abortion and maybe her timing hadn't been the best. For an instant after the words had left her mouth, she'd wished them back. But she couldn't stand to have the secret between them. She wanted their future to be bright and sparkling and free from that burden. She knew he'd be upset. She just hoped and prayed he'd eventually see it from her perspective too.

It was late. After midnight. But she couldn't sleep. She kept rewinding her conversation with Zac, trying to see how she might have handled it better. The thing was, apart from her choice of timing, she didn't think she could have done things any differently. No matter the circumstances or even different words, Zac was always going to react like he had. It was just the way he was.

That was one of the qualities she loved in him. His sense of honor, loyalty, his devotion to his family. Family was important to him. Even though she hadn't really thought of the small fetus as a baby, she knew Zac saw it differently. She only hoped they could get past this. Then again, it was better to know now if it were a deal breaker.

The sound of her phone ringing was loud in the silence of her apartment. In her rush to leave, she hadn't given any thought to Leo. Hopefully he was snug and safe in his bed at Zac's house. Climbing out of bed, she padded over to her dresser and picked up her phone.

Zac.

Her heart stopped. A rush of nerves clogged her throat. She didn't want to answer the call. What if he were still angry? What if he told her she'd been wrong? That she'd had no right to abort their baby, at least not without telling him?

She drew in a deep breath in an effort to calm her racing heart. The only way to find out how he was feeling was to talk to him. Taking hold of her courage, she answered the call.

"Zac."

"Emily. Thank God," he breathed. "I wasn't sure if you'd answer."

"Where are you?" she asked, pleased that he sounded more in control than the last time they'd spoken.

"Um… Where am I? I'm not sure. Somewhere between Richmond and Broken. Are you still at the party?"

"No. I… I came home. I'm in Sydney."

"Okay."

A beat of silence passed before Zac spoke again. "Do you mind if I come over?"

"Now?" she asked with surprise. "It's already midnight and you're at least an hour away."

"I know. But I'm not going to sleep until I talk to you and I'm guessing you feel the same."

His quiet admission resonated. She compressed her lips. He was right. There was no way she could sleep until they'd cleared the air, sorted things out one way or the other. She breathed out a heavy sigh.

"Yes. Okay. You can come over." She gave him the address and ended the call, not sure if she'd done the right thing, but knowing she had no choice. If Zac was ready to talk to her, he must have come to a decision. Putting it off wasn't going to change anything. It would only prolong her misery. Whether she'd be happy about his decision, that remained to be seen, but there was nothing she could do about that now. Except wait. And hope. And pray. In that order.

Zac pulled into the curb beside Emily's apartment block. She lived in a high rise that reached for the sky. The building looked like it had been recently gentrified, along with most of the other houses and apartment blocks in the street, but as stylish and new as it looked, he couldn't imagine not having a yard to play in and green grass under his feet.

Taking the lift up to the seventh floor, he found her door and knocked, his heart thumping. He'd come there with the best of intentions, but what if it all went wrong? He'd never forgive himself if he lost her a second time.

She met him at the door looking just as scared and uncertain as he felt. He stepped forward and gave her a hug, grateful when she hugged him back. It was a good start.

"Hey," he said quietly.

"Hey."

"Thanks for seeing me."

She merely shrugged and stepped back to let him enter. He looked around at the spacious open plan kitchen and living area. The walls were painted a cheerful yellow. He bet they looked great in the sunlight. The kitchen cupboards and island bench were a crisp white. There were potted plants on the windowsills, a decent view of the city, colorful cushions on the navy-blue couch. A framed picture of her brother and another one of her parents stood on an antique dresser.

"You have a nice place," he said.

"Thank you. Can I get you a drink?"

"Sure." He'd passed on the drink at Callum's, but right now he could do with some Dutch courage.

"Is beer okay, or would you rather a coffee?"

"Beer's fine."

She handed him a bottle out of the fridge. He twisted off the lid and gulped down a mouthful. He looked at her. "You're not drinking?"

"No. I'm fine."

He noticed she looked like she'd been crying. Her eyes were red and swollen, her skin blotchy. It reminded him of the way they'd parted and how angry he'd been. Regret washed over him. He took another gulp of beer and then set it aside.

"I'm sorry, Emily. I shouldn't have stormed off like that."

She gave another half-shrug, as if she didn't trust herself to speak.

"I was shocked and angry and... I thought the best thing I could do for both of us was to walk away until I'd had a chance to cool off."

"And have you?" she asked quietly.

"Yes."

"Okay."

"I drove around for a while. Then I called in and spoke to a friend. He helped me get some perspective."

Curiosity flickered to life in her eyes. "What did he say?"

"He told me how brave you were for telling me."

She bit her lip and looked away, but not before he saw tears glinting in her eyes.

He kept his gaze on her. "Why did you tell me, Em?"

She wrapped her arms about her waist and drew in a deep breath. "I love you more than I thought possible. I didn't realize it could be so good between us. I didn't want our lives going forward yet tainted with my secret. It was selfish of me. But that's the way I felt. If it meant losing you, then I needed to have that happen before I was completely invested in our future."

"I would never have found out if you didn't tell me. You could have kept it to yourself."

"Maybe. Maybe not. Secrets have a way of coming out. I didn't want to take that risk. I wanted you to know the unvarnished truth and make a fully informed decision about our future. If I hadn't told you and you'd found out somewhere down the track, you would have despised me."

Zac drew in a deep breath, taken aback by her honesty...and courage. "I hate to think I could ever despise you for anything," he said quietly. "But you're right. Finding out something like that years down the track would have been devastating. It's hard enough finding out now."

Fresh tears hovered on her lashes. Her lips trembled with the effort to hold back her emotions. Zac's heart turned over. He hated seeing her hurting.

"I love you, Emily Wilson. I always have and I always will. I'm sad about the loss of our baby and the fact you didn't think you could tell me about that, but I understand. You did what you thought you had to do, and you've lived with that decision ever since. I know you. It can't have been easy. I don't want to add to your burden by never forgiving you."

He heard her sudden intake of breath and saw the flash of hope in her eyes. "You... You forgive me?"

He closed the distance between them and took her in his arms. "Yes. I forgive you. I love you. I love you so much. How could I love you this much and not be willing to forgive you? That would make me a hypocrite."

"Oh, Zac!"

She covered his face with kisses, laughing and crying and loving him all at once. His heart swelled with love and tenderness.

Their kisses soon turned passionate and they tore at each other's clothes. His expensive suit hit the floor, along with his shirt and tie. Her pajamas quickly followed. Before they could draw breath, they stood naked in her kitchen, drinking each other in.

Then Zac bent and hoisted Emily up in his arms. Her legs went around his hips. He walked the short distance to the counter and set her down on top of it. She framed his face with her hands and kissed him over and over again. The heat of her passion drove his desire to fever pitch. His cock was thick and hard and throbbing. He yearned to bury himself inside her.

Breaking away from her, he gasped for breath and retrieving his discarded pants, he fumbled for his wallet. He pulled out a condom and quickly sheathed himself and returned to her side. She gazed at him with hooded eyes, dark and stormy with desire. As he positioned himself between her legs, she brought her arms up around his shoulders and clung to him.

With one hard thrust he was inside her, enveloped in her moisture and warmth. She met his thrusts in perfect rhythm, crying out with passion each time. They'd never made love so fast and furious, but somehow it felt right. Instead of anger and hurt, he poured all the passion and love he felt for her into his movements, imprinting her on his very soul. He didn't want to spend another moment without her. He wanted to fall asleep in her arms for the rest of his life.

They reached the peak together and cried out their joy and relief. Afterwards, they clung to each other as they caught their breath and slowly drifted back to earth. Hours later, after making love a second time—this time in her bed—Zac threaded his fingers through hers and pressed a soft kiss on the back of her hand.

"I love you so much," he whispered.

She looked at him, her expression rapturous. "I love you too."

"No more secrets?"

"No more secrets."

Zac sighed with contentment. "I can't wait to spend the rest of my life with you. Starting now. I don't know if you're willing to move to Broken, but I don't care if you're not. I just want to be with you. If that means selling my house and getting a job closer to the city, I'm happy to do that. Whatever you want. All I want is to make you happy and wake up next to you every day for the rest of my life."

She cupped his cheek and smiled tenderly and then pulled him to her, kissing him gently, lovingly on the lips.

"I think that can be arranged."

THE END

Get a free book when you sign up for Chris Taylor's newsletter at: http://www.christaylorauthor.com.au

If you enjoyed Zac and Emily's story don't forget to leave a review at your favorite digital retailer. Every review is really appreciated and helps with visibility so that other readers can find and enjoy my books.

Broken Hearts is the next book in the Barrington Family Series. Keep reading for a sneak peek at *Broken Hearts*:

CHAPTER ONE

Intensive care paramedic Molly Barrington groaned as the phone on the wall of the crib room began to ring again. She glanced across at her colleague, Benson Pitt, who sat opposite her at the dining room table in the ambulance station. He looked equally unimpressed. As paramedics attached to the busy Sutherland Hospital situated about nineteen miles south-west of the city of Sydney, it wasn't unusual for them to attend ten or twelve callouts each day, but they'd exceeded that many already that day and they still had four more hours before their shift ended.

Most of the cases had involved suspected heart attacks. One had been for a suspected broken collarbone of a child who'd fallen off school playground equipment. Another had been for a suspected broken hip when an elderly lady living on her own had taken a nasty fall. But now the dispatcher had advised them of a single vehicle accident on a busy city street. Only one person injured, thank goodness, but according to the onlooker who'd made the ooo call, it was bad. The male driver was still trapped in his vehicle. He reportedly was seriously injured and was in a lot of pain.

With a sigh, Molly pushed away from the table and poured the rest of her coffee down the sink. She rinsed her hands before heading to the plant room where the ambulance vehicles were kept. Benson followed beside her.

"Guess we'd better hop to it," Molly murmured.

"Guess so," Benson replied. His teeth flashed white against his dark skin.

She tucked an errant strand of hair behind her ear and climbed into the passenger's seat of the ambulance. She and Benson had decided at the beginning of their shift that he'd be the driver for the day. His job was to get them to any callout and back again safely and deal with all communications whilst at the scene. As the treating officer, her role was to deal with the patients.

They'd already cleaned the inside of the ambulance from the last patient, including wiping down the surfaces and changing the sheets. As Molly downloaded the address of the site of the accident from the mobile data terminal, Benson drove out of the ambulance station. Once he was clear of the building, he activated the beacons and siren and floored the accelerator.

A familiar surge of adrenaline poured through her. Her mind was already on the upcoming accident and what decisions she might have to make: The amount of damage to the vehicle, the difficulty of getting the victim out, the extent of the victim's injuries, whether he was still alive...

By the time they arrived, the scene was already crowded with onlookers; spectators all keen to get a look at the carnage. It never ceased to amaze Molly how people gathered at an accident for no other reason but to satisfy their curiosity. It was like some macabre side of their personality that was only placated by witnessing someone else's tragedy.

The police arrived about the same time and were in the process of cordoning off the area surrounding the accident with blue-and-white checked police tape. Benson parked perpendicular to the road a safe distance away, helping to block the traffic from the accident scene. Molly spied a white late model Toyota Corolla wrapped around a steel power pole. It had suffered extensive damage. The driver's side had taken the brunt of the impact. She looked at Benson, feeling grim.

"Looks bad."

He nodded, looking equally grim. "Yep."

Benson switched off the siren but left the beacons on. In silence, Molly quickly pulled on her protective clothing – high visibility vest, helmet, safety glasses, mask and climbed out of the vehicle. While Benson radioed their exact location and other details of the accident back to their control center, Molly took stock of any potential dangers, including fallen power lines, and then hurriedly made her way over to the victim.

She was relieved to discover he was conscious. His face was covered in blood from a large laceration on his forehead, most likely as a result of coming into contact with the side of his car. The front of the car had folded in on itself and was crushed against the driver's legs, along with the steering wheel that pressed against his chest. Both the driver's and front passenger's airbags had been deployed and further restricted the amount of space the driver had. In an effort to reassure him, Molly shot him a friendly smile.

"Hi, I'm Molly. What's your name?"

"Shane Lucas," he hissed through gritted teeth.

"How old are you, Shane?"

"Thirty."

"Do you know what day it is?"

"Um…Monday?"

"Where are you?"

"In Sutherland."

"Have you been drinking?"

"No."

"Drugs?"

"No."

"I'm not a cop. I don't care whether you have or not, but I need to know if you've taken anything."

"I don't do drugs. Ever."

"Okay. Well, we're going to get you out of there as fast as we can. Can you tell me where it hurts?"

"Everywhere," he rasped.

"Can you be a bit more specific? I can see you've cut your forehead. Where else have you been injured?"

"My legs. My chest. My lungs. I can't breathe. It hurts too much."

"On a scale of one to ten, with ten being the worst pain imaginable, how would you rate your pain?"

"Ten."

The driver's side door was pulverized. She tried the handle, but the door was stuck fast. The passenger side had also sustained serious damage. There was no way she was going to be able to get either door open without help. She peered through the driver's side window. The glass had been broken into a million splinters, most of which were embedded in the man's clothes. Shards were also stuck in his face. They glinted in the mid-afternoon sunlight.

Mindful of the broken glass, she reached in through the window and checked the pulse in the side of his neck. It was weak and erratic and fast. His skin was pale and clammy. His startling green eyes, though focused, were glazed with pain. With the steering wheel jammed so tightly against his chest, there was also a strong possibility of internal bleeding.

"Can you squeeze my finger?" she asked, leaning in again.

He shook his head. "Can't move."

She pinched the skin at the back of his neck hard. "Can you feel that?"

"Yes. I think so."

"Good. Just keep breathing, Shane. Slow, deep breaths. That's it. You're doing well."

"When...can you...get me...out...of here?" he gasped.

"Soon. The door's stuck and you're wedged pretty tightly against the steering wheel. We might need to bring in a rescue crew with the jaws of life."

"How long?"

Molly looked around her at the now-chaotic scene. The crowd of onlookers had swelled. People held up their phones, presumably recording the carnage before them. Several more police vehicles had arrived, along with her duty operations manager, Raoul Kumar. She was relieved to see him.

He nodded a greeting as he approached her. "What have we got?"

"Thirty-year-old male. High speed crash into a power pole. Major vehicle deformity. Patient is alert with a GCS of eight," she said, referring to the universal Glasgow Coma Scale that was used to measure a person's level of consciousness. "He's also trapped. We're going to need some help to get him out."

"I'll speak to the police commander and see what we can organize." He switched his attention to the man who remained trapped in the car, his face a mask of pain.

"Hang in there, mate. We're going to get you out of there as soon as we can."

With that, Raoul walked away, headed in the direction of the police commander. Molly moved closer to her patient and offered him another smile of reassurance. She wanted to keep him talking. Not only to take his mind off his injuries, but to help him maintain consciousness.

"You sound like you have a British accent. Are you a local, Shane?"

"No. Born...in the UK. Came out...backpacking. Liked it so much...I stayed."

"What about your family?"

"Parents still live...in the UK. A sister...in the US. No one else."

He grimaced as another wave of pain hit him. She reached for his hand and squeezed it. "Is there anyone we can call? A wife? A partner?"

"No wife. No girlfriend. Just me."

"Okay. But we're going to have to notify someone. Do you have a friend we can contact?"

His answer was swallowed up by a moan of pain. Gasping for breath, his eyes glazed over. His grip on her hand tightened.

"Oh, God. Please. It hurts so much."

"Breathe, Shane. Slowly in and out. As big as you can manage. In. Out. In. Out."

Slowly, the pain in his eyes eased, along with the pressure exerted by his hand. Molly resisted the urge to pull her hand away and flex her fingers to ascertain they were all still working.

"What do you do for a living?" she asked in an effort to keep him talking.

"Lawyer."

"Wow," she said, impressed. "What kind of law do you practice?"

"Family law."

"That must get tough sometimes," she murmured.

"Yeah."

Raoul came up to her again and drew her to one side. "I've spoken to the police commander. He's put in a call for the jaws of life. Unfortunately, the closest police rescue team were called out on another job only twenty minutes earlier. Someone's fallen over a cliff at Bondi. They're going to be caught up for the rest of the afternoon. The commander's trying to source another team. It might take a while."

"How long?" Molly asked.

"An hour or two. Maybe more."

Molly's heart sank. Though it wasn't unusual for a specialized police rescue team to take that long to attend an accident, particularly if they were otherwise engaged, it meant that her patient would remain trapped for all that time. It made treating him all the more difficult and further delayed his transfer to a trauma center where he could receive more specialized medical and surgical care.

"I'll see about some pain relief then," she murmured.

She moved back to the car. Shane's expression twisted with pain.

"How long?" he gasped.

"I'm afraid it's going to be a while yet," she answered.

"How long?"

The desperation in his eyes filled her with dread. She hated having to tell him the truth, but she'd never shied away from that, not even when the news was bad.

"An hour or two."

Shane's eyes flared wide with surprise. His expression quickly turned to one of despair. "An hour or two?"

Molly held his gaze. "Yes."

"Fuck."

The quiet expletive held a wealth of emotion. She hurried to boost his spirits.

"They'll be here as soon as they can and then we'll get you free. In the meantime, I'm going to administer some pain relief. Are you allergic to anything?"

"No."

"Are you taking any medications?"

"No."

"How much do you weigh?"

"Ninety-five kilograms."

"When did you last eat?"

"Lunchtime."

"So, a couple of hours ago?"

"Yeah. I guess."

"Do you remember what happened?"

"Yeah. A vehicle ran the red light. Came out of nowhere. Clipped my car and spun me around. I slammed into the power pole."

Molly frowned. She'd seen no evidence of another damaged vehicle. Still, that was for the police to sort out. Her only priority was her patient.

"Can you stretch your arm out for me?"

With gritted teeth, the man did as she asked. It was awkward in the cramped confines of the driver's seat, but he managed it.

"That's great," she encouraged. She opened her kit and pulled out a blood pressure machine. Wrapping the cuff around his arm, she quickly took a reading. Though it was low, it wasn't as bad as it could be.

She released the blood pressure cuff and tucked it back into her kit. She squeezed his arm reassuringly. "I'll go and get that pain relief. I'll be back in a minute."

Hurrying back to where Benson remained with the ambulance, she slid open the door to access the rear of the vehicle and stepped inside.

"How's he doing?" Benson asked.

"He's conscious, at least. There's a two hour wait on the jaws of life."

Benson winced. "Shit."

"Yeah. I'm going to give him some pain relief."

"Morphine?"

"No. He's not alert enough for that. There's a good chance he has internal injuries. His blood pressure is low, but stable, which is a good sign. I'm worried his level of consciousness might decrease the longer we have to wait."

"So, ketamine then?"

"Yep."

Molly opened a drawer and pulled out IV equipment, along with the ketamine. It would help with the pain without making him drowsy. It was the best option in the circumstances.

She double-checked the medication with Benson and then wrote it up on the patient's notes. She added his name and age and then climbed out of the van.

"You need some help?" Benson asked.

Molly smiled. "No. All good. But thanks."

With that, she turned and strode back to Shane's crushed vehicle. The crowd of onlookers had begun to disperse. No doubt the lack of immediate action meant their attention had waned. It also helped that the police who'd gathered at the scene were actively encouraging people to move on. Molly was glad.

"Hey, Shane. You still with me?" she asked, leaning in through the car window.

He gave her a wan smile. "Still here."

"Great. I've organized some pain relief. I'm going to give it to you intravenously. That means inserting a needle into your vein. Are you okay with that?"

"Just do it," he replied through clenched teeth.

Quickly and efficiently, she inserted the cannula into a vein on the back of his wrist. She was relieved that his veins hadn't yet collapsed. That gave her hope that if there was internal bleeding, it wasn't severe enough to affect the volume of blood in his veins.

"How're you doing?" she asked as she taped the cannula in place.

"Great." He gave her a lopsided smile.

It transformed his face. She suddenly became acutely aware of how attractive he was beneath the blood and pain. Thick hair the color of ripened wheat. Olive complexion. Vivid green eyes. A strong jaw.

Impatient with the direction of her thoughts, she quickly pushed the revelation aside and focused on her job. She prepared the syringe of ketamine and injected it into him through the cannula port.

"That will take a few minutes to take effect. Keep breathing, nice and slowly. Try and relax."

He shot her a wry look. "You're kidding, right?"

She grinned. "Do I look like I'm kidding?"

Chapter Two

Shane Lucas had never been in so much pain in his life. Not even when he'd come off his motorbike at full speed when he was seventeen and had skidded fifteen yards along the asphalt on the seat of his pants. The road had torn through the leather and had shaved several inches of skin off the back of his thighs. One of his wounds had required a skin graft. But even that was no match for the agony that consumed him now.

He hurt in every part of his body. Every time he moved, it was like a red-hot poker searing through him. Every breath was agony. He worried about broken ribs, punctured lungs – any manner of injury for that matter. His legs were immobile. His chest was jammed against the steering wheel. His face stung from a variety of cuts. God knows what other injuries he'd sustained.

Panic nipped at his consciousness. It took a gargantuan effort to rein in his imagination. At least he was still alert. Kind of. That was a blessing. Or maybe not. If he were unconscious, he wouldn't feel the pain. Then again, if he were unconscious, he wouldn't be talking to the pretty paramedic.

Molly. That's what she'd said. It suited her. Glossy dark hair pulled back off her face. Bright blue eyes. Kind eyes. Compassionate. Friendly. She was a nice distraction. Kept him from thinking about the pain. Her gentle yet confident voice filled him with hope even as the pain raged through his nerve endings and he lost feeling in his legs.

His mind shied away from what that might mean. God, he couldn't stand the thought he might be paralyzed. That would be unthinkable. He'd always loved adventure sports: cycling, motorbike riding, abseiling, hiking. Not to mention team sports. They were only halfway through the football season. He was their top try scorer. He couldn't bear the thought of letting his side down.

But even if his legs still worked, it was obvious he was out for the rest of the season. He only hoped that was the extent of it. He tried to remember back to the accident, but it was all a bit of a blur. He could remember the lights changing green and accelerating into the intersection before the other car came from nowhere and T-boned him. He remembered seeing a flash of silver. He thought the other car was a 4WD – maybe a Toyota Prado or a Landcruiser. There was no doubt it had been much bigger than his Toyota.

The other driver had come at him fast. He'd been a sitting duck. He'd taken a direct hit to the driver's side. The awful screech of the impact of metal-on-metal still rang in his ears. He was spun around several times before his car took to the air and flipped. Finally, it landed on its wheels, wrapped around a power pole. Thank God he'd been wearing a seatbelt.

There was broken glass all around him, filling his hair, covering his clothes. Shards had punctured his cheeks and his bare arms. Warm blood trickled from a cut on his forehead. All in all, he felt like shit. But at least the pain medication appeared to be working. The pressure in his chest had eased, along with the pain in his legs. Still there, but bearable. Just.

"How are you feeling, Shane?"

His angel was back, regarding him with concern. He tried for a smile that felt more like a grimace.

"A little better. Thanks. Whatever you gave me has taken the edge off."

She smiled, showing a row of even, white teeth. "That's great."

"How much longer?" he asked, desperation tinging his voice.

"A little while yet, I'm afraid. Tell me more about yourself. How long have you been in Australia?"

He swallowed a sigh and did his best to answer her.

"Ten years. Came out on a working holiday. Had a great time traveling around Australia, driving tractors, picking fruit, meeting the local women. There's nothing quite like the Australian women." He managed to wink.

He was amused to discover her blushing. It made her look younger. He wondered how old she was.

"Ah. So it was the women who made you stay," she said with a grin.

"That and the weather. Months and months of sunshine. I applied for permanent residency. And here I am."

"What about your family? Don't they miss you?"

He drew in a breath and was relieved to discover it didn't hurt as much as it had. "Of course. But they're getting older now. They're both retired. Mom was a high school teacher. Dad was a defense lawyer."

"Did he inspire you to go into the law?" she asked.

"Yes, I think so. He never put any pressure on me. It was something I always saw myself doing."

"You said you had a sister. What does she do?"

"Harriet's studying fashion design in New York. She says she's never going to leave."

"How old is she?"

"Twenty-five."

Molly's eyebrows rose. She slowly shook her head. "Your poor parents! Neither of their children close by! Not even living in the same country! My parents would hate that!"

"Tell me about your family," he urged. The sound of her husky voice was soothing. It also helped distract him from his pain.

"Well, for a start, there are nine of us."

His eyes widened in surprise. "Nine?"

She grinned cheekily. "Yep. I have six brothers and two sisters."

"Six brothers? Are you kidding?"

She laughed. "I'm afraid not."

He smiled. "Wow. I can't imagine what that was like growing up."

"Loud. Boisterous. Crazy. But so much fun. I'm actually a triplet."

He blinked. "A triplet?"

"Yes. We're not identical. One boy, two girls."

"Wow. Do you have a special way of communicating, like they make out in the movies?"

She laughed. The husky sound of it washed over his battered body, bringing a moment of relief.

"No, not really. I think that's only for identical siblings. But all of us get along, including the other six. There's a lot of love between us."

The wistfulness that had crept into her voice told him a lot about how she felt about her siblings. He liked that she cared about them so much.

"Are you still close?"

"Yes. Unlike you and your sister, we all still live in the country of our birth. Most of us live in or around Sydney. One brother lives in the country about six hours' drive away from here. The rest of us get together fairly regularly for family dinners at our parents' house. They live about ninety minutes south of Sydney."

"Wow," Shane murmured again.

He could hardly comprehend that. Though he and his sister were close enough, they'd both been keen to leave home and strike out on their own. The fact they'd made their lives on the other side of the world was just how things worked out. He couldn't imagine returning to live in the UK just because his parents were still there.

Lucky, they felt the same. Or at least, they understood his decision. They'd encouraged both of their children to spread their wings and find their own way in life. They might have preferred he and his sister stay closer to home, especially now they were getting older and more infirm, but they'd never asked them to change their plans. He'd never thought that much about it before but he could see how selfless it had been of his parents to let their children do what they wanted where they wanted and without feeling guilty about it. That went to show how much they loved them.

All of a sudden, he was hit with a wave of homesickness. It had been three years since he'd last been to the UK. Though his parents had visited him in Australia a few times over the years, it had been even longer since the whole family had been together. It was times like this that he missed them. When he hurt in every part of his body. When he wasn't sure what the prognosis would be. When he didn't know if he'd ever walk again...

The yearning for his mom hit him like a sledgehammer. He gasped aloud from the impact of it. Molly's face immediately reflected concern.

"What is it? Where does it hurt?" she asked.

Tears of pain and helplessness burned in his eyes. "Everywhere."

"Oh, Shane. Hang in there, buddy. We're going to get you out of there soon."

He stared up at her, pleading with his eyes. "How bad is it?"

She regarded him somberly. "It's hard to say. The fact you're still conscious is a good sign. Until we get you free, I can't do a proper assessment."

"What's going to happen when they remove this steering wheel? What if it's controlling the bleeding and when they release the pressure, I end up bleeding to death?"

"That's not going to happen."

She said it with so much certainty, he believed her. Staring into her clear blue eyes, he took courage from her confidence.

"Specialist retrieval teams have already arrived to help. They're just waiting for the police rescue team to arrive with the jaws of life. Once they've removed the barriers to your release, my partner and I will move in and do whatever needs to be done to stabilize you. Then we'll get you to the hospital."

He looked at her, wanting to believe her. Wanting to take reassurance from the hope and certainty in her voice. She was his only link to the future. He had so much left to do! So many mountains to climb! So many goals to achieve. His life had already been put on hold for two years. He didn't want to waste another moment.

"Okay, time for twenty questions," she said with a smile, interrupting his thoughts.

He blinked. "Twenty questions?"

"Yes. I ask you a question. You give me an answer. Then you get to ask a question."

He looked at her, intrigued. "And will you answer it?"

She grinned. "That depends."

She has such a nice smile...

He grinned through his pain. "On what?"

"On whether I want to."

"Oh. I see. So do I get to choose whether I answer or not?"

"Of course not."

He chuckled and then winced as pain rippled through his chest. "You don't play fair, Molly."

She shrugged and smiled again. "You wouldn't be the first person to accuse me of that. You ought to be there when I play Monopoly." She winked.

Despite the pain he was in, his belly clenched with instinctive desire. Before he could contemplate that any further, she cleared her throat and clapped her hands.

"Okay, so are you ready to play?"

He smiled. "Do I have any choice?"

"None at all!" She gave him a triumphant grin. "First question: What's your favorite color?"

He looked into her eyes. "Blue."

Her cheeks turned pink. She looked away momentarily, appearing flustered. She cleared her throat.

"Favorite song."

"That's easy. Anything by Cody Johnson."

Her eyes widened with surprise. "You like Cody Johnson?"

"Dear Rodeo..." he managed.

She grinned. "Oh my goodness! You really *do* like Cody Johnson."

He widened his eyes in mock innocence. "Would I lie to you?"

"Okay, next question."

"Hang on. It's my turn now."

She smiled. "Go ahead."

"The name of your first boyfriend."

He wasn't sure she was going to answer. Then she said, "Wayne Stanford."

"Did you kiss him?"

She held his gaze. "Yes."

"Did you like it?"

She screwed up her nose. "I was twelve. Not so much."

He laughed, enjoying their conversation.

"My turn," she said. "What's more important? Love or happiness?"

"Who says you can't have both?" he shot back.

She shook her head. "Nope. You have to choose. Love or happiness?"

He thought for a while. "Happiness."

Her eyes went wide. "Not love?"

"What good is love if you're unhappy?"

She gave him a searching look. "Interesting. I guess I'd like to think if I was in love, that would make me happy." She paused and then her expression turned cheeky. "Okay, first person you had sex with."

He started in surprise. He hadn't expected her to get so personal. This was getting interesting. "Marley Matthews."

"How old were you?"

"Sixteen."

"Were you in love with her?"

"No. But I wanted to have sex with her."

Her eyes flared with emotion. "Was she in love with you?"

"I think so."

"And you didn't think to tell her you were only there for the sex?"

He deadpanned her. "I was sixteen."

"How long did you date her?"

"Who said anything about dating?"

Her mouth turned down. He could tell he'd disappointed her. Somehow, he wished he'd been able to give her a different answer. Then again, he was being honest. If she didn't want the truth, she shouldn't have asked the question.

"My turn," he said. He kept his gaze on hers. "First lover."

Her cheeks turned crimson. She wouldn't meet his eyes. "Pass."

"Oh, come on!" he protested. "That's not fair."

"I already warned you I don't play fair." She smiled to soften her words.

He smiled back. Their gazes locked. Something passed between them, something foreign and unidentifiable. He could tell she felt it too. Her blue eyes darkened. Her mouth parted on a quick intake of breath. The knowledge that she was just as affected as he was left him feeling good. Though the pain was still there, somehow she'd managed to make him forget about it for a bit. He could nearly kiss her for that. He focused on her mouth. Full bottom lip. Soft and plump. Sensuous. So ripe for the kissing...

As if aware of the direction of his thoughts, she cleared her throat again. "Okay, let's keep going. Favorite holiday destination."

Okay, so now she's going to play it safe... He sent her a knowing look but answered anyway.

"That's easy. The Great Barrier Reef."

She nodded. "I've heard it's beautiful."

He looked at her in surprise. "You've never been?"

"No. In fact, you've probably seen more of my country than I have. After graduating from university, I went straight into full-time work. I haven't had the luxury of doing much sightseeing."

He thought about all the places he'd traveled while he'd been backpacking around Australia. He'd spent time in every state apart from Tasmania. From the tropics of Queensland to the dry deserts of Western Australia. Each part was different, but all had something to offer. He wondered if he'd ever get to travel like that again.

Not if you're in a wheelchair...

The thought came from nowhere and snatched his breath. At the same time, a pain so severe it made him cry out ripped through his chest. He gasped, but it only made things worse. Molly's expression filled with concern.

His eyes now felt so heavy he could barely keep them open. The angel in front of him went blurry. He could only just make out her features.

"Shane? Stay with me, mate."

He heard the elevated anxiety in her voice, but there was nothing he could do to stave off the encroaching darkness. The pain swirled through him, surrounding him, draining him. He wanted desperately to keep his eyes open so he could keep looking at her, but he was fast losing the battle.

Just let me sleep... Please, just let me sleep...

Chapter Three

"Patient is now red label!" Molly shouted, looking about her for help.

Benson came running over, along with Raoul. Both were wearing full PPE.

"What's wrong?" Benson asked.

"He's lost consciousness," Molly supplied.

"What happened?" Raoul asked.

"I don't know. We were just talking. Then he cried out in pain. God, I hope it isn't a blood clot."

Her fingers were pressed against the pulse in Shane's neck. It was so weak. She quickly applied the blood pressure cuff and took a reading. Her heart sunk. It had also fallen dangerously low.

"We need to get him out of here," she cried.

"I'll get an updated ETA on the jaws of life," Raoul muttered and strode away.

"What can I do?" Benson asked.

"Nothing. Until we get him out of there, we can't do anything. We can't even administer CPR the way he is."

Benson looked grim. Molly hated the feeling of helplessness that seeped into her veins. This wasn't the first time she'd been in a life-and-death situation with a patient, but somehow with Shane she felt more desperate. He was more than just another patient. They'd developed a bond, a special connection. There was no way she could lose him now.

She leaned in through the shattered window, mindful of the glass. His skin was a sickly pallor. His breathing shallow and uneven. She checked his blood pressure again. Dread filled her stomach. It had fallen even lower.

Urgency swept over her. It was all she could to do maintain a professional calm.

"I need some help over here!" she yelled. "Where the hell is everyone? We need to get this man out of here."

And then chaos erupted around her. The police van arrived with the jaws of life. Rescue police hurried toward her. They surrounded the car. She stepped out of the way, giving them the room they needed to do their job. Until Shane had been released from the car, there was nothing else she could do.

She found Benson and Raoul standing a short distance away. Both men watched on solemnly as the rescue team got to work. First the driver's side door was removed. Then they cut away the roof of the car. It was discarded to one side and a hydraulic ram brought in to lift the dashboard and steering wheel away from Shane's body. Endless minutes ticked by. Molly watched on, feeling helpless, praying for Shane to hang on.

Finally, he was clear enough from the wreckage that they could move back in and attend to him. Benson hurried to bring forward the stretcher. Molly crouched beside Shane. His eyes remained closed. His skin was now chalky. She felt for his pulse and was relieved when she found it. Weak and erratic, but still there.

"Shane! Shane! Can you hear me?" She slapped his cheek. To her relief, he slowly opened his eyes.

Shane woke to the feel of excruciating pain. He tried to focus on what was going on around him. The roof of his car and the driver's door was gone. The dashboard and steering wheel were no longer pressing in on him, but he still couldn't move. It was like he was glued to the seat.

Panic surged through him. He looked around for Molly and found her. She was crouched low beside the car, staring at him. Her expression was tense, her cheeks were pale. Concern darkened her blue eyes. When she realized he was awake, her expression changed. She gave him a strained smile.

"Hey, Shane. You're back with us. How do you feel?"

"Terrible," he managed.

She smiled again. "We're going to get you out of here. Just hold in there, okay? Big, slow breaths."

He tried to do as she asked, but it hurt too much. The red-hot poker was back, and it was burning a hole in his chest. Whatever she'd given him for the pain had worn off.

"It hurts," he gasped.

"I know, Shane. We're working as fast as we can."

The face of an aboriginal man dressed in the navy-blue uniform of a paramedic filled his vision. Then Molly spoke again. "Shane. This is my partner, Benson. He's going to help me get you out of there."

From the corner of his eye, Shane spied a stretcher. It had been brought down to his level. It looked like a simple matter to slide across onto the mattress, but Shane knew the effort was beyond him.

"Can't," he croaked.

"That's all right, Shane. You don't have to do anything," Molly reassured him. "Benson and I are going to move you. But first I'm going to give you another shot for the pain."

With that, she fiddled with his hand. He felt cold liquid slide into his veins. Within minutes, the pain had subsided enough that he felt he could breathe again.

"Oh, God. That's good stuff." He sighed.

Molly smiled and patted his hand. "Okay, Shane. We're going to move you now." She looked at her partner. "On three. One. Two. Three."

"*Arghhhh!*" The involuntary cry of pain was ripped from his body. The paramedics lifted him out of the car and settled him down on the gurney. If he thought the pain had been bad before, now it was beyond excruciating.

"More!" He gasped. "The pain. Please. I need more."

Tears sprang to his eyes. He was beyond feeling embarrassed. All he wanted was to be rid of the pain.

"I can't give you anymore right now," Molly replied calmly. "You're doing so well, Shane. Big, slow breaths. That's it. We're taking you to the hospital. They'll be able to give you something else for the pain there."

Her calm and professional manner helped contain his panic. He tried not to think about the fire that coursed through his body or the kind of injuries that could cause such excruciating pain. As he was loaded into the back of the ambulance, he held back another cry of agony. Though he could tell Molly and her partner were trying their best to minimize the jostling, it wasn't possible to load him without some movement. Each bump was excruciating.

"Sorry about that, Shane. How are you hanging in there?" Molly asked.

He grimaced, beyond words. It was all he could do to keep breathing through the pain. Molly and her partner moved quickly and efficiently inside the vehicle, strapping him in securely, checking his cannula, starting an IV. It was obvious they'd done this sort of thing many times before. The knowledge brought him a measure of comfort.

On a ragged sigh, he closed his eyes again. There was nothing he could do but put himself in their hands and pray for the nightmare to be over. As the darkness descended once again, he let himself be consumed by it with barely a whisper.

Molly saw Shane's eyes drift closed and knew he was once again on the verge of losing consciousness. A wave of urgency washed over her. His skin was so pale it was almost translucent. He was cold and clammy to the touch. She'd hooked him up to the monitor and now had a constant read on his vital signs. His blood pressure remained alarmingly low.

Benson had climbed behind the wheel. He started the ignition and called out to Molly.

"All good to go?"

"Yep. Step on it. Let's get this guy to the hospital."

With lights and sirens blazing, they arrived at the hospital. Benson had radioed ahead with details of their patient. The Emergency Department staff worked like a well-oiled machine. As the ambulance pulled up in the ambulance bay and Molly and Benson wheeled Shane through the plastic doors, doctors and nurses appeared from nowhere and surrounded the gurney. Molly brought the ED doctor up to speed on the patient's condition, including a brief description of the accident, injuries she'd observed, his vital signs and what pain relief had been administered. Shane was transferred onto another bed and taken straight to X-ray.

All of a sudden, Molly's part in the emergency was over. Her shoulders slumped with relief. They'd managed to get Shane to the hospital still breathing. The adrenaline that had been pouring through her veins slowly eased. She drew in a deep breath and tried to recalibrate.

"I'll attend to the gurney," Benson offered and wheeled it out of the way where he could wipe it clean and change the sheets in anticipation of their next patient.

"Thanks," Molly said. "I'll deal with the paperwork."

Finding the nurse who'd been put in charge of Shane's care, Molly went through the details of the accident she had to hand.

"Any drugs or alcohol in his system?" the nurse asked.

"He said no. I couldn't smell any alcohol on his breath and he didn't appear to be under the influence of illegal drugs."

"Allergies?"

"No."

"Next of kin?"

"None in Australia. He moved here from the UK. His parents are still there. He has a sister in New York. That's all I know."

She thought back to their conversation. The twenty questions game. She actually knew more about him than she'd let on. Okay, so they hadn't gotten to twenty questions, but she'd found out some interesting things about him in that short time. His favorite color, holiday destination, first lover...

She couldn't believe she'd asked him something so personal. At the time, she hadn't given much thought to her questions. She'd just been trying to keep him from sliding into unconsciousness. She'd been surprised he'd told her about his first sexual experience. She sure as hell hadn't been prepared to share hers. And then his intriguing answer to her question about love and happiness...

All of a sudden, she wished she'd met him under different circumstances. Not only was he good looking, but he was also interesting. Despite the pain, his green eyes had shone with intelligence and good humor. He'd told her he was a lawyer. That all amounted to a tidy package and one she would have enjoyed exploring further if they hadn't met the way they had.

For now, he was seriously injured, possibly on the brink of death. If he'd suffered internal injuries, there was always a chance they wouldn't be able to stem the flow of blood in time. Despite all the advancements in modern medicine, some patients still lost their life. She could only hope and pray Shane wasn't one of them.

"You ready?"

Benson appeared behind her. She turned and nodded. "Yep. All done. Let's get out of here."

Time to go back to the station and wait for the next call.

Shane felt like he was swimming through molasses. It was like the time he jumped off a cliff about fifty feet above a deep, natural pool. He'd hit the water hard and had sunk down, down, down. He'd panicked when he realized how deep he'd gone. Kicking frantically, he'd fought to find his way back up to the top, plowing desperately through the water. By the time his head broke the surface, his chest was on fire, his lungs burning for air. He felt that way now.

Every part of him hurt. His chest felt like there was an elephant sitting on top of it. He tried to breathe, but it was too painful. There was something on his face. An obstruction in his throat. He wanted to claw at it, but he couldn't find the strength to lift his arms. He must have made a sound, but he couldn't remember speaking.

Suddenly, someone was there, talking to him in low, soothing tones. *Molly?* He couldn't tell. In the background, he heard the beeping of machines and the hum of conversation. It all sounded so far away. And then he felt a coldness slide into his veins and the pain began to fade, along with everything else. He surrendered once again to the darkness...

Broken Hearts is due for release in August, 2022. It's available now for preorder from your favorite digital retailer.

Other books by Chris Taylor

The Munro Family Series (in order)

The Profiler
The Investigator
The Predator
The Betrayal
The Deception
The Negotiator
The Christmas Vigil (A novella)
The Ransom
The Defendant
The Shooting
The Maker

The Sydney Harbour Hospital Series (in order)

The Perfect Husband

CHRIS TAYLOR

The Body Thief
The Baby Snatchers
The Final Bullet
The Debt Collector
The Lab Test
The Stolen Identity
The Cliff-top Killer
The Likeable Fraudster

The Sydney Legal Series (in order)

An Accidental Murderer
At the Hand of her Father
A Woman Scorned
Lies and Deception
Ordinary Evil
The Ties that Bind
The Perfect Crime
A Toxic Inheritance
Malicious Love

The Craigdon Family Series (in order)

Callum
Joel
Isabella
Nicholas
Sophia

Flynn
Noah
Logan
Elizabeth

The Barrington Family Series (in order)

Broken Lives
Broken Promises
Broken Bonds
Broken Spirits
Broken Minds
Broken Vows
Broken Hearts
Broken Dreams
Broken Homes

The Fairfax Family Series (in order)

A Cattleman in Disguise
A Cattleman's Quest
A Cattleman's Daughter
A Cattleman's Secret Baby
To Catch a Cattleman
The Doctor and the Cattleman
To Rescue a Cattleman
A Cattleman's Heart
For the Love of a Cattleman

Bachelors and Brides Series (in order)

Matilda
Austin
Farrah
Benjamin
Verity
Denver
Ebony
Tyrone
Willow

Books by Chris Taylor
Writing as Bella Christian

This Is Where It Ends Series
(in order)

Jessie's Story
Ryan's Story
Holly's Story
Sarah's Story
Veronica's Story

Love audiobooks? Check out Chris Taylor Books on audio
iTunes Amazon   Audible

Join Chris Taylor's Facebook reader group/fan page and be among the first to receive news of book releases, read and review books prior to release and other amazing offers.

Join Now!

Acknowledgments

As usual, no book comes into being without a lot of help and support by my friends and family. A world of thanks must go to my wonderful editor, Pat Thomas. Thank you for everything that you do to make my stories even more amazing than I could ever dare to dream. I'm so sad this is our last book together. We had a great time! To former Detective Superintendent Michael Kilfoyle, thank you for lending my story credibility. Any mistakes are wholly my own.

To Justin Mendez and all of the team at 100 Covers, thank you for the fantastic book cover. To my sister, Nicole Guihot and to my friend, Ally Thomson, thank you for your excellent editorial comments, proof reading skills and suggestions. I hope you like the final result.

To the fantastic writer organizations such as Romance Writers of Australia, Romance Writers of America and Romance Writers of New Zealand for all the help, support and encouragement they offer new and aspiring writers, including me.

To my readers, thank you for your support and love for my stories. Your encouragement and enjoyment make this journey all worthwhile.

And lastly, to my friends and family, especially my husband and children. Thank you for putting up with late dinners and even later conversations as I've emerged day after day from the sometimes scary but always enthralling world I've created on my computer.

About the Author

Chris Taylor grew up on a farm in north-west New South Wales, Australia. She always had a thirst for stories and recalls writing her first book at the ripe old age of eight. Always a lover of romance and happily-ever-afters, a career in criminal law sparked her interest in intrigue and suspense. For Chris to be able to combine romance with suspense in her books is a dream come true.

Chris is married to Linden and is the mother of five children. If not behind her computer, you can find her doing the school run, taxiing children to swimming lessons, football, ballet and cricket. In her spare time, Chris loves to read her favorite authors who include Richard North

Patterson, Sandra Brown, Kathleen E Woodiwiss and Jude Devereaux.

353

You can find out more about Chris and get a free book when you sign up for her newsletter at her website:

http://www.christaylorauthor.com.au

Join Chris on Facebook at:

https://www.facebook.com/christaylorauthor/